THE AWARD

France, 1940: When the German army invades, sixteen-year-old Gaëlle de Barbet loses her family, and her closest friend is sent to a detention camp. Joining the Resistance, Gaëlle takes terrifying risks to fearlessly deliver Jewish children to safety, and later to help save France's art treasures. But when the war draws to a close, she is falsely accused of collaboration, and flees to Paris in disgrace. There, she begins a new life that eventually takes her to New York, from a career as a Dior model to marriage and motherhood, unbearable loss, and mature, lasting love when she returns to France. No matter where she goes, however, her label as a collaborator remains — until her granddaughter, a respected political journalist, embarks on a journey to see Gaëlle recognized as the war hero she was.

SPECIAL MESSAGE TO READERS

Although Danielle Steel was born in New York, she spent her formative years living in Paris. She decided to make the journey back to New York after she had finished her education. One of her first jobs in the city was for the pioneering PR firm, Supergirls Ltd, where she was involved in creating PR campaigns and hosting parties for clients. During a spell working in advertising, Steel started publishing poems in women's magazines. Since then she has written at a furious pace and has enjoyed huge success, with 57 bestsellers, over 100 international bestselling novels in print, and more than 600 million copies sold.

You can discover more about the author at www.daniellesteel.com

Facebook
www.facebook.com/DanielleSteelOfficial

Twitter @daniellesteel

DANIELLE STEEL

THE
AWARD

Complete and Unabridged

CHARNWOOD
Leicester

First published in Great Britain in 2016 by
Bantam Press
an imprint of
Transworld Publishers
London

First Charnwood Edition
published 2017
by arrangement with
Transworld Publishers
Penguin Random House
London

The moral right of the author has been asserted

A catalogue record for this book is available
from the British Library.

ISBN 978–1–4448–3468–0

Published by
F. A. Thorpe (Publishing)
Anstey, Leicestershire

Set by Words & Graphics Ltd.
Anstey, Leicestershire
Printed and bound in Great Britain by
T. J. International Ltd., Padstow, Cornwall

This book is printed on acid-free paper

To my beloved and very brave children,
Beatrix, Trevor, Todd, Nick, Sam,
Victoria, Vanessa, Maxx, and Zara,

We each have our battles to face,
the wars we must survive,
the losses we must endure and accept,
the times we are accused falsely,
and must rise again from the ashes.

Be as brave as you can be,
fight with courage, kindness, compassion,
   and forgiveness.
Love with all your might,
give each other strength,
and remember how much I love you,
and how proud I am of you. Always!

With all my heart and love,
Mommy/D.S.

A TOUS LES FRANÇAIS

La France a perdu une bataille!
Mais la France n'a pas perdu la guerre!

Des gouvernants de rencontre ont pu capituler, cédant à la panique, oubliant l'honneur, livrant le pays à la servitude. Cependant, rien n'est perdu!

Rien n'est perdu, parce que cette guerre est une guerre mondiale. Dans l'univers libre, des forces immenses n'ont pas encore donné. Un jour, ces forces écraseront l'ennemi. Il faut que la France, ce jour-là, soit présente à la victoire. Alors, elle retrouvera sa liberté et sa grandeur. Tel est mon but, mon seul but!

Voilà pourquoi je convie tous les Français, où qu'ils se trouvent, à s'unir à moi dans l'action, dans le sacrifice et dans l'espérance.

Notre patrie est en péril de mort.
Luttons tous pour la sauver!

VIVE LA FRANCE !

18 JUIN 1940

C. de Gaulle

GÉNÉRAL DE GAULLE

Translation of General Charles de Gaulle's message (on posters around Paris) on June 18, 1940, when France became occupied by the Germans:

TO ALL FRENCH PEOPLE:

France has lost a battle!

But France did not lose the war!

Opportunistic governors have capitulated, giving in to panic, forgetting honor, delivering the country into slavery. However, nothing is lost!
Nothing is lost, because this war is a world war. In the Free World, immense forces have not given in. One day, those forces will crush the enemy. On that day, France must be present for victory. And France will then reclaim her freedom and grandeur. That is my goal, my only goal!
That is why I exhort all French people, wherever they may be, to unite with me in action, in sacrifice, and in hope.
Our country is in peril of death.
Let us all fight to save her!

LONG LIVE FRANCE!

Charles de Gaulle

'Courage [is] nothing less than the power to overcome danger, misfortune, fear, injustice, while continuing to affirm inwardly that life with all its sorrows is good.'

— DOROTHY THOMPSON

1

Delphine Lambert, a dark-haired, serious young woman, was reading *Le Figaro* intently in her apartment on the rue du Cherche-Midi on the Left Bank in Paris, on New Year's Day. She was reading a list carefully, as she did every year on that day, and had for several years. At twenty-nine, a political journalist and historian, she had two books to her credit that had done well, and frequently published articles in the press. Her long straight hair concealed part of her face as she pored over the newspaper, as Georges Poitier, the man she lived with, watched her and smiled. He had already guessed what she was reading. She had been chasing a dream since she was seventeen years old.

'What are you looking for?' he asked her gently. The list was published twice a year, on New Year's Day, and the fourteenth of July.

'You know . . . my grandmother,' she answered without looking up, not wanting to lose her place. There were five hundred names on the list, and she feared that the name she hoped to see wouldn't be on it yet again. It hadn't been so far, despite all of Delphine's efforts for the past dozen years, and she had worked tirelessly on the project. 'How long are they going to wait?' she muttered, fearing disappointment again. Her grandmother, Gaëlle de Barbet Pasquier, was ninety-five years old, and she was far less concerned about it than her granddaughter, to whom it had become a sacred cause. The list was of the upcoming recipients of the Légion d'Honneur, the most distinguished award in France.

Gaëlle had never expected to be decorated, and had none of the aspirations Delphine had for her, and thought it entirely unnecessary. Delphine insisted it was only right. The entire family knew how hard Delphine had worked to get her grandmother exonerated and recognized. Gaëlle was at peace about her life. The events she would have been acknowledged for were all so long ago, during the war. They were chapters of her life that were a distant memory now. Gaëlle rarely thought about it, except when Delphine questioned her, which she seldom did anymore. She knew the whole story, and her grandmother's bravery had been a powerful motivating force in her life, and an inspiration to her. Her grandmother was a shining example of everything Delphine thought a human being should be. And whether the government came to its senses, righted the wrongs of the past, and honored her or not, she was a hero in Delphine's eyes, and had been to countless others during the Occupation of France seventy-nine years before.

And then, as she read, Delphine sat still for an instant, and her eyes flew open wide. She read it again, to be sure she had seen it correctly, and she looked at Georges across the breakfast table with amazement.

'Oh my God . . . it's there . . . she's on it!' It had finally happened. All her letters and years of

2

careful research, and haranguing every member of the chancellery she could lay hands on, had finally done it. Her grandmother was being decorated with the distinguished Legion of Honor Medal, as a knight.

There were tears in Delphine's eyes as she looked at Georges, and her hand was shaking as she showed him the newspaper. Gaëlle de Barbet Pasquier. She read it over and over to be sure there was no mistake. It was there at last. He smiled broadly at her, and leaned over to kiss her, knowing how hard she had worked for that. And her grandmother knew it too, and had always said it was a futile project. And now it had finally happened, thanks to Delphine.

'Bravo! Good work,' he said, proud of her. There was no question that her grandmother was an amazing woman, and now the world would know it, as her countrymen recognized her.

Delphine got up from the table a minute later to call her. She could hardly wait to get her on the phone and tell her. She was sure that her grandmother hadn't bothered to read the paper that morning, or pounce on it as she had. Gaëlle hadn't been optimistic about it. She had always said it would never be possible. And Delphine had proved her wrong. Persistence had finally won the prize.

Her hands were still shaking as she called the cellphone she had given her grandmother, and it went straight to voicemail, as it did most of the time.

'She never uses the cellphone I gave her,'

Delphine complained to Georges over her shoulder. Her grandmother claimed it was too complicated and she didn't need it, and preferred to use her phone at home. Delphine called that number next, and let it ring for a long time, in case she was busy or in the bath. There was no answer on that line either, the message machine was off, and Delphine went back to the breakfast table in total frustration. She couldn't wait to tell her that it had finally happened.

'She probably went to church this morning,' Georges reminded her.

'Or she's walking the dog. I'll try her again in a few minutes.' But she had no greater success ten minutes or half an hour later. Delphine didn't know how she would contain herself until she reached her, and she finally called her mother instead, who was as thrilled as her daughter and burst into tears when she heard the news. It had been their fondest hope for her, however modest she was about her accomplishments. And it frustrated both of them not to be able to find her. But despite her age, Gaëlle was healthy and independent, an early riser, and usually had plans that took her out for the day or the evening. She was in remarkably good shape, of sound mind and body, and she enjoyed seeing friends, going to museums or the theater, or taking long walks with her dog in her neighborhood or along the Seine.

'I'll call her later,' Delphine told her mother, and went back to stare at the list again, to make sure that her grandmother's name was still there and it hadn't been an illusion. It was the culmination of a dream, for all of them, and so greatly deserved by Gaëlle.

★ ★ ★

Gaëlle Pasquier had risen early that morning, as she always did. She did her stretching exercises, made toast and a large cup of café au lait, which she savored with pleasure, enjoying her daily habits. She bathed and brushed her well-cut snow-white hair, which she wore in a chic bob that framed her aristocratic features, and then dressed to visit her friend Louise. They both lived in the seventh arrondissement, and it was a healthy walk from the Place du Palais Bourbon, where Gaëlle lived in a small but elegant apartment, to Louise's home on the rue de Varenne. Gaëlle's neighborhood was fashionable, but the building wasn't showy. She had beautiful paintings, and the apartment was decorated with handsome antiques. The atmosphere she created was warm and inviting, and when she went out, she took her small long-haired brown dachshund Josephine with her. Gaëlle and the dog were inseparable, her grandchildren had given it to her, and Josephine was instantly ecstatic when she saw her leash and Gaëlle put it on her, talking to her gently, and promising her a nice walk.

Despite her age, Gaëlle lived alone and had no problem doing so. A housekeeper came in the daytime during the week, but she cooked her own dinner, and as often as possible went out with friends. She had finally retired seven years

5

before at eighty-eight, and had been reluctant to do so. She had loved her job as curator of a small, distinguished museum that she had helped establish and had been devoted to for almost fifty years.

She saw all the important new art exhibits in Paris, and usually went with her friend Louise, who was ten years younger, and in excellent health too. Louise had a daughter who lived in India and a son in Brazil, so she was grateful for Gaëlle's company, and the two women had been friends for fifty-seven years, since Gaëlle came back to France, after living in New York for sixteen years. Louise had been a patron of the museum Gaëlle had helped to set up, and they had been devoted friends and allies ever since.

Gaëlle had two daughters, one in New York and one in Paris, and three grandchildren. She was luckier than Louise, with family nearby. Louise only saw her children and grandchildren once a year when she traveled to see them, but was a cheerful person nonetheless. Her husband had been in the diplomatic corps, and they had lived abroad in their youth too.

Gaëlle's older daughter was an investment banker and financial wizard like her late father, in New York. And her younger daughter, Daphne, was an obstetrician, married to a cardiologist, and they both loved their work. They were busy but invited Gaëlle to join them whenever she wished. She always said she didn't want to intrude on them, and managed to keep busy with her own activities and friends, most of whom were younger than she, since few people her age were as active as she was, and still as engaged in the world.

Gaëlle's granddaughter, Delphine, was a journalist, her younger brother was in medical school, studying to become a doctor like their parents, and the youngest grandson was in business school at HEC, the best school of its kind. Gaëlle was proud of all of them.

She had fun with Louise, and they planned activities and trips together and occasionally went away for weekends, to see an art exhibit in Rome or an opera in Vienna, or to attend some cultural event in London or Madrid, or to walk on the boardwalk in Deauville. Gaëlle still managed to lead an interesting life, more so at times even than her younger friends. She walked with a firm step, as she headed toward Louise's home on the rue de Varenne, with Josephine on her leash, trotting along beside her. Gaëlle always liked the idea of a new year, and said it gave her much to look forward to. She had a positive attitude about life, and lived in the present rather than the past. She saw no benefit in dwelling on what lay behind her and preferred to look ahead.

She still had a lithe figure, and an eye for fashion, although she dressed conservatively and appropriately for her age. And something about her style and the way she put herself together was decidedly French, despite the sixteen years she had lived in the States. She was unmistakably Parisian to her core.

When Gaëlle reached Louise's street, she walked past the Rodin Museum and Matignon,

7

and stopped in front of the heavy old doors, painted a shiny dark green, outside Louise's home. She lived in one of the grand old eighteenth-century houses with an interior courtyard, carriage stalls that had been turned into garages, an elegant home, and a well-tended garden. The guardian opened the heavy outer doors when Gaëlle pounded the brass knocker, and greeted her politely. And a maid answered when she walked up the front steps and rang the doorbell of the house. She left her coat in the front hall, and took off Josephine's leash, who bounded into the living room where Louise was sitting by the fire with her impeccably groomed white Pekingese Fifi at her feet. The two dogs were thrilled to see each other and began playing immediately, and Louise smiled broadly when Gaëlle walked in.

'Happy New Year!' Gaëlle said to her friend, as she bent to kiss her, and then sank into the comfortable chair next to hers. They had spent many a pleasant afternoon and evening in front of the fireplace in those two chairs, talking about the museum, their children, or their latest plans.

'Congratulations!' Louise responded with a look of obvious delight for Gaëlle.

'What for?' Gaëlle looked startled, with no idea what she meant. 'Being alive at ninety-five for another new year?' she said, laughing. 'In that case, congratulations to you too,' although Louise was only eighty-five. She was smaller and rounder than Gaëlle, and looked cozy and grandmotherly, and more her age, although she was lively too, which was why they enjoyed each other, and the two dogs were chasing around the room, Josephine having absconded with one of Fifi's toys.

'You didn't read the paper this morning?' Louise asked her. It was the first thing she did every day, and both women were current on world events and well informed. They read all the latest books, and shared them. Daphne always said her mother put her to shame, since as a busy physician she had no time to read novels, only medical journals. Gaëlle was a voracious reader, as was Louise.

'I hate reading the paper over breakfast,' Gaëlle commented. 'It depresses me, all the tragedies around the world, the crimes against humanity and natural disasters. I didn't bother today.'

'You should have,' Louise said cryptically, visibly pleased for her friend.

'Did the president have another affair? Did I miss the latest scandal?' Gaëlle asked her, looking amused.

'No, my dear,' Louise said fondly. 'Then I am particularly pleased to be the first to congratulate you, as Madame Chevalière.' Gaëlle stared at her for a minute expressionlessly, unable to believe it.

'You're not serious. You can't be. Poor Delphine has been hounding the chancellery for years, but I never thought it would be possible.' Louise knew that Gaëlle had worked for the Resistance in her teens and risked her own life heroically during the war. And then had been falsely accused of collaborating with the Germans. It was a shadow that had followed her

9

all her life, which her granddaughter had fought valiantly to dispel and clear her name. And finally she had.

'Well, apparently you've been cleared. Whatever Delphine said to convince them worked. You're getting the honor and recognition you deserve.' Louise was visibly proud of her, as she knew Delphine would be. She must be over the moon.

'How do you know that what they said isn't true?' Gaëlle asked her sadly, remembering back so many years. 'Maybe I've been lying to you.'

'I've never doubted what you told me. I know you. It's justice, Gaëlle. For everything you did.'

Gaëlle sat silently, staring into the fire for a quiet moment, and then looked at her friend. 'It was all so long ago. What does it matter now? I've always known the truth. And there were so many lives I couldn't save, or change . . . ' *Like Rebekah's*, she thought to herself. It had all started with Rebekah, the friend she'd lost when they were both seventeen. She still had a wisp of her hair ribbon in a little leather box in her desk, and she looked at it from time to time . . . Rebekah . . . her beloved friend.

'I should call Delphine to thank her,' Gaëlle said in a voice filled with memories. 'She worked so hard on this.' Gaëlle was overwhelmed by the news, and Louise could see it, as she gently reached out and patted her hand.

'You deserve it, Gaëlle,' Louise repeated reassuringly. 'You have nothing to feel guilty about. You did everything you could, for all of them.'

Gaëlle nodded, lost in thought. She only wished that that were true.

2

In December 1940, six months after the Germans occupied France, Gaëlle de Barbet had turned sixteen a few weeks before. She lived with her parents in the family château at Valencin, in the countryside outside Lyon. Her brother Thomas was studying at the École Polytechnique in Paris, and was two years older than she.

Life had been difficult since the war had begun fifteen months before, food was growing scarce, and the Occupation had been stressful for everyone. Her brother reported that there were German soldiers and officers all over Paris, and they were enforcing strict rules for the Parisians, and curfews for everyone at eight P.M. There were checkpoints to verify people's ID papers, everyone over the age of sixteen had to carry a national ID card, and two months earlier, in October, an edict called the 'Statut des Juifs' had made clear the occupying army's position about Jews. Many or even most Jewish French citizens had lost their jobs, as they were excluded from the army and government positions. Jewish journalists had been fired, and were banned from liberal professions. Many Jewish students had been expelled from the universities, and large numbers of Jews had been arrested, without reason, as undesirables. Detention camps had sprung up in the countryside, where Jewish families were being held, and their businesses and homes were seized by the Germans. The atmosphere was one of fear and unrest in the cities, though less so near Lyon, where the persecution of Jews was less acute than what Gaëlle's brother reported in Paris. And their father had sternly told Gaëlle not to linger on her way to school, and not to talk to the soldiers, although her ID papers identified her as a Catholic. They were aristocrats who had lived in the region for three hundred years, and the occupying army had no quarrel with them. And her father continued to oversee their estate and tenant farms without problem. The wealthier Jews in Lyon had not been touched so far. But her father had told Gaëlle that the Jews would be wise to move before trouble started in the region. It all seemed unreal and hard to believe. But nothing unpleasant had happened to the Jewish families they were acquainted with.

Gaëlle's closest friend was Rebekah Feldmann, whose father was the richest and most respected local banker. Their family had come from Germany originally, but the Feldmanns had been in Lyon for three generations, and had nothing to fear, or so they thought. Gaëlle had reported to Rebekah what her father had said, and Rebekah told Gaëlle her parents had discussed it too, but her father wasn't worried. In fact, several of the German officers deposited their money in her father's bank. But they'd all heard rumors of poorer Jewish families being forced from their homes in other towns, and of the detention camps in the area. Neither of the girls had heard of anyone they knew who'd been sent there, and for the moment it was all whispers and gossip.

It was no secret that the Feldmanns were far more prosperous than the Barbets, whose fortune had been dwindling slowly for years. Gaëlle had overheard her father say that they were land rich and cash poor, but they had everything they needed, and their château was one of the oldest and finest in the region. And aside from her parents' warning not to talk to the soldiers, they hadn't curbed Gaëlle's activities, and she was still riding to school on her bike every day, and stopped to meet Rebekah on the way. Gaëlle always tried to leave enough time to spend a few minutes in the Feldmann kitchen, where the cook and two maids served them freshly baked croissants and brioches, and rolls filled with melted chocolate. It was Gaëlle's favorite time of the day, and their friendly cook always gave them a few extra rolls to take to school with them. The two girls had been best friends since nursery school.

Rebekah had two younger brothers who were twelve and fourteen, and a five-year-old sister, Lotte, who Rebekah insisted was a pest, but Gaëlle had loved her since she was a baby, and Lotte worshipped Gaëlle. And her brothers went to the same school they did. The Feldmanns had a large home, not as big as the Barbets' château, but much fancier, with beautiful furniture, art, and decorations, and Rebekah's mother bought beautiful clothes in Paris, and wore jewelry and furs. Gaëlle loved visiting them, they always made her feel so welcome. Her own mother was

13

shy, more reserved, and somewhat austere. Gaëlle had more fun at Rebekah's house than she did at her own. Before Thomas left for university, he loved to tease both girls, but had been far more serious for the past year, and concerned about the Occupation. He and their father talked about it for hours whenever he came home, and now he spent little time with Gaëlle, whom he treated like a child.

Two weeks before Christmas, she headed to Rebekah's house on the way to school, and as she rounded the bend that brought the Feldmanns' house into view, she saw two police trucks parked outside, and a flock of gendarmes standing beside it. When she slowed to see what was going on before she approached, she saw Rebekah's father dragged from their home by two of the policemen, with his wife being pulled by two more, as she clung to Lotte's hand, and the terrified five-year-old was screaming. They pushed the two boys down the stairs, and they landed in a heap at the bottom, where two more gendarmes threw them into one of the trucks, and then she saw Rebekah, with her long blond hair flying, she hadn't had time yet to braid it, and one of the soldiers tossed her into the truck like a rag doll. She was a slight girl, and her hair was the same color as Gaëlle's. People at school often said they looked like sisters, although Gaëlle was taller, but just as slim. And for an instant as the gendarme grabbed her, her eyes had met Gaëlle's, and then she was flung into the truck and disappeared. And Gaëlle saw one of the men take the elegant homburg from Mr.

Feldmann's head, throw it to the ground, and crush it under his boot. She heard him say, 'You won't need that where you're going.'

Gaëlle's heart was pounding as she watched the scene with horror, not daring to approach, and a moment later she saw the trucks pull away, and a police captain's car follow. She wanted to run after them but knew she couldn't. It was impossible to understand why French gendarmes and local policemen were dragging them from their home. They weren't German soldiers but their fellow countrymen. She was crying a moment later when she rode her bike up to the house and ran up the back stairs and into the kitchen. The cook and both maids looked terrified, and there was the smell of burning baked goods coming from the oven, as no one moved.

'What happened? Where are they taking them?' Gaëlle shouted at them, sobbing, and the cook turned on her in a fury.

'Get out of here! Go! You don't belong here! Go now!' She pointed to the door and spoke to her in a way she never had before, and Gaëlle could see that the two maids were crying. They had all been told that they would be arrested for working for Jews if they did not leave the house immediately, and the gendarmes had said they would be back later. There was the sound of footsteps running upstairs, as the other maids gathered up their things to leave.

'Where are they going?' Gaëlle asked the cook in desperation.

'I don't know . . . to detention probably. They

should have left before this,' she said, looking distraught herself, and slightly less fierce with Gaëlle than she had been at first. 'You must go now, and don't come back. The officers said that Germans are taking over the house this afternoon. The Feldmanns won't return.'

'I have to find her,' Gaëlle said, looking frantic.

'No, you don't,' the heavyset woman said, grabbing her arm roughly and shaking her. 'Leave it alone. They won't let you see her.'

'How could they do this to them?' Gaëlle choked on sobs as the cook who had always been so kind to her pushed her toward the door.

'They're Jews. Forget you know them. You can only get trouble from this. Now go — ' She shoved her firmly out the door then and locked it behind her, and Gaëlle stumbled down the stairs, grabbed her bike, and rode away, shocked by everything that had happened, and worried sick for her friend. The police had treated them all so roughly, as though they were so much garbage they were throwing into the back of the truck. And Gaëlle had no idea where they'd gone. She was so shaken by it that she fell off her bike twice on the way to school, tore her dress, and arrived late with a scraped arm and bleeding knee. She looked a mess.

'What happened to you?' a boy she'd never liked asked her as she limped in, looking dazed.

'I had an accident on the way to school,' she said, and didn't want to tell him what had happened to the Feldmanns. She didn't trust anyone now. In an instant, everything had changed.

'Where's Rebekah?' he asked her as she

16

started to walk away, and she didn't answer, and then murmured over her shoulder.

'I don't know. Maybe she's sick.' *Or dead*, Gaëlle thought with a wave of terror. She had to find her, no matter what the cook had said. She wasn't going to forget her, or any of her family. Wherever they were being held, she was going to locate them.

She sat blindly through school all day, and afterward grabbed her bike and rode home alone, and went to find her father as soon she got there. He was just coming back from the stables, leading a lame horse. She had ridden past the Feldmanns' home and had seen soldiers and an officer parked outside, and some of the men were carrying trunks and suitcases. They were moving into the house.

She told her father what had happened that morning, and he frowned as he listened.

'Did anyone see you there? The soldiers, I mean?' he asked harshly.

'No, I waited until they left.' But she didn't tell him Rebekah had seen her, and for an instant their eyes had met, before they threw her into the truck. 'Then I went in and talked to the cook. She didn't know where they took them.'

'To a detention camp,' he said with certainty, and he was visibly shocked too. He had been afraid of something like this. He had heard stories like it happening in Paris, but not in Lyon yet, or the surrounding area. And if they were taking people like the Feldmanns, no Jew would be safe anywhere. 'I don't want you going back to the house, or trying to find out where she is.

17

You can't go to see her, Gaëlle. Is that understood? They won't tell you anyway. And it's dangerous to even ask.'

'I have to find her, Papa,' Gaëlle said miserably.

'No, you don't!' he shouted at her. 'Now go to your room.' Gaëlle was crying when she walked into the house, and lay down on her bed, as the hideous scene she'd watched that morning played again and again in her head. And her mother was just as stern with her that night. She knew how much the two girls loved each other, but that was over now. All it could bring was trouble to them if Gaëlle persisted in attempting to locate her.

'Promise me you won't try to find her,' her mother said, looking pale and sick. She didn't know the Feldmanns well, except from school events, but it was obvious that they were dangerous people to know now. And if they'd been taken away, it was reasonable to assume they'd be sent to a detention camp, where Jews were being held, or even a labor camp somewhere, possibly in Germany or the east. But for now, the Jews being rounded up were being detained in France. But there was talk, and rumors, of worse to come.

Gaëlle refused to come downstairs for dinner, and when her parents insisted, she couldn't eat. There was no school the next day, so she stayed in bed, thinking about Rebekah. And two days later, she heard two of her father's tenant farmers talking about Jews being picked up the week before, and taken to Chambaran camp in

18

Vienne, thirty-five miles south of Lyon and eleven miles from Valencin. Gaëlle felt as though God had wanted her to have that information, and the following day, instead of riding her bike to school, she rode almost two hours into the countryside on back roads, and she saw an encampment that she had never seen before. It was a vast area, surrounded by high metal and wood fences, with some huts and tents inside, and a large barn or stables, where she could see people coming in and out, carrying their belongings. There were men and women and children of all ages milling around, and guards with guns patrolling them, but there were not as many as she had feared there would be, and she saw no dogs with the soldiers, and no guard towers, which was a relief.

She rode along a rutted lane on her bike, and no one noticed her, and at one point the narrow country lane came close to the fence, and she stood watching for a while, and by sheer miracle she saw Michel, one of Rebekah's brothers. She waved to him, and he saw her and approached the fence.

'What are you doing here?' he said, looking shocked.

'I came to see how you are. Where's Rebekah?' He smiled at the familiar face with the long blond braids, although at home he would have teased and tormented her with pleasure.

'She's inside, with Mama and Lotte. Papa had some money they didn't find, and he paid someone to get us a place inside the barn. It's freezing cold outside at night.' It was nearly

19

Christmas, and there was ice on the ground.

'Can I see her?' Gaëlle asked nervously.

'You're crazy to be here. If they catch you, they'll throw you in with us.'

'No, they won't. I'm not a Jew,' she said sensibly, and he nodded and promised to tell his sister she was there. Gaëlle waited ten minutes and wondered if he was coming back, and then she saw her, in a thin dress with no coat. She hadn't had time to put on her coat when they took them. Only her father had been wearing one, and he had given it to his wife when they arrived at the camp, and Lotte was huddled under it with her in the barn. The boys had sweaters on, and Rebekah only the wool dress she was going to wear to school. She was shivering when she approached the fence with a look of wonder to see Gaëlle. She thought her brother was playing a joke on her when he told her Gaëlle was there.

'You shouldn't have come,' Rebekah said, seeming frightened, as Gaëlle took her coat off hurriedly, and pushed it through the wires at her. Rebekah grabbed it as it fell to the ground. 'You'll get sick,' she protested, feeling guilty for taking it, but it was warm, and she was grateful to have it.

'Put it on,' Gaëlle insisted, as their eyes met and held, and everything they felt for each other was there. 'Don't be stupid. You need it more than I do. I'll come back tomorrow,' Gaëlle promised.

'What if they catch you?' Rebekah asked with a look of terror.

'They won't. I love you, you stupid thing,' Gaëlle said, and Rebekah smiled.

'You're the stupid one for coming here. I love you too. Now go before they catch you.' She had put on the coat and was shivering less violently.

'See you tomorrow.' Gaëlle smiled at her and got on her bicycle.

'It's all right if you don't come,' Rebekah said, hoping that she would. And then Gaëlle turned her bike around and pedaled away, trying to look normal as she did, but no one saw her.

It took her two hours to get home, and she was shaking from the cold when she got there. She went to her room before anyone could see that she had come home without her coat. And she sneaked up to the attic that night, to find some of her old clothes so she could bring a coat for Lotte the next day. She found one that looked as though it might fit, and she rolled it up as small as she could to put it in the basket of her bike. The coat was black velvet with an ermine collar, and Gaëlle could remember wearing it one Christmas a long time ago, when her grandmother was still alive and had come to visit.

She was quiet at dinner that night, but her parents didn't seem to notice. There was nothing much to say these days, all the news was bad. Her mother had had a letter from Thomas, and most of it had been blacked out by the censors, but her mother said it sounded like he was fine.

And the next day Gaëlle skipped school again and went back to see Rebekah. She was outside watching the fence, and came over as soon as she saw Gaëlle approach and stop under a tree. She took the coat for Lotte, and Gaëlle gave her some apples and chocolate bars and some chunks of bread wrapped in a napkin, in case they were hungry. She hadn't dared take more, but Rebekah grabbed the food gratefully. She was wearing Gaëlle's coat, which was too long for her, and she said the conditions in the camp were awful, people were sick and cold and had too little to eat. They just gave them soup and stale bread and a few vegetables, and people were fighting over food. And there were only outhouses and far too few of them. They had met a few families they knew at the camp, and two of her father's employees from the bank, who'd been shocked to find the Feldmanns there. It told them just how bad things were.

And from then on Gaëlle rode to the camp directly after school every day. She stopped eating her lunch and brought it all to Rebekah. Going there got her home close to dinnertime every night, and she told her mother they had kept her at school to help with the younger children and clean up afterward, and she believed her. Gaëlle went faithfully every day, except on Christmas day and one week in February, when she was sick with the flu. And miraculously none of the guards at the camp ever noticed her. There weren't many of them, and most of them were young. And given the nature of their prisoners, mostly families with children, they weren't particularly vigilant and focused their attention on the residents milling around, not on the fence.

It was May, and Gaëlle had been visiting Rebekah for five months, when a guard spotted her for the first time. Gaëlle had just passed a pale blue ribbon through the fence to her, it was the same color as their eyes, which were the same, like their pale blond hair. The ribbon snagged on the fence as Rebekah took it, and a little piece was left on the barbed wire. Gaëlle snatched it back and put it in her pocket, as the guard shouted at her to stop, and Gaëlle froze.

'Hey! What are you doing here?' he said, pointing his gun down, and trying to sound fierce. He was barely older than they were, and seemed like someone they would have known at school.

'I just stopped to ask what this is,' Gaëlle said innocently, smiling at him. Her heart felt as though it would fly out of her chest, it was pounding so hard.

'It's a summer camp for families,' he answered, smiling at her. She was a pretty girl, and so was Rebekah, but he paid no attention to her, since he knew she was a Jew. 'Do you live near here?' She nodded, and he pointed his gun back down the path. 'Then go home. This place isn't for you, it's for poor people. They send them here from the cities to get some fresh air.'

Gaëlle tried to look as though she believed him, and headed down the path without glancing back at Rebekah, and she heard the guard tell her roughly to go back to the others in the barn. It was too dangerous to turn back, so she didn't. The camp was out of sight when Gaëlle stopped to catch her breath and calm down. She pulled

23

the little piece of blue ribbon out of her pocket and held it in her fingers for a minute, thinking of Rebekah, and she was glad nothing worse had happened. It seemed incredible that they had already been there for five months, and more people were arriving all the time, but they hadn't sent them anywhere. They were just keeping them at the camp. Rebekah said that there were rumors that they would be sent away, but nothing had happened yet. Rebekah's father had tried to meet the commandant to find out where they would be sent, but he wouldn't see him. And the population of the camp had grown from hundreds to thousands by June. And Gaëlle and the others had noticed that several of their classmates had vanished from school. One by one the Jewish families were disappearing, and no one talked about where they'd gone. No one knew for sure, and it was too dangerous to ask.

And that summer the commanding officer of the local German army took over the château. Gaëlle's mother took to her bed as soon as they were notified, and her father warned Gaëlle again to steer clear of the soldiers. And when the time came, and the officers moved in, the Barbets were moved upstairs to maids' rooms in the attic, while the officers lived downstairs in their rooms. And the family's servants worked for the officers and soldiers now. The Barbets were allowed to come downstairs at night to cook their food. Agathe, Gaëlle's mother, stayed in her room almost all the time. Her nerves were shattered from living in constant fear, under the same roof with the occupying army.

The commanding officer was polite, and at her father's instructions, Gaëlle stayed upstairs most of the time too, except when she went to school, or went to see Rebekah, which she still did almost every day. She had brought her a few cotton dresses when the weather got warmer, and some for Lotte. Rebekah said her mother cried all the time, and had had a cough since the winter that wouldn't go away. And they had Mr. Feldmann serving food, and cleaning the latrines with the other men. It was hard to imagine, and Gaëlle knew there were German officers living in the Feldmanns' house too. But at least the ones at the château had been nice to them so far. One of them had left some chocolates for her in the kitchen, which her father wouldn't let her take upstairs. Her father, Raphaël, was out frequently now visiting their farms and tenant farmers. He said he had to work with them, since they were short of men. And he was relieved that the commanding officer kept his men in good control. No one had bothered Gaëlle so far.

It was a long, hot summer, and Gaëlle went to see Rebekah whenever she could. Agathe was sick a lot, and Gaëlle had to stay to help her. And Rebekah said that her mother was sick all the time too, a lot of the people in the camp were. There were several doctors, but no medicine. And Gaëlle noticed how thin Rebekah had gotten, she was skin and bones, but she wore the blue hair ribbon all the time. Gaëlle had brought her a red one too, but Rebekah preferred the pale blue one, and Gaëlle still had the little piece of it at home in a drawer.

In September, Gaëlle started her last year of school. After she passed her baccalaureate degree the following June, she was supposed to go to university in Paris in the fall, but her father had already told her that she wouldn't be going. He didn't want her in Paris alone, with German soldiers everywhere. It was bad enough having Thomas there, but not a girl. He said she would have to wait until after the Occupation to go to university, and he needed her at home, to take care of her mother. Thomas had only come home for a few weeks in August, and then went back to Paris. He had a job in a restaurant, to help pay for his expenses. They had no money coming in, since all the food they grew and normally sold was being requisitioned by the Germans, so they had nothing to sell and barely enough to eat. Their old housekeeper Apolline kept something back from the officers' meals occasionally, and hid it in a drawer for them, but there was never enough, and they were all growing thinner by the day.

Conditions in the camp got worse as the weather turned cold again, and it was a hard winter, and snowed early. In December, the Feldmanns had been at the camp for a year. It seemed like an eternity, and the rumors were continuing that the detainees would be sent away, but nothing changed. There were five thousand people in the camp by then, in terrible circumstances. Some had been sent there from Paris and Marseilles, and there were other camps like it springing up everywhere, as more and more Jews were taken from their homes and ordinary lives and sent to camps, waiting to be shipped to labor camps. Their final destinations were still unknown, and a source of worry for all.

Both girls had turned seventeen by then, and Rebekah asked Gaëlle one day if she thought life would ever be normal again, and Gaëlle assured her that it would. It had to be. The insanity couldn't go on forever. She wanted to believe it too. But at least none of the Feldmanns had gotten seriously sick, and hadn't been sent anywhere. Gaëlle was beginning to wonder if they were going to just keep them there. At least she could see Rebekah almost every day, and there were so many people in the camp now that the guards paid even less attention to the fence. In the warm weather during the summer, Gaëlle had sat on the ground sometimes, holding hands with Rebekah through the fence while they talked, and a few times her brothers had come to say hello too. Their parents didn't know that Gaëlle was still visiting them. Nor did the Barbets. Gaëlle's mother no longer cared what was happening beyond her room, and her father was never there, always doing something somewhere else on the estate. It left Gaëlle free to do what she chose.

It was still freezing cold in March 1942, fifteen months after they'd gotten to the camp. Rebekah had a bad cold when Gaëlle went to see her, and she looked like she had a fever. Gaëlle kissed her cheek through the fence, and felt how hot she was, although Rebekah was shivering severely. And two days later Gaëlle was sick too, and must have caught it from her. Her mother made her stay in bed for a week, and the housekeeper brought her soup to their rooms in the attic. Gaëlle was weak when she finally got on her bike to visit Rebekah at the camp on the first day she was strong enough to do so. Her legs felt like cement as she rode her bike, and it took her longer than usual. Things looked different when she arrived at the camp. She noticed it from the distance, and wasn't sure why, and as she got close to the fence, she realized with horror that the camp was empty. Everyone who had been detained there was gone, and there was no one she could ask where they'd been sent, possibly to another camp nearby, and Gaëlle wasn't sure how to find out. She was exhausted from the ride, after being sick for a week, and she stood there in silence, staring at the empty barn and tents, panicked over what had happened to them. And then finally she rode away, with tears streaming down her face. All she could think of was the last time she had seen Rebekah and kissed her, but she had never thought it was goodbye.

She stopped at a small café in the first village on the way back, and asked for a cup of tea. It was cold and she was shivering, and the woman who served her let her have it for free when Gaëlle said she'd had the flu, and then she casually asked the woman about the camp, which was why she had stopped there, hoping for news more than tea.

'What happened to all the people at the detention camp?' she asked innocently, and the woman frowned at her immediately.

'You shouldn't ask about that,' she said in a whisper. 'They're just Jews. They sent them away. They deported them last week. I hear they've started sending some of them to labor camps in the east. They're deporting them from Paris too. Good riddance. All they've done is bring trouble down on us. I'm glad they're gone. I hear they're bringing in more soon, but they won't keep them here long anymore. They put them on trains and shipped them out. I don't know why they put that camp here anyway. There are too many of them, and they breed disease.' She walked away then when a soldier sauntered in and ordered a beer, and a minute later Gaëlle got up and thanked her, put her empty cup on the bar, and rode away.

She cried all the way home that day, and when she got back to her room, she opened the drawer and took out the little wisp of blue ribbon from the one she'd given Rebekah the summer before. It was all she had left of her, just that tiny shred of satin, the same color as her eyes. Tears rolled down her cheeks as she put it away in the drawer, and she prayed that her friend was safe, and they would find each other again one day. She didn't know it, but it was a defining moment that would forever change her life.

3

The days after the Feldmanns and the others disappeared from the detention camp were a blur. Gaëlle feigned a relapse of the flu, and stayed in bed for another week, where she thought of Rebekah day and night, continued to pray for her safety, and cried herself to sleep. She looked as though she'd been sick for a year by the time she got out of bed. And her mother was no better. She had developed terrible migraine headaches, and rarely got up anymore. She couldn't cope with the collapse of her world as she knew it. She was terrified of the Germans, and everything she heard from Apolline, their housekeeper, when she brought her meals.

At her father's insistence, Gaëlle went back to school. She had to prepare for her baccalaureate exam in June, but there seemed to be no point to it, since he wouldn't let her go to university. And her brother Thomas said it was all different now anyway. Many of the professors, who had been Jewish, had disappeared and been sent away, along with the masses of Jews who were being picked up in all the cities and deported. They didn't stay long in the detention camps anymore and were being sent to labor camps in Germany and the east. And all of the Jewish students had long since been removed from Gaëlle's school as well. Only Christians were allowed to attend school. Jewish shops and businesses were closed, as their owners vanished. There was no pharmacy in their village now, and Gaëlle had to ride a long way to get medicine for her mother's headaches, and the only remedies she could find for her were the old natural ones, which didn't work anyway. Her mother was in pain all the time, and grew weak and pale from never going out. The doctor who came to see her said it was her nerves.

The commanding officer who had taken over the château offered to have her seen by one of the German doctors who was in the area to tend to their men, but Gaëlle's father had refused. He wouldn't let a German doctor touch her, no matter how obliging and seemingly well intentioned the commanding officer was. When he asked Gaëlle about her mother, she barely answered and scurried upstairs whenever he spoke to her. He left sweets and chocolates for them occasionally, and her mother said they only made her headache worse. Gaëlle couldn't swallow them, remembering what had happened to Rebekah and her family. There had been no news of them, and Gaëlle didn't expect to hear from her, and just hoped that they were all alive and well, and maybe even in a better place than the overcrowded detention camp where they had spent fifteen awful months, but she missed visiting her.

Gaëlle thought of her constantly and hoped to see her again soon, or hear where she'd gone. She passed her exams in June, and got decent grades, and in August Thomas came home for a visit, and told them tales of deportations in Paris, and horrific stories of some instances where they only took children. And the deportees were paraded through the streets, being marched to the railway stations with soldiers guarding them, as they dragged their belongings with them, and the men were frequently shot if they said anything impertinent to the soldiers, or tried to protect their wives and children. It made Gaëlle cry as she listened.

Thomas was relieved to see his friends again, and to be home for a few weeks. Like his parents and sister, he stayed out of the way of the soldiers, and sneaked out at night, despite warnings not to, to drink with his friends after curfew, and visit an old girlfriend of his in a nearby village. His father had cautioned him to be careful. No one could be trusted anymore, and the soldiers got rowdy at night and tormented the locals. But Thomas said he was used to it, and dealt with it all the time in Paris. They had all learned to live below the radar, and pass unnoticed. Gaëlle did that herself, keeping her eyes down, and going to her room in the attic whenever she came back to the château after doing errands for her parents. She was a quiet, good girl, and never caused them any trouble. And they still had no idea that she had spent fifteen months visiting Rebekah at the detention camp, and would have been horrified if they knew, but nothing bad had ever happened to her. The villages were still less dangerous than the cities, as long as one wasn't a Jew. And her father made no trouble for the commanding officer either, and kept out of the way, always somewhere on the estate until after dark, helping the farmers and making sure the produce they grew was given to the Germans. He occasionally sneaked some fruit or lettuce or vegetables, and potatoes, which he took directly to their rooms upstairs, and they ate it as quickly as possible, so there was no evidence of what he'd stolen.

And Apolline would throw away any trace of it the next day. She was loyal to the family, and to France, even though she was forced to work for the Germans now, whom she hated passionately. She had a son in the Resistance, which no one in the family knew, until he was shot and killed shortly after Thomas came home. They had known each other as boys, and Apolline was inconsolable, he was her only child. But she was proud of him too, for what he had done for France before his death. Others may have capitulated, but in her heart she never would. They had interrogated her after he was shot, but the commanding officer vouched for her, and she convinced them that she knew nothing of her son's activities, which was not entirely true, but they left her alone after that, to mourn him in peace.

Gaëlle heard her brother sneak out late one night, to join his friends. She peeked out her door, and saw him carrying a bottle of wine. He winked at her and put his finger to his lips. In many ways, although he was nineteen now, he was still a mischievous boy. When he was younger, he and his friends were always up to some prank. Now all they wanted to do was drink and talk, and share the rumors they heard of what was going on in nearby towns. He was going out with his friends that night, and she didn't blame him. She had no friends herself now that Rebekah was gone and she was finished with school. She had nothing to do except nurse her mother. She spent a lot of time reading and hiding in her room, to stay out of the soldiers' way, as her father had ordered her to do, and she wouldn't have dared sneak out at night like her brother. But he was older and bolder than she, and a man, and had less to risk.

She never heard him come in that night, and later assumed he had slipped back into his room after she fell asleep. She had been reading by candlelight, until it flickered out and she drifted off, and all she heard were her mother's screams in the morning when she woke up. Gaëlle rushed out of her room, and saw her father consoling her mother as she collapsed in his arms.

'What happened?' Gaëlle asked, and went to help him as a shiver of terror ran up her spine. She sensed instantly that it was Thomas.

'Your fool of a brother went out after curfew last night,' her father said through gritted teeth, with tears on his cheeks too. 'He must have gotten drunk. He ran his bicycle straight into an army truck on patrol. They hit him before they saw him. He was killed instantly.' It was such a senseless, stupid death, not a hero's death, but a boy's thoughtless meeting up with old friends to talk and kick up their heels as best they could. The commanding officer had given Raphaël the news early that morning, with his apologies and deep regret. He had lost his own son and daughter, and his wife, in a bombing raid in Germany, and his eyes had been damp when he told Raphaël the terrible news.

There were grim days afterward when they prepared Thomas's body for burial. Gaëlle helped her father wash him, and the commanding officer allowed them to bury him on the estate, after the priest said the funeral mass in the local church. Agathe could barely stand up at her son's funeral, and Gaëlle and Raphaël had to half carry her from the church, one of them on each side of her. And Apolline was there too, sobbing for the boy she had taken care of as a baby, who had died only days after her own son. Thomas's death was one of those terrible, needless casualties of the Occupation. There was some question that the soldiers driving the truck that hit him might have been drunk too. They were all about the same age. The commanding officer had looked into it, but found no conclusive evidence, and it didn't change anything. Gaëlle had lost her best friend and her brother, and Agathe didn't come out of her room again. She became rapidly too ill, and the doctor said there was nothing he could do for her. She didn't have the emotional stamina to cope with what they were living through. She became delirious at times, and would ask Gaëlle where her brother was, or if he was home yet, and Gaëlle stopped trying to explain it to her, and just said he was out. It was the most depressing summer of Gaëlle's life.

And the worst blow of all came in September. Gaëlle heard loud men's voices in the courtyard, and tried to see what was happening from her window and couldn't at first, and then her father came into view. He was wearing the clothes and boots he wore when he visited their farms, and worked the fields with the other farmers, and there were two men with him. He was deeply tanned from being outside all the time. There were soldiers shouting at him and pushing them, as they pointed rifles at all three men. She could hear her father saying something, but couldn't understand the words. She ran down the back stairs as quickly as she could, and looked out a tiny barred window, just in time to see them shoot her father and his body crumple to the ground in a pool of blood. They shot the others seconds later, and then dragged them out of sight, as other soldiers came running.

Gaëlle was so shocked, she didn't know what to think, except to wonder if they were going to kill her and her mother now too. She didn't know whether to run upstairs to protect her mother, or out to the courtyard to see if she could help her father, but when she saw them load his body onto the back of a truck, she knew for certain he was dead. She heard the word 'Resistance' spoken by the soldiers in their heavy German accents, but she couldn't believe her father had been part of it. He had been so adamant about their not doing anything to enrage the soldiers, keeping their heads down, and not getting involved with what was happening. He couldn't have been in the Resistance, but then she remembered all the times he hadn't been at home in the last year

36

and wondered if it was true.

In the end, she didn't dare go out into the courtyard, in case they killed her too. She tiptoed up the back stairs, went to check on her mother, who had slept through the gunshots, with some sleeping powder they had found for her, and Gaëlle went to her room to lie on her bed and wait for what would happen next. She couldn't believe she had just lost her father. It didn't seem real to her yet.

Apolline came up a little while later with her eyes brimming with tears, to check on her. Gaëlle sat up as soon as she saw her and the housekeeper hugged her as they both cried at the terrible losses they had suffered in this awful war.

'He was in the same cell as my son,' she whispered to Gaëlle, who pulled away from her, looking shocked. 'He was very brave.' Gaëlle couldn't believe it, and she was certain then that she and her mother would be next. Apolline whispered that she was afraid they would be too, but she said that if they tried to escape and were caught, it would be worse.

'What should I do?' Gaëlle said softly so no one could hear. 'Should we try to run away?' But where would they go? And her mother was too sick, mentally and physically, to go anywhere or for Gaëlle to move. And she knew of no one who would take them in. Her father had shared none of his Resistance contacts with her, or even the fact that he was engaging in illegal activities. He had been well aware of the dangers, and had risked them. None of them had any idea of what he'd been doing, except Apolline, who had heard it only once from her son, but she was a faithful, honorable woman, and would never have done anything to put Raphaël and his family in danger, or her son.

'Maybe they'll let you stay here,' she said hopefully, knowing how ill and disoriented Gaëlle's mother was. She was having fewer and fewer moments of lucidity, all she wanted to do was sleep now. The reality of their life and what was happening around her was just too much for her.

'I don't think they will,' Gaëlle said thoughtfully, but she couldn't abandon her mother and run. She had to stay with her till the end. Apolline went back to the kitchen, so they wouldn't suspect that she knew anything or had talked to Gaëlle, and she came back with their lunch a few hours later, and together they told her mother the terrible news. She didn't even scream this time, she just lay in her bed glassy-eyed, still under the influence of the sleeping powder, and they gave her more. Gaëlle hoped that if they came to kill her, she would be asleep in her bed. It would be better for her. She whimpered softly and drifted off to sleep, murmuring her husband's name.

Gaëlle was called to the commandant's office that afternoon, and there were two officers with him in the room. She tried not to look as overwhelmed by fear as she was. Her eyes met the commandant's bravely and he looked very grave.

'I know you must be aware of what happened

this morning. There was an unfortunate incident involving your father on one of the farms. They were hiding a family of Jews. I'm not certain that your father was aware of it, but the men who discovered it believed he was. They are exploring all the other farms now. They found a second family an hour ago. We are not certain if his farmers acted independently, or if he was in charge of a clandestine operation to smuggle Jews out of France. These are very serious crimes against the army of occupation, and your own country,' the commandant said severely. 'These are acts of treason against the law today.' Gaëlle said nothing, waiting for the death sentence they would impose on her. She fully expected them to take her outside and shoot her as they had her father that morning. She didn't even know where they had taken his body, or what she and her mother were going to do now without him. 'Were you aware of your father's activities, Mademoiselle de Barbet?' he asked her, looking deep into her eyes, and she looked very young with her slim childish figure, her big blue eyes, and blond hair in braids. She reminded him of his lost daughter every time he saw her and it tore at his heart, and it made him more inclined to be lenient with her, which the other officers didn't know. And he had liked her father too. At another time in history, they might have been friends.

'No, Commandant, I wasn't aware. He never told me,' she said in a shaking voice. He could see her shoulders tremble, although she faced him bravely. The others watched her for any sign of guilt. To them, the French had turned out to be extraordinary liars and capable of incredible acts of destruction and treachery while appearing innocent, even young girls her age. The Resistance was becoming a powerful and alarming force, which they were doing everything in their power to crush. The government had given up easily, without a fight, but its citizens were doing everything they could to undermine the Germans, and throw obstacles in their path wherever they could.

The commandant hesitated for a long moment and then nodded. He could see in her eyes that it was true. And she had known nothing about her father's activities in the Resistance until the soldiers killed him. She looked shocked as she stood in the room trembling, trying to be courageous. It was not guilt, he felt certain, but pure fear.

'I am aware of the state of your mother's health,' he said in a stern voice, 'and the hardship it would be for her to be sent elsewhere.' He doubted that she'd survive it, and so did Gaëlle. And he was sure that Agathe knew even less about her husband's activities, in the condition she was in. He would have never told her what he was up to, or it would have put her over the edge, where his sudden death was likely to send her now, as the commandant and Gaëlle both knew. 'Out of compassion for her, I will let you both continue to stay here. But I warn you, if there is even the slightest suspicion that you are engaged in subversive activities of any kind, you will both be removed and deported immediately. I recognize that this is your home, and we are very pleased to be here. But you must respect us, obey us, and follow the new laws in France.'

Gaëlle nodded silently. She had no intention of doing otherwise, and for her mother's sake, and even her own, she was more than willing to agree. Her mother would never have survived deportation, or prison, and Gaëlle did not want to face that either. Their rooms in the attic were the safest place for them to be, and she knew that it was what her father would want for them too. And without her father and brother, they had no one to protect them now. They were at the mercy of the occupying forces, and the Germans who had taken over their home. 'Do you agree?' the commandant asked her solemnly, and she responded respectfully. They had killed her father, but she and her mother had nowhere else to go.

'Yes, sir. I do,' she said, her eyes huge and her face pale as she looked at him.

'Very well, and you may hold a proper burial for your father in the cemetery on the estate.' The other two officers looked unhappy about that, and objected strenuously in German. He had been a criminal against the Reich, and he didn't deserve a hero's death. The commandant answered them in clipped tones and turned to Gaëlle again. 'Do it quickly and quietly. Is your mother well enough to attend?'

'I don't believe she is,' Gaëlle said seriously, and he nodded, and dismissed her from the room. She felt sick as she walked back to the top floor of the château, up the dark staircase that before the war only the servants had used, and she was obliged to use it now, while the army occupied the rest of the house. But she was grateful that he had spared their lives. All she wanted was peace for her mother now, she had already been through too much.

Gaëlle sat down on her bed and gave in to tears of relief and grief after the meeting. She had lost her father that morning, her brother a month before, and her mother was barely more than a ghost. And her beloved best friend was gone. Gaëlle was entirely alone in the world.

She went through some of her father's things that night while her mother was sleeping, after going to see the priest late that afternoon. He had heard what had happened to her father, news traveled fast. And several others had been shot that day on the estate, for concealing Jews, to spare them from being sent to deportation camps. But they had been sent anyway now, and the benefactors had been killed. They had paid a high price for courage and compassion, and the tides of evil could not be stemmed.

The priest had agreed to bury her father the next day, with a graveside service that only she would attend, at the commandant's request.

And as she went through Raphaël's books and papers, she came across a letter, and an envelope of money with it. It was a small amount, but he had put it aside in case something happened to him. It wouldn't get them far, but it had been the best he could do. And he had been well aware that if Gaëlle was reading the letter, he would already be dead, and he urged her to take care of her mother and to be careful, wise, and safe herself. He had written it only a month before, and made no reference to his activities in the Resistance, lest it incriminate her and her mother, but now she knew. She was devastated that he had died, but proud of him too. She wished that she had known before, and wondered if he could have helped the Feldmanns if she'd asked him to. But once they were in the detention camp, there was little anyone could do.

There had been a few escapes from the camps, but not many, and most of the internees were too frightened to resist or try to flee. A few young men had tried, but most had been shot and killed as an example to the others. And the camps were full of women and children, young boys, and many older men, heads of families, who thought that less resistance once captured would be less dangerous for their loved ones. And they were French after all, they weren't foreigners. They were citizens, and how could their own country turn on them in this way, and turn them over to the occupying forces to be deported? They were respectable people, many of them with good jobs and money, and fine homes, and had led exemplary lives. They were lawyers and doctors, bankers like Mr. Feldmann, and professional people who had been responsibly engaged in their communities. But they were Jews — the worst crime now of all. No one had fully understood until then how vast the hatred against them had grown. They were to be shunned and feared, and all association with

43

them avoided. Their money and property had been seized, their jobs and professions taken from them, and they had committed no crimes at all. It was impossible to understand.

Gaëlle put the envelope with the money under her mattress, determined not to use it for anything except medicine for her mother, or some unseen emergency she couldn't predict. It was all they had.

Apolline came to check on her again that night, and Gaëlle didn't tell her about the money. She trusted no one now, not even their faithful servant. They all had too much to lose, including their lives. And the next day she met the priest at their small chapel and cemetery, and they buried her father in an unmarked grave with a simple wood cross. She vowed to herself to bury him more respectfully after the war, but for now there was no other choice. At least they had returned his body to them, so they could bury him at home. She could have a headstone made for him later. They buried him next to her brother. It had been a summer of heavy losses.

Gaëlle turned eighteen two months later, and Apolline baked her a small loaf of bread, a great luxury now, and put a candle in it, and other than that, the day went unnoticed. She didn't mention it to her mother, who hadn't gotten up since her husband's death, and took the sleeping powder twice a day now, when Gaëlle brought it to her. Gaëlle herself never went far anymore. She took long walks on the estate and visited the farms occasionally. And she went into the village to get small things for her mother, and their food rations. She had to bicycle two villages away to a pharmacy, for the sleeping powder her mother used to avoid reality and lose herself in her own fantasy world, where nothing bad could touch her.

It was a lonely life for Gaëlle, and she was riding her bike back from the village late one afternoon, thinking about her father and brother. She missed them both. But she and her mother had food and a place to live, thanks to the mercy of the commandant, and she was grateful for that.

She was halfway home, when she saw a police truck outside a house, and gendarmes, and she slowed before they could see her, and got off the road for a moment. She didn't want to be questioned by them, and as she watched from the distance, she saw a familiar sight that brought back painful memories for her. A man and a woman with two small children, and the woman was carrying an infant and crying, as they were forced from their home at gunpoint and got into the truck. And as she watched the agonizing scene that reminded her of the Feldmanns, although they looked like simpler people and the house was small, the déjà vu was agonizing for her, and she saw a sudden movement out of the corner of her eye. When she looked more closely, she saw a small child climb out a side window from what must have been the basement. It was a little boy, and he was cowering behind some rusty pipes. They seemed to have forgotten him as they drove away. She saw that he was wearing short pants and had no

45

coat on, and he was shaking as he hid, barely visible except if you knew he was there.

Gaëlle watched and waited, and he didn't move as she stared at him from where she stood. She wondered if the soldiers would come back for him, but no one did. And after she thought she had waited long enough, she leaped on her bicycle and rode past him, stopped a few feet away, and went back to look behind the pipes where he was hiding. He stared at her in terror, too frightened to move. He looked about four years old. She reached a hand out to him and he shrank into the shadows, desperately afraid of her.

'Come. I won't hurt you,' she said softly.

'Will you take me to my mama?' She nodded, lying to him. And he took a step toward her, and came out from where he had stayed hidden since climbing out the window. She lifted him swiftly into the basket of her bike, and covered him completely with her coat, which she took off hastily. She looked around to make sure no one had seen them, and was satisfied that no one had.

'Don't talk, don't make any sound,' she said, loud enough for him to hear her, and he didn't respond. He was curled up in a ball in the basket, which was just big enough for him. It was cold riding home, and she pedaled as fast as she could, with her precious cargo, with no idea what she would do with him or where she would go. But she knew what she had to do. It had been an instant decision as soon as she saw him, and she tried to think of where she could hide him until she figured it out. She remembered an old shed past their orchards on a back path of the estate where no one ever went. It was near the cemetery, and she had been there recently to tend her father's grave. It was a small shed for equipment, and there was a cellar underground where they had kept cider in better days. It was the only place she could think of where he'd be safe, for now anyway.

She rode past the château on the back road, toward the cemetery, and no one noticed her. It was dark when they got to the shed. She wheeled her bike inside, and it smelled of apples. It had a dirt floor, which was frozen hard, and a trap door to the cellar she remembered, although she hadn't been inside it in years. She and Thomas used to hide there when they played games. She lifted the boy carefully out of the basket and set him on his feet, as he looked up at her in the moonlight coming through the windows. His face was pale, and his eyes were huge in the small face.

'What's your name?' she asked him in a gentle voice, bending down to talk to him. He looked clean, and his clothes were neat, his hair had been brushed, and she could see that he was a child his mother loved and took good care of. She wondered if she had told him to escape through the window, or if he had figured it out himself. The other two children had looked slightly younger than he was, and the baby was very small. He was the oldest of the four children.

'I'm Jacob,' he said softly, still afraid of her,

and not sure what she was going to do with him, nor was she.

'I'm Gaëlle,' she said solemnly, and ran a gentle hand across his hair and kissed his cheek.

'Where's my mama?'

'I don't know,' she said honestly, and then she asked him to do something she knew would be hard for him. 'I need you to be very brave. I have to leave you here for a little while. You can't go outside. I'll come back later. No one will find you here. Will you do that for me? Stay in this little house in the dark?' For a child of his age, it was a terrifying prospect, but his safety depended on it. He nodded after a minute.

'Will the bad policemen come back, with the guns?'

'Not if you're inside here and are very quiet. I'll bring you something to eat.' He nodded again. She stroked his head, smiled, and wheeled her bike back outside, and then rode back to the château. She had left her coat with him in case he was cold, and as she headed toward home, with her cheeks flaming from how fast she was pedaling, she prayed that no one would find him, and she would think of a way to keep him safe. She was doing it for Rebekah, and her family, and all the people she couldn't save. She wanted to save this one life now, to make up for the rest.

She left her bike in the courtyard and went upstairs to check on her mother. She was asleep, as usual, and had grown disastrously thin. She looked almost like a cadaver as she slept. Gaëlle left the sleeping powder next to her bed in case she woke up, and went back to her room, thinking about what she had to do. She had to get to the kitchen, and steal some food for him, and then she wanted to go back and settle him in for the night, and in the morning she would have to decide what to do. There was no one she could ask, she had no idea where to go, or how to hide a child for a long period of time, as others did. And she couldn't leave him in the orchard shed forever. She prayed to find an answer, just as Apolline showed up with some food for her, and a tray with soup and a small crust of bread for her mother. There was another crust for Gaëlle, from the commandant's table, and some dried meat and a little stew, and a small sliver of cheese. Gaëlle thanked her and wrapped the bread, meat, and cheese in a napkin, and put some water in the thermos she kept in her room, and she quickly ate the stew herself since she had no way to carry it to Jacob. And an hour later she went out again, with the food in her basket, and a blanket she had taken from the linen cupboard they used upstairs.

At first she couldn't find him when she wheeled her bike into the shed. There was no sound, and he didn't answer her when she called his name, and she suddenly panicked thinking that they had found him and taken him, and then she saw his eyes in the moonlight, staring at her.

'Hi, Jacob,' she said. 'I brought you some dinner.' She took it out of the basket and held it out to him, and slowly he approached. He ate all of it, and drank some of the water she had brought for him. She stayed with him for an hour, wrapped him in the blanket with her coat, and left the thermos of water with him. She told him that in the morning, he would have to go down into the cellar in case someone came, and she showed him how to open the trapdoor. 'I'll be back for you first thing tomorrow,' she promised him, and he pulled something out of his pocket right before she left and handed it to her. It was a piece of paper with an address on it, and looked as though it had been written in haste. 'What is that?' Gaëlle asked him as she stared at it and then back at him. She could read it in the dim light but didn't know what it meant.

'I don't know. My mama said to go there if someone found me.' He hadn't mentioned it till then. But it told her that his escape through the window must have been orchestrated by his mother as the gendarmes entered their home.

'We'll go there tomorrow then,' Gaëlle said calmly, wondering what she had gotten herself into, but there was no turning back, and she didn't want to. She wanted to do this for him, and for his mother, and all the others like them.

'Will my mama and papa be there?' he asked her with a look that went straight to her heart.

'I don't think so. But if your mama said to go there, I'm sure it's a safe place.' He nodded, satisfied with her answer, and she tucked him into his makeshift bed on the floor before she left, and then rode back to the château, sure of herself now.

Jacob had become her mission, and she would get him to safety for this woman she didn't know. It seemed like a small thing to do for them, and she didn't care about the risk to herself. What difference did it make? What future did any of them have, and who were they as human beings if they didn't at least try to help? She slept in her clothes that night, so she didn't have to waste time getting dressed in the morning when she got up, and she fell into a deep sleep and dreamed about Rebekah. She was smiling at Gaëlle in the dream, and Jacob was standing beside her. In the dream, Rebekah said they were waiting for Gaëlle to come.

4

Jacob was still asleep when Gaëlle slipped into the shed just after dawn the next day. She had stolen a few more crusts of bread for him on her way past the pantry when she left, and no one would miss it. She had brought some gardening tools so she could say she was tending to her father's grave if someone asked where she was going, but she saw no one on the way, and she woke the little boy gently. He looked startled when he first saw her, and then he remembered. She let him relieve himself from the doorway, and then gave him the crust of bread. She hadn't dared consult any maps, but she knew that the address hastily scrawled on the piece of paper was in a small town two villages away, and she knew how to get there.

'Do I have to go in the cellar now?' he asked her, and she shook her head.

'No, we're going to go to your mama's friends.' She helped him into the basket, and covered him with the blanket, and left the gardening tools in the shed. She had decided that going in broad daylight would look less suspicious, and she estimated that it would take them a little over an hour to get there. She had her identity papers, and her permission to circulate freely in the county, and as long as he didn't make a sound or move in the basket, she thought they would get there without any problem. The local soldiers never bothered her, although she was a pretty girl, since they had been warned to treat the local women respectfully. The commandant of the area didn't want reports of abusing women to get back to headquarters in Paris, and he had been strict about it. And it was obvious that Gaëlle was from a respectable family, and her address was at the Château de Mouton-Barbet, where the commandant was billeted.

She checked on Jacob in the basket one last time before they left the shed, and she took off then on the back roads, and eventually joined the road that was traveled more frequently, where she would be less noticed among others going to the next village, to work, or to market. A few people smiled at her along the way, and she saw no soldiers until they'd been on the road for almost an hour, and they didn't stop her or ask for her papers and just waved her on. She was so Aryan looking, no one was ever suspicious of her.

It took them less than two hours to get to the address on the scrap of paper. There was no name on it, and she rang the bell at the gate when she got there. A tall young man came to answer it a few minutes later, and looked at her suspiciously.

'Yes? What is it?'

She wasn't sure what to say. She had no code word, no instructions, or the name of who to ask for. 'I have a package for you,' she said simply, glancing at the basket on her bicycle, and he stared at her with a question in his eyes that she didn't dare answer.

'What kind of package?' he pressed her, as she fished the piece of paper out of her pocket and handed it to him, in case something about it looked familiar to him, and he reacted immediately. 'Come inside,' he said curtly, and once they all were inside the gate, he directed her to a garage behind the house. He followed her, and in the garage she prayed that she was doing the right thing, as she gently lifted the blanket off of Jacob, and he sat up and stared at them. The fierce-looking young man smiled as soon as he saw him, lifted him out of the basket, and held him in his arms. 'Welcome,' he said to the little boy. 'We're going to take good care of you,' he assured him.

'Are my mama and papa here?' Jacob asked anxiously, and the tall boy shook his head.

'No, they aren't. But you have friends here who want to help you.'

'His name is Jacob,' Gaëlle explained to him, and smiled at the child she had delivered. The young man said his name was Simon.

He brought him farther into the garage then, with Gaëlle following them, and knocked on a door, which opened a moment later and a pretty young woman smiled and took the child from his arms. 'This is Jacob,' he introduced the boy, and she looked ecstatic, as though she had been waiting for him to arrive. Gaëlle could see that there were other children in the room, and then the door closed behind them.

'You're just in time,' Simon explained to her. 'We're taking five others to Le Chambon tonight. He can go with us.' She knew that Le

54

Chambon sur Lignon was in the Haute Loire in Auvergne, in south-central France, but she knew nothing else about it, and he acted as though she should. 'We've taken more than two thousand children there in the past two years, all Jewish refugees like Jacob. Friends and neighbors have been hiding them in homes, hotels, farms, and schools.' He explained it to her for a few minutes.

Le Chambon and the neighboring villages had made a deep commitment, three months after the Occupation began, to bring Jewish children to safety. The movement had been founded by Huguenots, led by Pastor André Trocmé, whom everyone thought was a saint. There were safe houses all over France now, with people like Simon and the woman who'd taken Jacob waiting to help the children reach safety. And by some miracle, Jacob's mother had heard about them, and wrote the address down for Jacob to give to whoever found him. 'We get them to the Swiss border when we can, or hide them with locals, or keep moving them around. We give them new papers, and new identities.' Pastor Trocmé had given a speech a few months before, in Paris, accusing his fellow countrymen of cowardice for giving in to anti-Semitism. He was an outspoken pacifist, determined to undermine the local authorities whenever he could. And so far they hadn't touched him. Trocmé was working closely with American Quakers of the American Friends Service Committee, and their leader Burns Chalmers, who had been trying to negotiate the release of interned Jews for two years, but they had nowhere to go. And Trocmé had turned his entire village into an underground network to protect and harbor Jewish children, and two or three of the neighboring villages were involved now too. Simon said they were the bravest people in France, and that the Swiss Red Cross was assisting them as well. And the Swedish government had recently begun sending funding to assist Trocmé's efforts in Le Chambon.

'Are you a church group of some kind?' Gaëlle asked him, mystified by what he told her.

'We work for the OSE, Oeuvre de Secours aux Enfants, the Children's Aid Society. If anyone gets the children to us, we get them to Le Chambon. We work hand in hand with Pastor Trocmé, and the American Quakers, and whoever else will help us. Would you ever carry a package for us again?' he asked her directly. She hesitated and then nodded. She had never thought of it before, but it seemed like the right thing to do, and she wanted to help. She thought Rebekah would be pleased, and it was a way of making penance for what Gaëlle hadn't been able to do for her. All she had managed to do was visit her, she couldn't free her. She wondered if she could have saved her, if she'd gotten her to Le Chambon. But it was too painful to think of now. 'Jacob will be in good hands,' he reassured her, as he walked her to the gate.

'I just happened to see him escape from a window when they took his parents and their three other children.'

'It was lucky for him you did.' She found it hard to believe that an entire town was successfully defying the Germans. Pastor Trocmé must have been an extraordinary individual to get everyone to rally, to help save so many children, and even enlist the help of foreigners for their cause. 'He'll have a new name and identity by tomorrow.'

'And his family?' Gaëlle asked sadly, but already knew the answer.

'Once they're deported, it's much more difficult. Burns Chalmers has done some successful negotiations, but very few. They're sending the families away to camps in Germany now, and they don't come back. Most of the children we hide will be orphans by the end of the war or already are,' he said seriously. And she knew it applied to Rebekah too, who had been with her family and had been sent to God knew where. 'We'll be in touch,' Simon said as she got on her bike. He looked a little like her brother, and she tried not to think about it.

'I live at the Château de Mouton-Barbet,' she told him shyly, 'but so does the commandant of the Gestapo for our region. They let us live upstairs.' He nodded, and realized they'd have to be cautious approaching her, but she was obviously a brave girl.

'You did a great thing today,' he said quietly to encourage her.

'He's only one boy, and they've taken so many,' she said sadly. Too many that she knew of, friends from school, families from her village, the Feldmanns, and others she'd heard about.

'There's a saying in the Talmud that to save one life is to save a world entire. That's true. If you saved Jacob, that's a miracle for him.'

'Are you Jewish?' She was curious about him.

'No, I'm Protestant, a Huguenot like Pastor Trocmé. But it really doesn't matter. Protestant, Catholic, Jewish, Huguenot, we all want to save these children. They deserve it. What the Germans are doing is an abomination, trying to turn a whole country, even all of Europe, against one race. We can't stop them, but hopefully we can save as many of the children as we can. So welcome to the OSE. Have a safe trip back,' he said seriously as she got on her bike.

'Give Jacob my love,' she said softly, and took off a minute later, musing about the extraordinary quirks of destiny that had led her to be there in time to see Jacob escape, and be able to help him the night before. Everything Simon had told her about their organization, the town of Le Chambon sur Lignon, and Pastor Trocmé had amazed her. It was good to know that there were people like that in the world. She smiled as she rode back to the château. And even seeing soldiers on the way didn't faze her. She had nothing to hide now. She wondered when she'd hear from Simon or his colleagues at the OSE again, or if she ever would.

★ ★ ★

The next weeks were relentlessly depressing and hard. It was their first Christmas without her father and brother, and her mother's health was

58

deteriorating visibly. Agathe kept herself sedated most of the time, which left Gaëlle totally alone. Christmas was bleak, and she spent part of it tending to her father's and brother's graves. She was on her way back one day when she had the feeling that someone was following her, and she was afraid it was one of the German soldiers. She pedaled faster, and a few minutes later a man stepped onto the road and blocked her path. She was frightened the moment she saw him. He looked angry, had a shock of dark hair and a beard, and looked menacing. Before she could turn back or run or speed away, he said the words 'Simon sent me, from the OSE,' and then she realized why he was there. 'We have another delivery for you. A nine-year-old girl. We need to get her to St. Chef quickly. Will you do it?' Gaëlle didn't hesitate and agreed.

'Where is she?' she asked.

'She's at a farm nearby, but she can't stay. They had trouble yesterday.' She wondered if the farm was on her father's land, but she didn't ask.

'There's a shed near the cemetery, with a cellar and a trapdoor,' Gaëlle explained, feeling a rush of adrenaline, knowing what lay ahead.

'If I get her there, can you move her tomorrow?' he asked, and Gaëlle nodded. The town he had mentioned was three hours away, and a nine-year-old was too big to hide in a basket. She was thinking quickly about how to do it.

'Will your farmer lend me his tractor?' Gaëlle asked him.

'I don't know. I think so. I'll ask him.' He

59

looked startled by what she'd said. 'You're going to travel three hours by tractor?' She nodded, and he smiled. No one had tried that before, but sometimes the most obvious escapes were the smoothest and worked best.

'Leave it next to the orchard,' Gaëlle said to him.

'I'll have her at the shed sometime tonight,' he promised.

'I'll pick her up early in the morning. And tell them to dress her in work clothes,' Gaëlle told him, and a moment later they both got on their bikes, and rode off in opposite directions. Gaëlle had all night to think about the plan, and worry if her idea was too bold.

She rode to the shed just before dawn the next morning, and found a little girl in overalls and a heavy sweater, shivering in the cellar under a blanket Gaëlle had left after Jacob had been there, and Gaëlle was relieved to see that she had pale blond hair. It would be easy to claim they were sisters if they looked something alike, and Gaëlle noticed immediately that she was a pretty little girl. Her name was Isabelle, and Gaëlle explained the plan to her after introducing herself. They were two farm girls, sisters, helping their father. Their brother was in Paris and could no longer help on the farm. 'How does that sound to you?' she asked the child, who had lively eyes and looked scared.

'I don't know anything about farms. We live in the city,' she said nervously. Her whole family had been deported, and she'd been at a friend's when they were taken away. Friends in a nearby town had been hiding her in their basement for the last five months, but felt they could no longer take the risk. They were afraid the authorities were on to them, or would be soon. And the OSE wanted to get her to Le Chambon and out of harm's way as soon as they could.

'Don't worry, they won't ask us to plow a field for them,' Gaëlle reassured her, and they took off on the tractor a few minutes later. Isabelle said very little on the trip.

The ride on the tractor was uncomfortable, and they passed groups of soldiers three different times, and each time they glanced at the two girls, dismissed them as farm girls from the neighborhood without checking their papers, and never suspected that the tractor was a ruse. They waved them on their way each time. Gaëlle was stunned by how easy it had been when they reached the safe house in St. Chef, and Isabelle thanked her politely and disappeared inside. The man she had met on the road the day before was waiting for her when they arrived.

'Everything went smoothly?' he questioned her.

'Perfectly.' Gaëlle smiled at him. 'If you ever want to do something illegal, do it on a tractor, no one pays any attention,' particularly since they were two young girls, and were the portrait of innocence, and neither of them looked Jewish. They looked Aryan to the Germans.

'I'll have to remember that,' he laughed at her, and then grew serious again. 'We have another package for you. In a few days, not yet, he's sick.'

'How sick?' Gaëlle looked worried. She wasn't

61

a nurse, but she wasn't experienced at this either, so maybe it didn't make a difference.

'We thought he had pneumonia, which would have been serious, but the doctor says it's just bronchitis. We want to give it a few days. We'll let you know when he's ready.' Gaëlle agreed and set out on the long journey home on the tractor a few minutes later. She arrived at the shed just before nightfall, left the tractor where she had found it, and rode her bicycle back to the château. She went to her room upstairs as soon as she got there, and lay on her bed, exhausted. It had been a long stressful day, worrying about getting caught, and traveling for six hours on a tractor, but everything had gone well.

She didn't hear from her contacts at the OSE for another two weeks, and wondered what had happened to the child with bronchitis. And although she had only transported children twice so far, it had given new meaning, purpose, and depth to her life, and she was excited to do it again. It was even more meaningful to her, knowing that an entire village had committed themselves to saving these children, and she wanted to join them in their efforts and do whatever she could.

It was two weeks after her tractor trip with Isabelle to St. Chef, when the same man rode his bike past her in the village, and all he said to her while appearing not to pay attention to her was 'Same place, six A.M. tomorrow.' She showed no sign of acknowledgment and rode on to the bakery, where the shelves were mostly empty, but she bought part of a loaf of dark bread and the owner gave her a cinnamon roll for her mother, from an order they had filled for the commandant. Agathe hardly ate anymore, and Gaëlle and Apolline were worried about her. She was too weak to get out of bed now, and the sleeping powder she took decreased her appetite even more. But her migraines were too severe without them. And sometimes they made them even worse.

Gaëlle got up at five-thirty in the morning the next day, and rode out to the shed to meet the child with bronchitis. It was dark and cold and dreary. And a few minutes after she got there, Simon let himself in carrying a basket that looked like he had groceries in it, and she heard a whimper, as though he had a kitten hidden somewhere. She looked startled and glanced up as he pulled aside the blanket, and there was a tiny infant in it. Gaëlle looked shocked.

'Oh my God, how old is he?' she asked, wondering how she would transport him.

'He's eight weeks old. David is our youngest client so far. His mother left him in a garbage can when he was a month old, the day they got deported. She had a note pinned to his blanket to bring him to us. Their maid brought him, and he got sick almost immediately. He's better now, though.' The baby was looking up at both of them and puckered up his lips to cry. It nearly broke Gaëlle's heart to watch him, and realize that he had already lost his mother so young. 'His father is a doctor and delivered him at home. They wouldn't let her deliver at the hospital because they're Jewish, even though her husband had practiced there for twenty years.' The stories were always shocking and agonizing, and Gaëlle picked the baby up and held him, and he nuzzled her neck, wanting to nurse.

'How am I going to transport him? And what if he cries?'

'Maybe you just have to carry him in a sling and act like he's yours. You can say you don't have his papers yet. I don't think he'd be a good candidate for the tractor.' Nor for the basket on her bike. She looked pensive as she thought about it, trying to decide how to do it. This was no easy mission.

'How far does he have to go?'

'A couple of hours.' Simon had just picked him up at a nearby farm but didn't want to risk getting him back to the safe house himself. He would have had a much harder time explaining a two-month-old infant than Gaëlle. And they couldn't count on him remaining quiet. He would cry whenever he was hungry, tired, or wet. And he still had a nasty cough, although he seemed healthy otherwise and was a good size.

Simon left her a few minutes later, with the formula they were feeding him, which the Red Cross had provided, and she fashioned a sling to put him in, from the wool muffler she was wearing, tied it around herself, and got on her bike after she fed him, and sang to him along the way to keep him quiet. He seemed fascinated by her voice. And she got on the main road an hour later, and this time was stopped at a checkpoint, where they asked for her papers, and didn't ask for the baby's. Hers were in order, and the soldier asked her where she was going.

'To visit my grandmother. She hasn't seen him yet. He's been sick.' The baby let out a horrific cough as soon as she said it, as though to prove the point.

'You shouldn't have him out in this cold,' the soldier scolded her, and said he had three children himself. He said he could tell this was her first and looked disapproving because she was so young and not married. But he smiled as he looked at the baby and tickled his cheek, and then told her sternly to get him into a warm house as soon as she could. It was January and bitter cold. She had been frightened for a minute, and relieved when he sent her on her way. She reached the safe house an hour later, and was happy to turn him over to one of the female workers. She'd never taken care of a baby, let alone one so young, but he seemed to have endured the trip without a problem.

'We have an opportunity to get him over the border tonight. We're leaving with him right away,' they told her. A couple in Switzerland were taking him, to live with seven other children they had helped rescue in the last year. There were remarkably brave people everywhere. And Gaëlle just hoped she didn't meet the same soldier on the way back, who would ask her what she had done with her baby. She was going to say she left him with her grandmother. The soldier had already thought her a bad mother on the way there, taking him out with a cough at two months in freezing weather. But much to her relief, she didn't see that same man on the way back, and no one stopped her.

She didn't hear from the OSE again for a while after that, and in February there was bad news, which she heard from rumors in the village. The Germans had arrested Pastor Trocmé and his assistant, Pastor Theis, and the headmaster of the school in Le Chambon sur Lignon. The local authorities had sent all three of them to an internment camp in Limoges. But there was sufficient outrage over interning religious leaders, and support from the Swiss Red Cross, the American Quakers, and the Swedish government, that they released them a month later. And when Gaëlle heard from Simon after that, he assured her they were back at work on rescue missions all over France. They were undaunted, and Gaëlle thought they were saints.

But the German police and Gestapo got tougher once they were released. They raided a school in Le Chambon in June, arrested eighteen students, and discovered that five of them were Jews and sent them to a labor camp where they were killed shortly after they arrived, and news of it got back to France. They had also arrested Pastor Trocmé's cousin Daniel, sent him to the Lublin/Majdanek concentration camp, and killed him. It was a powerful message to the OSE workers in Auvergne and all over France. The German High Command was not going to tolerate their dissidence and disobedience forever, no matter who supported them outside France. It made all the OSE units increasingly careful, and their operations even more clandestine than before. And from then on, Gaëlle did missions for them with greater frequency, which became increasingly dangerous for her, but it didn't stop her. If anything, it made her more determined to make a difference and do all she could for them and the children. By the fall of 1943, she had transported dozens of children, all of whom were destined to go to Auvergne, and from there as many as possible were taken across the Swiss border, most of them via Annemasse, their preferred route, which had worked well for them so far.

The Gestapo in Lyon became particularly vigilant and hostile to anyone transporting Jewish children, and Gaëlle had several close calls but succeeded with her missions every time. It was the only thing that made her life worth living as the war droned on. Her OSE contacts said she led a charmed life. Her code name, once she became a regular transporter for them, was Marie-Ange. She was nineteen years old by then, and Rebekah had been gone for almost two years. It felt like a lifetime to Gaëlle now, and each time she delivered a child into safe hands, destined to be taken to Le Chambon, elsewhere in France, or over the Swiss border, she prayed that it would somehow be a trade with God, and that one day her beloved friend would come back alive. There had been no news of her since they left.

5

In the spring of 1944, the war was going badly for the Germans, and the Resistance was making inroads and causing havoc in occupied France wherever it could. The Allies were hitting them hard in bombing raids over Germany, casualties were high on both sides, and the tides had begun to turn. By June, with talk of the German army withdrawing from Paris, there was wholesale looting of museums, as important works of art were being stolen by German officers to take back to Germany. The High Command and its art commission had officially removed what it wanted from the Louvre for the past four years. And Hermann Goering, head of the Luftwaffe and famed art collector, had come to Paris twenty times and taken trainloads of art treasures back to Germany for himself. Hitler had come only once.

In addition, Jewish homes had long since been plundered and their possessions appropriated by whichever officer wanted them as spoils of war, their fortunes having been seized in the name of the German government. And now even lesser officers were taking whatever they could. The loss of France's treasures was a source of outrage to the French, though not as much as the loss of life, which was even more acute in the final battles.

But the only thing that interested Gaëlle were

the missions she was still doing for the OSE, to get Jewish children, some of whom had been hidden for years by then, safely to the Huguenots and the Red Cross and over the Swiss border. If anything, they had stepped up their efforts to save every child they could, and Gaëlle had become an important member of the Resistance since the first child she had transported a year and a half before. She had lost track by then of how many children she had smuggled to safe houses and into trustworthy hands. She had no idea how many children the various organizations dedicated to them had saved, but it was said to be well into the thousands most likely, and some said well over five thousand. And the war wasn't over yet, although the end seemed to be near. The panic of the German army was some indication that it was already planning its retreat, and grabbing everything they could before they left. In many cases it amounted to boldfaced theft, under the auspices of being the spoils of war.

Gaëlle had just completed a mission, transporting an eight-year-old girl, who had been hidden in a dirt basement for two years, and her benefactors were afraid she'd get caught before the Occupation ended, so they had asked for the OSE's help, and contacted the Quakers in Le Chambon. Everything had gone smoothly, Gaëlle had never lost a child or been caught yet, and she was lying on her bed, resting afterward, when Apolline came upstairs to tell her that the commandant wanted to see her. He never sent his soldiers upstairs to deliver messages and intrude on them. And he had remained respectful and polite. He still inquired about Gaëlle's mother, who had dwindled to a shadow of what she had once been. And although she was very thin, from the little food they had to eat, Gaëlle had grown more and more beautiful, and at nineteen she was lovelier than ever. And she was very grateful that neither the commandant nor his soldiers and officers had ever been inappropriate with her, which was contrary to the stories one heard in the village. Several of the local girls had gotten involved with the officers and enlisted men, and even had babies with them, to the outrage of their fellow countrymen, who spat on the women as they walked past and called them traitors.

'Do you know what he wants?' Gaëlle asked Apolline as she followed her downstairs, and spoke in a whisper. Her father had told her never to keep the German High Command waiting, and to always be respectful to them.

'He didn't say. He just asked for you to meet him in the living room.' And when she did, he was staring into space, as though his mind were a million miles away. He inquired after her mother as usual, and Gaëlle reported that she was no better, and was suffering from the heat, which made her blinding headaches worse.

'I'm sorry to hear it. The war has been very hard on her,' he said sympathetically, although they both knew that it had killed countless others. But it had clearly destroyed her mother's nerves and health, particularly since the death of her husband and son two years before. 'And you are all right?' he asked, looking at Gaëlle in a way he never had before. It made her feel strange for a minute, as though he was suddenly seeing her as a woman and an equal, which made her uneasy. 'You must miss your father and brother very much,' he said, as she grew increasingly nervous about what he had in mind. For the first time, she felt extremely unsafe and vulnerable with him, and she just prayed he wasn't going to rape her. She tried to look serious, respectful, and chilly all at the same time, but all she looked was beautiful and young, especially to him. Gaëlle knew that he had been widowed almost since the beginning of the war, and didn't appear to be a womanizer. Unlike many of the other officers, he never caroused with the local women, and was unusually discreet and polite.

'I do miss them,' Gaëlle admitted, trying not to open up to him. Her feelings and her losses were none of his business, since he was responsible for her father's death, and indirectly for the disappearance of the Feldmanns, and so many others.

'I believe that you are very loyal to your country,' he said carefully, and for an instant a tremor of terror ran through her, and she wondered if he had heard of her activities for the OSE, helping Jewish children all over France.

'Yes, I am,' she said quietly. Her face gave nothing away.

'And you've grown up with beautiful things here at the château. You are fortunate that your country has so many national treasures. Germany does too, but I'm afraid that my colleagues and countrymen have been greedy while they

71

were here.' She had no idea where he was going with the conversation, and he had a look of pain and regret in his eyes when he said it. He had thought long and hard before summoning her, but he could think of no other way to execute the plan he had in mind. There was no one he truly trusted on his staff, and he had been careful not to make any friends among the locals, so he couldn't be accused of disloyalty later. He was a German to the core, although he disagreed with many of the orders they carried out. 'How do you feel about your national treasures? The famous artwork of France?' he asked her directly, emphasizing the word 'treasures,' and she looked confused. She couldn't see the purpose of his questions. But at least he wasn't asking her about the children she had transported, which would have been the prelude to her being executed, like her father, although it was a risk she had long since decided to take. Their young lives, and so many of them, seemed worth more than hers.

'I think we're fortunate to have what we do in France,' she said benignly. She hadn't been in a museum since the war began, and their national treasures were the last thing on her mind, but they were very much on his.

'So do I,' he said, smiling at her, and he looked fatherly when he did, and as though they were allies somehow, which was clearly not the case. She wondered if this was some kind of ruse to entrap her, and hoped it wasn't. 'And unlike my countrymen, I believe that the art of France belongs in France, and should stay here, not be sent to Germany, where many important works and artifacts are being sent, particularly in recent months.' He deplored the trainloads of priceless art that had left France to be divided among the connoisseurs of the High Command. The Fuehrer had always been passionate about art and was designing a new national museum in Linz, Austria. 'Some of the pieces that are being sent to Germany have been taken from museums. Others are from private collections that have been seized by the Reich,' he explained. 'I don't believe that is right,' he said seriously. 'I would like you to help me with a project, Mademoiselle de Barbet. A friend of mine in Paris in the High Command of the SS wishes to rescue what artifacts we can, preserve them here, and return them after the war to your government, or the national museums they came from. Those that came from private collections could be returned to the owners who claim them. Your national museums could keep them until then. Would you be willing to help me with that?' She looked at him, stunned by what he said.

'Are you asking me to steal them for you?' she asked in a hoarse voice. 'I'd be shot.'

'Indeed you would. And 'stealing' is too big a word, when we are talking about preserving national treasures for the government and collectors to whom they rightfully belong. No, I don't want you to steal them. They've already been stolen once. My friend has been asked by fellow officers to ship a number of important paintings to Germany. He has been able to divert some of them, and even put many in a vault, which he will turn over to the French government before we leave. And there are others for which he wants to find a safe home in France, temporarily. If you join me in this, I would like to pass these paintings on to you, quietly, and ask you to return all of them to the Louvre in Paris when we're gone. They would return those from private homes, when someone tries to trace them. I think you're an honest young woman with high morals, and I trust you with these important works of art. And if you ally with me, no one must know what we're doing, or we'll both be shot,' he said bluntly, using her own words.

'Where would I hide them?' Gaëlle looked shocked.

'Somewhere on the estate. I leave that up to you. I will give you rolled-up canvases, preferably small ones. My friend has made arrangements for the larger works in Paris. You must conceal what I give you somewhere safe, and return them after we leave, because we will be withdrawing in the next few months. That's not official of course, but we all see it coming, which is why the men in Paris, and even here, are stealing everything they can, as final souvenirs. But these would be very important souvenirs, too much so for any individual to own. And we have no right to them as spoils of war. Will you do this with me, Mademoiselle? I think this could be very important for your country.' It was his private way of making restitution. She was silent for a long moment, as she looked at him, trying to decide if she should agree to go along with his

74

plan, or was it a trap to incriminate her? But it seemed dangerous to turn him down, and if he meant what he said, it was a brave and noble thing to do, and he rose in her esteem, particularly since many of the paintings that had been taken had belonged to deported Jews, and he seemed to hope that the Louvre would return them once they were claimed.

She hesitated before answering him.

'I will attempt to protect you if we get caught, and take the blame myself,' he promised her. She was in so deep for the children that taking an additional risk for the art didn't worry her. And he was right, their national art treasures belonged in France, and everyone knew that the Germans had been stealing them all through the Occupation. Whatever he could save now, at the end, was just a fraction of what they'd lost, but it seemed worth doing. She nodded in answer, and he smiled at her. 'Perhaps we can establish a little routine of having coffee together in the evening, and I will give you a loaf of fresh bread for your mother every night, as a token of my appreciation for having lived in your beautiful home for four years.'

She was immensely relieved he had made no sexual overtures to her, nor discovered her work for the OSE. Hiding art for him seemed like very little to ask, even if it was also risky, for both of them.

'I am very grateful for your collaboration on this. I think we're doing something important for France. I love it here, and I would like to give something back for all the damage we've done.'

He looked at her pointedly, and she understood. Returning artwork to the Louvre did not compensate for her father's death, and others, but it was something he could do. 'You must promise me that you will return all of it to the national museums once we leave. The Jeu de Paume or the Louvre. They will return it where it belongs, and trace the pieces that were privately owned.'

'Of course,' she assured him, and he was certain that she would do as she promised. He had watched her for almost four years, and had a good sense of her character and morals. He had no doubt that she would do as he asked. He was certain he hadn't misjudged her.

He gave her a loaf of bread when she left the living room then, and she carried it carefully up the stairs. Bread, and a baguette in particular, had become the forbidden food during the war, and nearly impossible to get with rationing. So it was an enormous treat. And once in the safety of her tiny attic room, she pulled the two halves apart that had been pressed together, and saw a small rolled-up canvas inside, wrapped in special paper, and she took it out, unrolled it, and spread it out on her bed. It was a small Renoir, of the head of a child. She stared at it for a long time, and then rolled it up again, and hid it at the back of a drawer. She knew she'd have to find a better hiding place, particularly once he gave her more canvases. She wondered what her father would think of what she was doing, but she had a feeling he'd approve, and she went to bed, considering all that the commandant had said, and the faith he had in her, and the Renoir rolled up in the drawer. She carefully preserved the bread with the hollowed-out inside to give to her mother the next day.

In the morning, she went for a long walk around the estate, until she reached her father's grave.

'So what do you think, Papa?' she said out loud. There were the children she had saved, and now the art. The children meant far more to her, and were tied to Rebekah and her family for Gaëlle, but hiding major artworks to be returned to the Louvre one day, after the war, was a worthy project too. She wondered how many he would entrust to her before the Germans would be gone. She liked looking forward to the day when their home would be their own again, and maybe one day her mother would return to health, and Rebekah would come home. It was nice to dream of seeing her again. On her way back from the cemetery, Gaëlle stopped at the orchard shed and found a good hiding place for the next paintings he would give her. It was in a cool dry spot, behind a cabinet where no one would find them. She thought of the children she had hidden there in the last eighteen months, Jacob and all the others. There had even been so many babies entrusted to them by mothers who were desperate to get their newborns and infants out of France to safety, not even knowing into whose hands they would fall. But anything would be better than being sent to labor camps that were openly being called extermination camps now for the elimination of Jews. Gaëlle could only pray that Rebekah and her family hadn't been sent to one of them.

For all of June and July, the commandant had Gaëlle come to his room after dinner. She went to her parents' bedroom, which he had occupied since he'd arrived, having realized that if he met with her in the living room, one of his officers could walk in, and he wanted privacy when he met with her, so no one would discover their exchange. All they would have seen would have been a loaf of bread, occasionally some cheese, some summer fruit from the orchards, or the dried meats the German soldiers loved. He had chocolates for her occasionally, and rather than sending his soldiers to fetch her when he had a painting for her, he sent Apolline, which seemed more discreet. But after two months of their private meetings, no one had any doubt of what was happening behind closed doors. She would emerge with her hands full of food, and a precious baguette of bread under her arm. He had his personal chef make it just for her, allegedly for her mother. And the commandant would conceal a painting in it himself, after he took it to his room, in preparation for Gaëlle.

Apolline looked at her in disgust one night when she came out of the commandant's room. 'So you're selling your body now for a piece of cheese and a loaf of bread. I never thought you'd come to that.' She stared with revulsion at the girl she had helped to raise. 'My son and your father died heroes' deaths, and you are whoring yourself out now to the Germans. I'm glad your mother is too sick to understand what you're doing. She doesn't eat the bread anyway. I don't know why you bother.' She considered Gaëlle as low as any prostitute, and there was nothing she could say to defend herself. Gaëlle was sworn to secrecy by the commandant, and she didn't dare tell even Apolline that there were more than forty important artworks hidden in the orchard shed. Renoirs, several Degases, Corots, Pissarros, two small Monets. All the great masters of France were represented among the canvases he had given her. His friend in Paris, whose name Gaëlle never knew, was instructed to ship the paintings safely out of France and instead was sending them to his friend in Lyon, to be hidden and eventually returned by Gaëlle. But no one could know, and she had no defense against Apolline's accusations. She had to accept being called a whore, and considered one. The officers and enlisted men in his command thought much the same, although they were amused that in the final days of the war, the commandant had started an affair with a nineteen-year-old French girl. As far as they were concerned, she was part of the spoils of war too.

The Americans had landed in Normandy in June, but they hadn't reached the area around Lyon yet. At the end of the month, they liberated Cherbourg. At the beginning of July, the British and Canadians captured Caen, and in mid-July the Americans reached St. Lô, and ten days later took Coutances. The Allied advance was slow and steady, and they had the Germans on the run. They took Avranches on the first of August

79

and two weeks later invaded southern France. Gaëlle completed her last mission for the OSE in mid-August, spiriting a six-year-old boy to safety, and a few days later the commandant told her they were leaving. She had forty-nine major works of art hidden in the shed by then, and promised him again, when she saw him for the last time, that she would return them as soon as it was safe to go to Paris. He had done a very major feat for France. And by the time his colleagues discovered that the paintings of the commandant and his friend had disappeared, they would have bigger problems to deal with, and he could tell them they had gotten lost in transit. All he wanted to know was that they were in the right hands, and he was convinced they were with Gaëlle.

'Thank you for helping me,' he said, the night he said goodbye to her. They were leaving in the morning, retreating from the area, and going back to Germany. The Allies were only days or weeks away, and none of the German forces wanted to risk getting caught by them. They were anxious to leave. And there were reports of a Resistance uprising in Paris.

'It was a very good thing for you to do,' she said quietly the last time she saw him, and they shook hands as he thanked her and wished her well. The truth was very different from Apolline's accusations and insults, assuming she was having sex with the commandant when she went to his room. Apolline never dreamed that Gaëlle was smuggling priceless works of art out of the room in loaves of bread. Apolline's contempt for her

80

knew no measure, and she would no longer even speak to her, even after they were gone.

Gaëlle tried to explain to her mother that the Germans had left and the Americans were coming, hoping to raise her spirits, but she no longer cared. She had nothing to look forward to, nothing to live for. Her husband and son were dead, and the years of Occupation had taken too great a toll.

The last days of the war for them were sad and eerie. The country had been pillaged, so many people killed or sent away. So many wonderful young people had died in the Resistance, and so many dreams had died with them, but somehow Gaëlle had survived. The war had made her stronger and more mature, particularly the missions she did. Having no one to care for her and protect her had rapidly turned her into an adult. Her dreams of going to university at the Sorbonne were over, it made no sense to her now, and she lay in bed at night, thinking of the children she had helped to save, wondering where they were now. Almost all of them were orphans, but at least they were alive.

By the end of August, the Americans had arrived. They washed across the countryside like a flood of clean water, bringing hope and victory with them, as people hugged them, kissed them, and threw themselves into their arms. Paris was liberated on the twenty-fifth of August, there was music and dancing, the GIs gave candy and chocolates to children and smiled at all the pretty girls. And in the ensuing days, city after city was liberated. The nation was exhausted, but in a final burst of energy, they celebrated the arrival of their saviors. France was free again at last!

6

When the dancing in the streets, parades of tanks and troops, and atmosphere of jubilation began to slow down, the final reckoning came for the people in the villages, towns, and cities all over France. In most cases, everyone knew who the traitors were, but here and there were surprises, and treacherous citizens who had betrayed their country in secret were denounced by their relatives and friends.

The mayor of the Vichy government was driven out of town, and a new one was named. He had been loyal to France, a member of the Resistance who had committed extraordinary acts of bravery. People began filing in, demanding justice, and often taking it into their own hands.

Apolline was one of the first to go to the town hall, when the new mayor was named. He had been in the same Resistance cell as her son, and she denounced Gaëlle for sleeping with the commandant, selling her body for food and sometimes just a loaf of bread. There was a group of citizens to list the villagers' complaints, to determine if they were war crimes or just acts of infidelity to France. Most of those denounced were women who had slept with German officers and enlisted men, lived with them, had babies with them, and had consorted with the enemy, but not been spies. They had betrayed themselves more than all else. And Apolline proudly submitted Gaëlle's name for the list. She wanted to see her publicly vilified for what she'd done.

A band of outraged hooligans and local citizens dragged the accused into the street, roughed them up, shoved them around, slapped them, beat them up in some cases, and then shaved their heads and forced them to parade through the streets to exhibit their shame to the entire town. People booed and jeered them, threw things at them, rotten food, garbage, empty bottles, whatever was at hand. It was a scene of total humiliation, and most of the women tried to weather it bravely, but it was an ugly scene with many minor injuries.

They found Gaëlle in the courtyard of the château, and dragged and pushed her to the main street, where men slapped her and women hit her with broomsticks. When it was over, Gaëlle went back to the château with a bruise on her face, a black eye, her shaved head, and a deep cut on her arm where someone had thrown a bottle with a jagged edge at her. She had foul-smelling garbage stuck to her clothes, and a look of devastation in her eyes. She was brokenhearted by what they'd done. There was no vindication or justification, no one to defend her. The workers of the OSE had gone back to Le Chambon and Marseilles, where they had loose ends to tie up, and the families of children to trace. No one came forward to acknowledge what Gaëlle had done for almost two years. No one knew of the paintings she was hiding to return to the Louvre, and she had promised not to tell anyone until she returned them, so they wouldn't be stolen, which seemed wise. She had millions of francs of the national treasure in her hands, and she didn't want them taken. She had to endure her undeserved shame in stoic silence, and went home sick and devastated after she was paraded through the streets. Even the American soldiers watching had jeered and hissed. No one liked a traitor, when the locals had explained who they were, and what they had done.

She met Apolline at the foot of the back staircase when she was home, and didn't want anyone to see her come in, but her shaved head spoke for itself. She looked with tragic eyes at the woman who had cared for her as a child. It was Gaëlle who had been betrayed, not France, in her case. The two women stood gazing at each other, and the old woman spat in her face. It was the final blow from someone she had loved, and Gaëlle walked slowly upstairs with tears rolling down her cheeks. She hadn't moved back to her old room, and stayed in the attic to be near her mother, who wouldn't go back to her room after the Germans had lived there for four years. She said she could never sleep there again.

Gaëlle didn't go in to see her mother that night, and waited until the next morning to check on her. Apolline was just leaving her room, after bringing her a tray, and she stared at Gaëlle again with hatred, as though everything that had happened the night before hadn't been punishment enough. And her mother lay in her bed and noticed her daughter's shaved head and black eye. Even she knew what it meant.

'What happened?' she asked with a look of horror. 'Why did they do that to you? What have you done? How did you betray your country? Who did you collaborate with?' She couldn't even imagine how she could have done something so terrible when her father had died in the Resistance.

'No one, Maman,' she said quietly. 'It's a mistake. I can explain it.'

'No, you can't,' her mother said with a look of outrage. 'They don't make mistakes about things like that. Were you sleeping with the Germans, while I was here sick in my bed?'

'No, I wasn't,' Gaëlle said in a dignified tone. 'I never slept with anyone. I'm still a virgin.' It was true. Nothing she had done had led her to sleep with anyone, and the German soldiers had left her alone, thanks to the commandant controlling them, and keeping them away from her. And he had done nothing wrong or disrespectful himself.

'I don't believe you!' her mother screamed at her. 'You've disgraced us! How will we ever face anyone here again? They know what you are. Look at you!' She pointed to her shaved head, as Gaëlle's eyes filled with tears that spilled down her cheeks. She knew her mother was too upset to listen to what she had done with the art treasures of France that had been entrusted to her care. Agathe was too hysterical to believe a word Gaëlle could say. Her shaved head spoke louder than her words.

She left the room quietly, intending to come

back later, and went downstairs to see Apolline in the kitchen.

'I never did anything wrong. I swear it to you,' she said, and the old housekeeper was stone-faced.

'I don't believe you, and no one else will either. You sold your body for food.' Others did, but Gaëlle didn't. And if she had, it would have been for her mother, but even that was not true. 'You slept with the enemy. No one will ever forget that here. You are tainted forever. You have disgraced your parents, and your family, and everyone who ever knew you.' Other than Rebekah being taken away, and her father's murder at the hands of the Germans, this was the third most defining moment of her life, and Gaëlle knew she would never forget it.

She went back upstairs to see her mother, and she had turned her face to the wall and wouldn't eat. For the next three weeks she ate nothing except her sleeping powder and a few crumbs of bread and sips of water. She was too weak to speak, but whenever she saw Gaëlle, she looked at her with hatred and shame. Gaëlle called the doctor, but he couldn't force her mother to eat more either. And after three weeks of self-imposed starvation, in her already weakened condition, she got pneumonia from never moving from her bed. And three days later, while Gaëlle was sitting next to her, Agathe turned to look at her. Gaëlle never had a chance to tell her the truth about the paintings, or the children. She tried to reach out to hold her mother's hand, and Agathe wouldn't let her. She pulled her hand away, and wanted nothing to do with her own daughter.

She thought Gaëlle was a traitor, which was the worst thing she could think of after five years of war, and the four years of German occupation. She closed her eyes and drifted off to sleep then. She sighed and said her husband's name, and then she was gone. It was all over. She had never recovered from her husband's death and was never going to. The war had been too much for her.

Gaëlle gently closed her eyes and covered her, and Apolline came upstairs a few minutes later and saw what had happened.

'You killed your mother,' she said coldly.

'No,' Gaëlle said angrily, 'the war killed her. It killed all of us. You, me, my father, my brother, your son, thousands of Jewish children. No one is the same, and I'm not what you think I am. It doesn't matter what you think. I know who I am.' She walked out of the room then, and they buried her mother two days later. She told Apolline not to come to the burial. She didn't want Apolline to spoil her mourning her mother. She was nineteen years old, and she'd been through enough.

'You can go now,' she told Apolline the morning after the funeral. And the old housekeeper looked at her, shocked.

'I've worked here all my life,' she said, her eyes begging for pity, which Gaëlle no longer felt for her.

'You should have thought of that before you reported me as a collaborator, threw garbage at me in the street, and accused me of killing my mother.'

'But you . . . I saw you . . . you went to his bedroom . . . ' The old woman's voice faltered.

'I may have gone to his bedroom, but I didn't do what you think there. I'm closing the house anyway. I don't want to be here.' The thought of staying in a town where they had paraded her through the streets as a collaborator was more than she could bear.

'Where will you go?'

'I don't know. I'll figure it out. Now pack your bags and go.' Apolline didn't argue with her. She still believed that what she had done, reporting her as a traitor, was right, but she hadn't thought about the consequences to herself, or that Gaëlle's mother would die, or that she would close the château and leave. But Gaëlle had no other choice now. She knew she couldn't stay here. Not now, after being accused as a collaborator. She had to go.

The door closed behind Apolline that afternoon when she carried her two suitcases out. She had been there for twenty-five years. The once-devoted servant knew she'd never see Gaëlle again, or the château. She was going to stay with her sister in Bordeaux. And after Gaëlle heard the door close behind her, she sat in their living room and cried. Gaëlle was totally alone.

★   ★   ★

It took a month for her hair to grow out to a length that looked presentable. It was short, and most people could guess why. But she trimmed it with scissors, and got it to look as fashionable as

89

she could. She was still a beautiful girl, even after everything that had happened to her. She had the resilience of youth.

She spent several hours in the shed, packing the rolled paintings with clean white cotton cloth and tissue paper into three suitcases. It was the end of October, and the weather was starting to get cool. And she wanted to return the paintings to the Louvre. She didn't want the responsibility of keeping forty-nine major works of art safe.

She had two more suitcases filled with her meager clothes, and the envelope of money her father had left. She had enough for a few weeks in Paris, and after that she didn't know what she'd do. Maybe Apolline was right and she'd become a prostitute, she said to herself sarcastically, but she knew that was something she would never do. She had to find a job somewhere, but she couldn't stay in her village now, after she'd been disgraced. Maybe she'd come back to the château one day, or sell it. She draped all the furniture and family portraits with dust covers before she left, locked everything up, and asked one of the tenant farmers to look in on it once in a while to make sure that nothing was broken or leaking. When she closed the door behind her, she never wanted to see it again.

She took the train to Paris with her five suitcases and arrived at the Gare de Lyon, and she asked a cab driver to take her to an inexpensive hotel in St. Germain des Prés. She called the Louvre from the lobby of the hotel, spoke to someone in the administrative office, and asked to meet with one of the curators. She didn't know who to ask for and wasn't sure what to do. And when she went to a nearby bistro for dinner, people stared at her short hair, and American soldiers jeered at her and propositioned her. No matter what she had done to it, they knew what the short haircut meant. And in most cases it meant easy women who would sleep with anyone in a uniform, or that was what they'd been told. She went back to her hotel in tears.

She had an appointment at the Louvre the next day. They had no reason to think the meeting was important, and as she suspected, when she arrived at the Louvre, she was led into the tiny office of a young woman who was only a secretary. Gaëlle had the three suitcases with her, and wanted to be sure she put the paintings into the right hands.

'How may I help you?' she asked coolly. She had noticed her hair too. Everyone did. No woman in France wanted to be seen with short hair now. Everyone wanted to show that their hair was long and they'd been loyal to France.

Gaëlle wasn't sure where to begin. 'I have paintings that were sent to a German commandant, who was the commanding officer for our region, near Lyon. He and a friend gained possession of these paintings from other officers who had taken them. He gave them to me when the German troops withdrew and asked me to return them to the Louvre. So here I am.' It sounded like a far-fetched story even to her, but it was the truth, as simply put as she could.

'Of course,' the young woman said superciliously. 'Just leave them with me.'

'I'm sorry,' Gaëlle said politely, 'but I don't think I can. They're extremely valuable. Could you please call someone else?' The young woman hesitated with a condescending look, but when Gaëlle didn't move, the secretary finally picked up the phone on her desk. She told someone on the other end that there was a woman in her office who claimed that she had paintings that had been taken by the Germans and she wanted to give them back. There was a long pause then, while she listened to the person on the other end, who was telling her that they were almost certainly forgeries or outright fakes. 'She won't leave them unless someone comes to see them.' Another pause, and then she hung up, and glared at Gaëlle, sitting nervously across from her. She hoped they wouldn't accuse her of stealing them, but the commandant had instructed her to give them his rank and name.

Five minutes later a woman with gray hair walked officiously into the room and glanced at Gaëlle impatiently. 'Now what's this all about? And where did you get the paintings you brought to us?' Gaëlle went through the story again in more detail, and something about the way she said it, hesitantly and carefully, told the curator that it might be true. Strange things had happened during the Occupation.

'May I show them to you?' Gaëlle asked politely, and the woman nodded, looking slightly less impatient, and suddenly intrigued. Paris had been liberated eight weeks before, and it was just possible the story might be true. Gaëlle carefully unwrapped one of the small Renoirs and laid it delicately on the desk as the older woman stared at it in disbelief. The second one was a Degas. The third a Monet. And then she picked up the phone and asked someone else to come in. He arrived a few minutes later. They were all there, all forty-nine paintings, just as Gaëlle had tried to explain. The woman turned to Gaëlle in amazement, as the man examined the paintings. He was one of their experts on forgeries, and he was staring at what she'd brought in astonishment.

'They're all real. There's no question of it,' he said, and the older woman turned to Gaëlle again.

'Do you know anything about the provenance? Where they came from? Who owned them? Who the Germans took them from?'

'No, I don't,' Gaëlle said honestly. 'All I know is that these two German officers wanted to stop them from being sent to Germany. Other officers had stolen them from museums, and maybe from Jewish families, I don't know, and the commanding officer asked me to bring them to you after the war ended. He smuggled them to me, in loaves of bread. I hid them, and now I've brought them to you, as I promised I would.' She gave her the name of the commandant and explained that he and his officers had taken over her family's château during the Occupation.

'Was he a friend of yours?' the female curator asked, looking for an explanation for the short hair that no French woman would have wanted to wear by choice.

'No, just the commanding officer for our

district. I was very surprised when he asked me to do it,' she said simply. She had nothing to hide.

The woman had another thought then, still suspicious of how forty-nine extraordinary paintings had wound up in their hands, delivered by a young girl out of three suitcases. 'Are you trying to sell them to us?' Maybe it was a scam of some kind. And Gaëlle looked shocked.

'Of course not. I'm returning them to you. I don't know who they came from originally, but he said you would.'

'I'm not sure we do. But eventually we can find out. Would you give us your name too?' she asked, more pleasantly than she had before. By some extraordinary stroke of luck, this was legitimate, and the girl had brought masterpieces to the Louvre that a German officer had prevented from being taken out of France. It was a miracle.

'Certainly.' Gaëlle wrote her name down, and the name of her hotel, and her address at the château. 'I don't know where I'll be. Both of my parents died, and my brother, and I came to Paris to find a job. I don't know how long I'll be at the hotel, but you can write to me at home, if you want to. Eventually they'll send it to me.' She could ask the farmer to forward her mail once she had a permanent address. But she wasn't expecting to hear from anyone.

'I don't know how to thank you,' the woman said, shaking her hand. 'These are very unusual circumstances.'

'Most things are, in a war,' Gaëlle said quietly.

'I'm just glad you got them back.'

'That was very honorable of the two officers, and of you to bring them to us.' She could have sold them just as easily. Gaëlle nodded. She couldn't imagine doing other than what she'd promised the commandant. And then the woman thought of something else, and wrote a name and address down on a card.

'What's that?' Gaëlle asked when she looked at what she'd written.

'Maybe a job,' she said, and smiled at her. She had children Gaëlle's age, and the poor thing looked so lost and was so young, and after Gaëlle was gone, she turned to the girl at the desk. 'The next time someone shows up and tells you they have forty-nine masterpieces in a suitcase, don't try to get rid of the person. Call me immediately.' Her voice was tart as she said it.

'Of course,' the girl said nervously. But who could have ever dreamed they were real and it would turn out like this? And Gaëlle was smiling when she left. She thought the commandant would be pleased. It had gone well. The paintings were back where they belonged, in a museum, and she hoped the others, from private homes and families, would be returned soon.

★ ★ ★

After the Louvre, Gaëlle went to another address she had gotten from her hotel that morning. It was the Red Cross office. The office was crowded with people when she walked in, all trying to locate relatives in Europe. She had to wait two hours to see someone, but other than the paintings, this was the most important thing she had to do. She had waited two and a half years for this, and she wanted answers now.

She explained to the woman who met with her who she was trying to trace. She gave her the names of the entire Feldmann family, the date when they had been first sent to the camp, and when they had been deported to Germany, or somewhere else.

The woman made careful notes and looked at Gaëlle sympathetically, and spoke to her in a kind voice.

'You realize, don't you, that it's possible that none of the Feldmanns are still alive. Very few people survived the camps. If we're lucky, we may find one or two of them, but we may not.' The camps had been liberated one by one in recent weeks, since the first camp at Majdanek was liberated by the Soviets in July, and the stories about them were shocking, inhumane, and upsetting beyond belief. The photographs Gaëlle had seen of them and the ravaged survivors made her cry each time they liberated another camp.

'I want to know what happened to them,' Gaëlle said doggedly of the Feldmanns. 'We should know. Maybe Rebekah's in one of those camps they just liberated and she's too weak to come home. I want to go to her if she's alive.'

'Of course,' the woman said gently, and told Gaëlle to check back in three weeks, which sounded like a long time to her. But it was worth the wait if they found her. Maybe she was one of the survivors. Rebekah had been young and strong. Gaëlle refused to believe she was dead. She was sure that with enough time they'd find her.

She went back to the hotel after that. It had been an exhausting, emotionally draining day. She was hungry but didn't want to go to a bistro and be propositioned by the soldiers again, so she went to her room, even though she was hungry, and as soon as she lay on her bed, she fell asleep.

★　★　★

She woke up ravenous the next morning, and went to a different bistro, and there were no soldiers there. She was wearing a plain black skirt and a black jacket that had been her mother's and was a little too grown-up for her, and flat shoes, because she was tall enough. She had café au lait and two croissants, and they were delicious, and then she remembered the card the woman at the Louvre had given her with the name and address for a possible job. She thought it might be for work as a secretary, or in an art gallery, and hoped she'd qualify. She had no training to be a secretary or a waitress or anything else, but she needed to find work soon, before her money ran out. She took it out and read it again. The name the curator had written was Lucien Lelong, which meant nothing to her, at an address she didn't know. She got a map at a newspaper kiosk and walked to the address, and stood in front of a small elegant building. A discreet sign said 'Lelong,' and two well-dressed women emerged. Gaëlle watched them, and then pressed the bell a moment later.

The door was opened by a man in a dark suit, who looked her over with some surprise and asked if she had an appointment. She could see a large reception room behind him, and still had no idea what kind of business it was. It seemed more like a home, and she wondered if the curator had sent her for a job as a maid. She was willing to accept any work she could find, as long as it was legal and not prostitution.

'I'm here for a job,' she said, trying to appear braver than she felt, and the man at the door smiled, and escorted her to a little sitting room, where he instructed her to wait for a minute, and then he disappeared. It was decorated simply with white furniture upholstered in gray silk. And there were drawings of evening gowns framed on the walls, and photographs of fashion shows with models from before the war. She wondered if it was some kind of store, but it didn't look like one. She was still wondering when the man reappeared with a tall, thin blond woman. She had a beautiful face, and looked very severe in a slim black suit with a fashionably short skirt just below the knee. Fabric had been rationed during the war, so styles had gotten shorter and narrower, closer to the body, in order to use less fabric. The woman was wearing her hair in a tight bun and was startled when she saw Gaëlle's clipped short hair, which appeared almost boyish but was flattering the way she'd cut it as it grew out. She was so pretty she could get away with it. The man in the dark suit went back to the door then, and left Gaëlle alone with the woman he'd introduced as Madame Cécile, who continued to observe Gaëlle intently.

'You've come for a job?' she asked, after she'd taken in every inch of Gaëlle, and the unfashionable suit she was wearing that looked to Cécile like a hand-me-down from her grandmother. 'As a *vendeuse?*' — a salesgirl — Cécile interrogated her.

'That would be fine,' Gaëlle said, feeling breathless under the sharp gaze of the blond woman, although she didn't know what she'd be selling. There was nothing to buy here. And transporting Jewish children for the OSE had been less frightening than being stared at by the woman in the chic black suit. Gaëlle knew nothing about fashion, but she could tell that the woman was stylish just by the confident, graceful way she carried herself, and she was watching every move that Gaëlle made, as though it mattered immensely. Gaëlle had never paid attention to clothes, her mother had had a local dressmaker, but nothing she wore had been remarkable or followed fashion. Mrs. Feldmann had shopped in Paris occasionally and had much nicer clothes, and a dressmaker in Lyon.

'Would you please walk across the room for me?' the woman asked her in an authoritative tone, and Gaëlle did as she was told, as the woman watched her and frowned. 'Again, please. Stand up straight now and look directly ahead of you.' Gaëlle crossed the small room again as

Madame Cécile nodded and seemed satisfied. 'That was better,' she praised her. It was all a mystery to Gaëlle, what she was doing there, what the job might be, and what they had to sell. 'You would have done well before the war,' she said cryptically. 'We don't have fashion shows since the Occupation, but we still make samples, and have girls wear them to show our clients.' And Gaëlle's hair didn't shock her, since they had been making clothes for the wives of German officers, as well as a few wealthy French clients for the past four years, and they had seen their share of shorn heads in Paris too, since August.

'Come with me,' she said then, and Gaëlle followed her out of the room, down a long hallway, and Madame Cécile unlocked a door with a key. They stepped into a large room full of women wearing white smocks. They were cutting fabric on long tables, fitting clothes on mannequins, and many of them were sewing by hand. Fabric was still being rationed and in short supply, but they seemed to have enough of it to keep a room full of women busy making clothes.

'Is this the store?' Gaëlle asked with wide eyes.

'No, my dear.' Madame Cécile smiled at her innocence. 'It's the atelier, the workroom. Monsieur Lelong makes haute couture clothes.' Gaëlle wasn't sure what haute couture was, but Madame Cécile made it sound very important, and the few garments Gaëlle could see nearly finished were beautiful. She was fascinated by what they were doing and the activity in the busy workroom. Lucien Lelong was one of the most

100

important designers in Paris, overshadowed at the time only by Coco Chanel, whose close ties with the German High Command had caused her business to flourish during the Occupation. Lelong had been more restrained, although he had dressed their women too.

Gaëlle was still glancing around when a slim young man entered the room, and all the women snapped to attention and appeared to be even busier than before. Madame Cécile introduced him to Gaëlle. It was Christian Dior, Lucien Lelong's star designer, and it had only recently been discovered that although he had important German clients, he had been passing information he gleaned from them to the Resistance for the entire Occupation. It made him a hero now, unlike Coco Chanel, who was not only accused of being a collaborator but was suspected of having been a German agent, and had rapidly left France for Switzerland when Paris was liberated. Dior's sister Catherine had been in the Resistance too, and had been caught by the Gestapo and sent to a concentration camp for her subversive activities. Her brother was hoping she would be freed soon when Gaëlle met him.

'What do you think of her?' Cécile asked him in an undervoice about Gaëlle as she chatted with the seamstresses who were embroidering an evening gown. Every stitch of the clothing was handmade.

'As what?' The head designer looked distracted. He was working on samples for their spring collection, and he was worried about getting enough fabric to meet their clients' demands. He gave Gaëlle a closer look then. 'Pretty girl,' he commented, 'beautiful actually. I wish we'd had her for our shows before the war.' But they still used models to show the clothes to clients. And with the Occupation over, once the rationing of fabric ended, Cécile was sure they'd do lavish fashion shows again. 'Do we need her?' he asked Cécile.

'We will. But for the moment, not as badly as she needs us. She just came from Lyon. She lost her whole family during the Occupation. Mother, father, brother.' Cécile had asked her about her family. 'She's in Paris to find a job. She's very young, just nineteen.'

'We can use her to model samples,' he said thoughtfully. 'She's beautiful and has a nice way about her. You can teach her how to walk and show the clothes. She has a natural ease and elegance I like,' he said, squinting at her as he appraised her. 'She can be our good deed for the day. She probably needs one,' he said and smiled at the head of haute couture for the house. And then he noticed her hair. 'Collaborator?' he asked in a whisper, with a worried expression.

'She says not.' Cécile had asked her that too, and then put in a good word for her. 'I don't know why, but I believe her. But someone in her home village didn't, given the hair.'

'I'd like to believe she's telling the truth,' the designer said, and Cécile nodded.

'Me too,' she agreed. There was an air of innocence about Gaëlle, good values, and poise beyond her years, probably due to the war.

'Why don't you start her immediately? I have

102

two new clients coming in this week. They've been here before but never bought anything. A fresh face always makes it more exciting.' She nodded, and he left the atelier then. A few minutes later Cécile took Gaëlle to her office, and they sat down.

'You start tomorrow, if you want to,' Cécile said, smiling at her. 'You're very fortunate. Monsieur Dior liked you, that's what it takes around here, and you have lots to learn about how to walk and move and show the clothes to advantage. And you *never* speak to clients unless they speak to you,' she said sternly. 'Where are you staying?'

'At a hotel, but I can't stay there for much longer. I have to find a place to live.' She looked anxious about it, but was shocked and excited about the job. It was like a dream come true!

'We have an apartment for the models. You'll be living with four other girls, and we expect you to behave like ladies and be nice to one another.' She said it like a school mistress, and she felt that way sometimes too, as Gaëlle stared at her in disbelief.

'How much will I have to pay there?'

'Nothing. It's free, as long as you're modeling for Monsieur Dior.' There were tears in Gaëlle's eyes as she thanked her. She had a job and an apartment. She was going to be a haute couture model, and as she left the building a few minutes later, she whispered to the man at the door that she got the job, and he smiled broadly at her and gave her a victory sign. She was floating on air as she walked back to the hotel, and when she got

103

there, she called to thank the curator at the Louvre who had given her the address. She sounded happy for her.

As Gaëlle packed her things at the hotel that night, she thought about how lucky she was. A whole new life had begun. The only thing missing was that she had no one to tell about it. No friends, no family. She knew that Rebekah would have been so excited for her. The only people she could tell were the doorman at Lucien Lelong, and the desk clerk at the hotel, who was busy and didn't seem to care. But all that mattered was that she had a job. She was going to be a model for their head designer, Christian Dior. Gaëlle could only hope that her parents would have been proud of her.

7

Gaëlle was up at dawn for her first day of work at Lucien Lelong. She didn't know what to expect, and she was nervous about it. She wore a gray pleated skirt she'd worn to school and a gray sweater, the same flat shoes, and her mother's black jacket. She never wore makeup, and there was nothing she could do to her hair yet, it was still too short.

She arrived at work with both her suitcases and put them in the models' dressing room. The other girls hadn't come to work yet, and Gaëlle was anxious about meeting them. Madame Cécile said they were all nice girls. She sent Gaëlle to the hairdresser then, much to her surprise.

'You want it shorter?' she asked in amazement.

'No, just better.' Cécile laughed. She had told the hairdresser what Monsieur Dior wanted. A stylish trim had been his suggestion, so that her short hair looked intentional and not the work of outraged villagers who had chopped it off.

She felt intimidated at the fashionable hairdresser where they sent her and was surprised at the effect they achieved with a few deft snips here and there. Her hair was a fashion statement now, not a mark of shame. Gaëlle returned to Lelong's haute couture house two hours later, and the other models had arrived by then and were excited to meet her and said they

105

loved her hair. Madame Cécile introduced them, and they were from eighteen to twenty-two years of age. It felt like going back to school to Gaëlle as they laughed and teased in the dressing room. They had no clients to dress for that morning.

They went to lunch together at a bistro nearby, as the girls and Gaëlle got to know each other, and that afternoon while the others modeled clothes for clients, Cécile taught Gaëlle how to walk and stand and give Monsieur Dior's designs 'allure.'

And after work, they took her to the apartment, and Elodie, a girl from Marseilles, helped her carry one of her bags. The building was small and chic, and there were five bedrooms in the spacious apartment. Gaëlle had the smallest room, which was much bigger than the attic cell where she had spent the last three years. As soon as she unpacked, Ivy, a British girl, broke out a bottle of champagne to celebrate. She had lost her parents and younger sister in one of the bombing raids on London, and had told Gaëlle about it over lunch. They had in common that they were both alone. And her boyfriend had been in the RAF and was killed two years before. They had paid their dues, and all of them were grateful for the jobs they had at Lelong, modeling for Monsieur Dior. They all liked him and said what a nice man he was. And the job paid well. Ivy had offered to practice speaking English with Gaëlle so she could speak to American clients when they spoke to her. She had learned in school, but hadn't practiced in several years, and her English skills were very basic.

Marie, the oldest of the group, who acted like the house mother, looked over Gaëlle's clothes that night and told her what to wear to work. They told her the house would dress her eventually, but until then she had to be as stylish as possible with what she had.

'There's not much here, is there?' Gaëlle said, embarrassed. They were all so sophisticated, in her eyes. She had brought her school clothes and a few things of her mother's, which didn't really fit her. She hadn't had new clothes since before the war, when she was fourteen. She didn't need them at home, but here she did.

'Don't worry about it,' Elodie said, poking her head in the door. 'You can borrow something from me.' They each contributed an item or two to her wardrobe that night, and Gaëlle was touched. She hadn't had anyone her own age to talk to since Rebekah left. And she'd never known girls like these. Living with them was fun. Everything in Paris seemed glamorous to Gaëlle, and they took her to their favorite bistro the following night. They went out together a lot, except Marie, who had a boyfriend, and was hoping to get engaged when they saved up enough money. Her boyfriend had been a law student before the war and was now a cabdriver, and had been in the Resistance in Paris. Monsieur Dior had seen her working as a waitress in a café, been struck by her beauty, and hired her as a model. All of them had happened into their employment by accident and felt extremely fortunate to be working at such a good job.

And although they enjoyed it, none of them planned to be models forever. Elodie wanted to go back to school, Ivy hoped to go back to England eventually, and Marie wanted to marry and have babies. Juana, the fourth of the girls, was Brazilian and wanted to go home too. She was shy and planned to study to be a nurse. She had a big family and missed them. Gaëlle didn't know what she wanted, except to get away from her village and the pain and losses she'd been through there. She couldn't think about her future yet, or how she would spend it, or with whom. The present, modeling in Paris for Christian Dior, was more than enough to keep her happy. She hadn't had this much fun in years, or felt as safe and welcome as she did with her new roommates. She was crazy about them, and they divided housekeeping chores between them, which seemed fair to her. She was happy to do whatever she could. It was such a blessing not to be living with enemy soldiers under the same roof, although there were plenty of men in uniform, French and Allied soldiers, in the streets, flirting with Parisian women.

She had her first photo shoot two days later, and Madame Cécile showed her how to pose in the shots. They did her makeup, and dressed her in an assortment of beautiful outfits that she wore well. Monsieur Dior came in himself and made a few comments and then left the studio. Ed Thompson, the photographer, was American, and said he had just gotten out of the army, and was glad he had been stationed in Washington for most of it, taking PR photos of the top brass.

The stories he heard of the fighting in Europe made him realize how lucky he had been. The Germans were still fighting in some areas. Hitler was trying to occupy Italy to keep the Allies out, and the French were still attempting to take Strasbourg back from the Germans. Life in Paris was better after the Liberation, but the war wasn't over yet by any means.

'I hear it was pretty rough over here,' Ed said to Gaëlle as she posed for him. One of the other models had said to her that he was a famous photographer, and they all liked working with him. And he told Gaëlle he enjoyed photographing her at the end of the session. 'You're going to be a big model one day,' he told her, and seemed sincere. 'You should try working in New York sometime.'

'I just got here, and I love it,' she said with a look of girlish ecstasy, and he laughed. Her school English was hesitant but adequate, and Ivy was already helping her.

'It's a tough business, but you're starting at the top. It doesn't get better than this.' And as he said it, she realized what had happened to her. She hadn't been in Paris for a week, and she was a model for Christian Dior, lived in a beautiful apartment, and had four new friends. She was stunned as it hit her. Her whole life had changed when she came to Paris. The war in France was almost over. Paris was free again. And she could hardly wait to see what was in store for her next in her glamorous new life. She suddenly felt as though she had a flock of guardian angels, Madame Cécile and Christian Dior among

109

them, and her four roommates.

The night after her shoot, the photographer and two of the models, Ivy and Elodie, took Gaëlle to the bar at the Ritz for a drink. Elodie explained to her that the beautiful hotel had been filled with German officers for the entire Occupation. The only civilian who had been allowed to live there was the designer Coco Chanel, due to her high connections. She had closed her shops at the beginning of the war, and knew everyone in Paris. She was rabidly anti-Semitic and became friends with Goering, Himmler, and Goebbels of the SS elite, and formed a romantic liaison with German officer Baron Hans Günther von Dincklage, which gave her free access to German social and military circles. And in a stunning coup, she attempted to get full control of Parfums Chanel from the Wertheimers, who owned the brand. She tried to wrest it from them by pointing out that they were Jews and therefore had legally abandoned the business, so she claimed full rights to their interests, only to discover that in May 1940, a month before the Occupation, they had protected their business by signing it over to Felix Amiot, a Christian. Coco Chanel's takeover of their business was unsuccessful, but she became one of the richest women in France from her share in their business, and the toast of Paris until the Liberation. She had already fled Paris by the time Gaëlle got there, but she was still much talked about for her strong ties to the Germans and allegiances during the Occupation. And with his work for the Resistance, Christian

Dior was at the opposite end of the spectrum, and deeply respected.

The girls and Gaëlle were talking about it with Ed at the bar of the Ritz when Elodie noticed a handsome American officer walk in and sit down at a table near them. He was alone and couldn't keep his eyes off the three beautiful women, and after exchanging smiles for a while, with the girls' permission, Ed asked him to join them. They introduced themselves, and Ed and Ivy spoke English, but Elodie and Gaëlle spoke very little. He said his name was Billy Jones from Houston, Texas, and he spoke surprisingly good French. He had just been released a week before from a prisoner of war camp in Germany, and had learned to speak French there from the French prisoners, he explained to the girls. And he had learned German from the guards.

'You must be anxious to get home,' Ed Thompson said sympathetically, after hearing the Texan's exploits. He had organized two escapes from the camp but had been recaptured both times and had spent two years in the camp. 'Why are you still in Paris?' Jones laughed easily in answer to the question.

'I'm here by the special invitation of General Eisenhower. He gave us a choice. Go home on the next flight, or accept a 'special mission' in Paris for two weeks, and do whatever we want, and they'll cover our butts with the folks at home. My girl got married to someone else when they declared me MIA for the first six months, so I figured what the hell, and took the general up on the 'special mission' here.' He grinned

111

broadly from ear to ear, and looked like he was enjoying himself, especially at the table with three gorgeous young models. He seemed to be having trouble deciding between Elodie and Gaëlle and was flirting with both, as they sympathized about his two years as a POW. 'I might have to thank the general personally for this,' he said as Elodie filled his glass with champagne. They were all in high spirits, and every night felt like a celebration to them, particularly this one. Ed was flying back to New York the next day, but Billy had another week to spend in Paris and intended to take full advantage of it. They left him outside the Ritz, and he promised to call the girls the next day at the apartment.

Gaëlle had just come home from work when he did, and she was alone at the apartment. The others were having fittings in the atelier with Monsieur Dior. And Billy didn't sound disappointed to reach her. He invited her to dinner at Maxim's. She offered to bring Elodie along, but he said he'd catch up with her another time, and wanted to have dinner alone with Gaëlle.

When he picked her up, they had an elegant evening together. Gaëlle had apologized to Elodie before she went out, who said she didn't care. They had a great time and went dancing after dinner. He tried to kiss her several times, and she explained innocently to him that she liked him a lot, but if they started a romance now, she'd be sad when he left and didn't know when they'd meet again. She had a point, but not one he wanted to hear after two years in a prison camp, or while in Paris for two weeks of unbridled fun, courtesy of the U.S. Army. But Gaëlle wasn't that kind of girl.

'Then maybe you'll just have to come see me in Texas,' he suggested after drinking most of a bottle of champagne himself, after wine with dinner. He'd had a lot to drink, but he was a nice guy, amusing to be with and not obnoxious, just more amorous than she wanted.

He took her home at four A.M. after more champagne and more dancing and a last attempt to kiss her. She would have liked him as a friend but doubted their paths would cross again. He was mustering out of the army when he got back, and had no plans to return to Europe. He wasn't looking for a bride, just a good time in Paris for two weeks before he went home. He'd earned it.

The next morning at breakfast, Gaëlle told Elodie she should go out with him.

'You wouldn't mind?' Elodie's eyes lit up like Christmas.

'Not at all,' Gaëlle assured her, and meant it.

He called that afternoon, and Gaëlle told Billy she was busy that night and handed the phone to Elodie. They went out later, and Elodie came home looking dazzled at six A.M. And when Gaëlle saw her dreamy look at breakfast, she smiled and guessed that Billy had gotten what he wanted, an unforgettable night in Paris, with a beautiful girl he would remember forever.

★　★　★

Within a few weeks of when she started to work for Lelong, Gaëlle had learned the tricks of the trade, how to walk, how to pose, how to do her makeup. Photographers loved working with her, the camera loved her. She was easy and good-natured and fun to talk to, and she did as she was told with no drama or attitude. She enjoyed her work every day. It was hard to believe that a few months before, her life had been one of deprivation, danger, and misery, and she'd been risking her life transporting Jewish children for two years, and now all she had to do was look beautiful, and they made it easy for her with gorgeous clothes, hairdressers and makeup artists, and even jewelry for her to wear.

Most of the other girls had been in Paris during the Occupation and had been modeling for a while, and all of them were impressed by how quickly Gaëlle adapted, and the five roommates got along like old friends. They all had stories to tell, although Gaëlle never talked about hers. The details of her father getting killed in the Resistance, her brother a month earlier, her mother withering away until she died, her best friend being deported because she was Jewish, none of them were stories she wanted to share, but she listened to theirs. And they sensed that there were things that were too painful for her to talk about, so they didn't press her. There were others who had suffered heavy losses too, and no one wanted to talk about the war years. They wanted to forget it now. Gaëlle preferred talking about what they were doing, modeling clothes for clients, the magazine shoots, and the beauty of Monsieur Dior's designs. It was exciting to see a whole new look emerge, always with the unmistakable stamp of Dior, as fabrics became more readily available.

By spring, six months after she'd come to work for the house, she was one of the hottest, most popular models in Paris, and they booked her for a cover shoot with *Vogue* in New York in June. She could hardly wait. Every day was a new adventure for Gaëlle.

The mood in France had lightened considerably too when Germany surrendered in May. The war in Europe was truly over, and the future looked very bright to Gaëlle.

She had been back to the Red Cross several times by then, and they still had no news for her, until one day in May, they called her at the apartment and asked her to come in. They had finally traced the Feldmanns despite the bureaucratic chaos in Germany, and the woman on the phone said she wanted to discuss it with her in person. Gaëlle didn't know if that was a good sign or not, but hoped it meant they had located Rebekah, possibly recovering in a hospital in Germany after being liberated from a concentration camp. She went to the Red Cross office on a warm afternoon, after work. She was wearing black slacks and a white silk shirt and looked very striking, and like a very different person from the first time she'd come in. But the moment she sat down across the desk from the Red Cross worker, she wasn't a Dior model, she was Rebekah's best friend, as she had always been. She looked intently at the woman

115

she'd been speaking to for months, and waited anxiously for news of her childhood friend.

'It's still incredibly difficult to get information in Germany. They did keep meticulous records, but they destroyed a lot of them at the end. We speak to everyone who comes through here for news of others we're looking for, who might have been at the same camp. And the survivors have begun to come home. Many of them have been too ill or weak to travel after they left the camps, and have been in hospitals there, which has made them harder to trace too. We got a report from Germany about the Feldmanns a month ago, and it's been corroborated by two survivors of the same camp. So I think we know the whole story now, and I want to warn you that the news isn't good.' Gaëlle had been afraid of that for three years, since they were deported from the Chambaran detention camp, and the last time Gaëlle had seen her.

'Where did they send them?' Gaëlle asked in a subdued voice.

'From Chambaran, they transferred them to the camp at Arandon in the northeast, and from there the whole family went to Auschwitz,' she said somberly. It was a name Gaëlle had learned to dread, after hearing stories once the camps were liberated, and seeing terrible photographs and films on the news. She'd seen a newsreel of soldiers liberating one of the camps and had to leave the theater. The freed prisoners looked like walking corpses and just stood there and cried, unable to believe they were free at last. Most of them were too weak to walk and had to be carried out. 'All of the Feldmanns' names came through on the report. They were all checked in on the same day, so they arrived together, by train.' She had all the details from the camp records, and some firsthand reports from Red Cross workers and a refugee organization they were working with as well. 'Mr. Feldmann and the two boys were put to hard labor in the men's camp. And Mrs. Feldmann was at the women's camp with the two girls. Lotte died a month after they got there, we don't know why.'

Gaëlle's eyes filled with tears as she listened intently to hear the rest. She had waited so long for this, and she wanted to know now, no matter how bad it was. 'Mrs. Feldmann and Rebekah were exterminated in October 1942,' the Red Cross woman said quietly. 'Many of the women were sent to the gas chamber then, to make room for fresh arrivals. And Mr. Feldmann and the boys died in January 1943.'

Her words hit Gaëlle like a building falling on her. Gaëlle knew it now for sure. Rebekah was never coming back. And all this time she had prayed that Rebekah would survive it, that she was still alive, and they would meet again. The whole family had died at Auschwitz, and she hated the Germans with every ounce of her being for what they'd done. And even all the children she had taken to safety didn't make up for this. The people she loved were gone. 'I'm sorry. I was hoping to give you better news. So many people were killed there, and so few survived it.' They had tried to destroy an entire race.

117

Gaëlle walked out into the sunshine feeling dazed. She walked back to the apartment, thinking about Rebekah and the last time she'd seen her, and all the years they had shared, and that terrible feeling of seeing the camp empty the last time she went. She had been afraid for them ever since, but had hoped anyway. And now there was nothing to hope for. It had been over for years. Rebekah had died at seventeen, right before her eighteenth birthday.

Gaëlle walked home blindly and nearly got hit by a taxi that honked furiously at her, and when she got back to the apartment, she went to her room and closed the door. She took the little box out of the drawer where she put it when she moved in. She always had it with her, and she pulled out the wisp of blue satin ribbon, and remembered how it had looked in Rebekah's hair when she gave it to her, and retrieving it from the fence for herself, as a souvenir of her friend. She could still hear her laughter, and see her smile, and feel the times she had kissed her cheek through the fence when she left. And poor little Lotte . . . and her parents . . . and the boys. All of them gone. 'Exterminated.' She hated the word. Exterminated was what you did to an insect, not a human. If only they had sent them to a different camp, maybe they'd still be alive, or if the Germans hadn't put them in detention camps in France at all and the French hadn't betrayed their fellow countrymen with such a cowardly act. She knew she was only one of thousands of people hearing terrible news from the Red Cross, and the other organizations helping to find their relatives and friends. Gaëlle had never felt worse in her life.

There was a soft knock on the door of her room, and Ivy, the English model, opened it and stuck her head in. Gaëlle was still sitting at her desk holding the ribbon, as she looked up with a ravaged expression.

'Gaëlle? Are you all right?' She didn't appear to be. She seemed devastated. Ivy had seen her come in and go straight to her room and close the door, and she looked as if she'd been crying, and she still was. 'Something wrong? Can I help?' She was a kind girl and Gaëlle liked her, they had become friends.

'It happened a long time ago, but I got bad news today,' Gaëlle said in a choked voice. She gently laid the ribbon back in the box, put it away, and closed the drawer. She knew she would keep the scrap of satin forever. It was all she had left of her friend, except for some photographs her parents had taken when they were little girls. And she had no photographs of the others, although they were engraved on her mind forever.

'War stuff?' Ivy asked. Gaëlle nodded and stood up.

'It's hard to understand how it all happened, and why no one did anything. No one ever tried to stop it.'

'I know. We had two Polish boys living with us during the war. Their parents died in the Warsaw ghetto. My parents adopted them, and then they were killed in the bombing with my family. It's all so terribly wrong.' Gaëlle nodded agreement.

The British had sent trains to Germany, Poland, Hungary, Austria, and Czechoslovakia to get Jewish children out right before the war. Most of them had lost every one of their relatives at home.

'That's a nice thing for your parents to have done. It's hard to balance that with our lives now, isn't it? This is so different.' Gaëlle felt guilty about it at times, the pretty clothes, the good times she was having. She often wondered if she deserved it when so many had died, like Rebekah. And others were still suffering in the aftermath of the war all over Europe.

'It's over,' Ivy said simply. 'We have to go on now. It won't bring them back if we keep crying.' She had a point, and Gaëlle followed her into the living room. They each had had losses, they just didn't talk about them. But Gaëlle knew they couldn't forget either. They had to remember the travesty forever so it never happened again.

Gaëlle was quiet that night, thinking about Rebekah. She went to bed early, and she knew Ivy was right. Suffering now wouldn't change it. They had to go on, for those who had died, for themselves, for those they didn't even know. All they could do now was honor them and remember how much they had loved them and let the scars heal in time. Gaëlle knew it was going to take time and the memories would linger forever. They would never forget them.

She went to sleep holding the little piece of blue ribbon that night, and dreamed of Rebekah. She was happy and laughing and Lotte was with her, and her parents and the boys. And wherever they were, Gaëlle hoped they were in a better place now, at peace, forever loved and always remembered. Rebekah would always be her most beloved friend.

8

The trip to New York for the *Vogue* shoot in June was dazzling. Madame Cécile's assistant went with Gaëlle, to help her, and also to make sure she behaved if necessary. It wasn't unheard of for young models to go crazy faced with an opportunity like the trip to New York, but Gaëlle was very circumspect, and totally overwhelmed at first.

They took a Pan Am flight from Paris, in first class, with stewardesses in trim blue uniforms, who looked like models, tending to them, and lavishly pouring champagne. The trip took fourteen hours with two stops to refuel. They landed at La Guardia Field, and stayed at the Waldorf Astoria Hotel on Park Avenue in the city.

Irving Penn, one of *Vogue*'s favorite photographers, had been hired to do the shoot. And the editor-in-chief, Edna Woolman Chase, was in the studio observing most of the time. She was very pleased with what she saw, and she called Christian Dior herself and told him Gaëlle was a new face, and she had a fresh innocence about her, and eyes that held the wisdom of the world. She was a wonderful combination of beauty and grace, and the clothes looked spectacular on her, with her long, thin body, and short sexy blond hair. She followed direction easily, and the proofs when they got them were exactly what they wanted.

The assistants at *Vogue* wined and dined her at night, took her to parties, and introduced her to famous people and other models. After the hardship of the war years, Gaëlle felt as though she had gone to heaven. She got offers from modeling agencies to represent her, and the editors at *Vogue* encouraged her to come to work in New York. Europe was still ravaged, money was scarce, and life was difficult in many ways. Business in New York was better, and the country hadn't suffered as they had in Europe. But Gaëlle wanted to go back to Paris, and she was loyal to the house of Lelong and Christian Dior, whom she respected deeply. And Madame Cécile's assistant was impressed by how well she behaved. Her good manners, integrity, and respectable upbringing served her well and made her a pleasure to work with. Everyone had wonderful things to say about her.

Two of the younger *Vogue* editors took her to a private party at the Stork Club one night. They always got calls asking them to bring models to glamorous social events, and the party at the Stork was to celebrate the premiere of a movie starring Rita Hayworth, and Humphrey Bogart was going to be there. Gaëlle wasn't even sure who they were, but she was excited to go. She wore a sexy white satin dress that was nearly backless and high-necked in front, and she wore a cascade of pearls Monsieur Dior had chosen for her. Bogart was bringing his gorgeous young bride, Lauren Bacall. They had just gotten married two weeks before. The press was excited about them as the fairy-tale couple. There were going to be a lot of important people there. And Monsieur Dior liked the idea of Gaëlle becoming a noticeable presence on the international scene. Madame Cécile had approved long distance every place Gaëlle would go. She was going to be on the cover of *Vogue* in September, and they wanted Gaëlle to be a star in her own right by then. It could only provide good press and PR and media attention for the house of Lelong and Christian Dior as the designer who had found her. She was a marketing tool for them now, like other big models before her, but there was something special about Gaëlle. She had more depth than the usual models, along with her exquisite face. And the makeup and hair they designed for her, as well as the clothes, only enhanced it.

The war in the Pacific was nearly over, and everyone in New York was in high spirits. Gaëlle and the two editors had just arrived at the party, with Madame Cécile's assistant, as chaperones, and the press went crazy when they saw her, and took dozens of photographs when she walked in. They wanted to know who the new beauty was, and they were writing down her name, when one of New York's best-known bachelors walked in. Robert Bartlett. He looked very handsome in white tie and tails. He was an important investment banker, and it was no secret that he was enormously wealthy. And all the prettiest women in the city appeared on his arm regularly. He came alone that night, and he noticed Gaëlle immediately, made his way through the crowd, and caught her eye from a few feet away as he hovered near her, waiting for the press to end their feeding frenzy. One of the *Vogue* editors told Gaëlle who he was, before he began speaking to her.

'Welcome to New York,' he said, smiling broadly as he handed her a glass of champagne. He had just learned that she was the latest model from Paris, and he recognized the women from *Vogue* and greeted them politely. Models were his stock in trade. He was considered a genius on Wall Street, and beautiful women were his hobby, as well as collecting modern art. He had one of the most important collections in the States.

Gaëlle thanked him politely for the champagne and was shy as he tried to engage her in conversation. He spoke to her in French and said he had just been in Paris a few weeks before and was sorry he hadn't met her then.

'How are you enjoying working for Christian Dior?' Her eyes lit up when he asked her. He could see that she was very young, and he thought there was something very touching about her that made one want to protect her. She responded in hesitant but adequate English that she loved her work and Monsieur Dior, who was very kind. Thanks to Ivy, she was learning better language quickly, with an accent Robert found endearing. He knew only too well that the sharks in her business would be after her shortly, people who wanted to exploit her in a variety of ways or take her money, although Lucien Lelong was a respectable house and she was well surrounded that night 'to protect her from men like me,' he said, and she laughed. He had perfect manners and was a total gentleman.

'You don't look dangerous to me,' she said with a schoolgirl grin.

'That shows how innocent you are in the ways of the world. Are you from Paris?'

'I'm from a small town near Lyon.'

'That explains it. Beware of the big city, whether Paris or New York. Where did you spend the war?' he asked with interest.

'At home, with my parents.' She didn't tell him that her whole family was dead now, and she was alone in the world. But in spite of her naïveté and small-town roots, she looked well able to take care of herself, which was an accurate assessment.

'Things weren't totally back to normal yet, when I was there recently,' he commented, 'but it seems to be recovering.' The Occupation had ended ten months before, and the country was doing well in spite of the hardships they'd been through, although he knew that Paris even during the Occupation had been lively and the Germans had taken full advantage of the beautiful city.

'It was very bad in my region when the Germans were there. We had very little food. And they were brutal.' She hesitated for a minute and then added, 'They killed my father for being in the Resistance.'

'And were you?' Bartlett asked her directly, and he found it interesting when she didn't answer his question. The subject was too vast to broach at a party, and she didn't want to. And what would she tell him? That she had transported Jewish children to safety, or rescued stolen paintings from the Nazis for the commanding officer of the district who had taken over her home? It was much too personal to discuss with a stranger, and she was too modest to do so. It was too complicated to explain, and too painful, like most war experiences. She hadn't mentioned her wartime activities to the girls she lived with either, though they had heard a rumor that she'd been accused of being a collaborator, and she didn't try to justify herself. Most real collaborators denied it now anyway, except Coco Chanel, who didn't seem to care what they called her. She was a very independent woman who paid no attention to what people said about her, but Gaëlle cared a great deal. She wanted to explain none of it to Robert Bartlett, and he could tell and changed the subject. 'How long are you planning to be in New York?' he asked her.

'I'm leaving in two days' was her response.

'What a shame,' he said, looking genuinely disappointed. 'I would have loved to show you the city, and some of my favorite nightclubs.' She guessed him to be somewhere in his late forties, but he seemed fit and athletic and was very handsome. They danced for a few minutes, but the dance floor was crowded. Having gotten all the press they wanted for her, her chaperones encouraged her to leave early. She didn't see Bartlett in the crowded room and didn't get a chance to say good night to him. He searched for her after she made a discreet exit. And she received three dozen red roses from him at the hotel the next day. The card said 'Until we meet again. Robert Bartlett.' And Gaëlle was enormously impressed. No man had ever sent her flowers, and surely not like that.

'Is he a playboy?' Gaëlle asked one of the women at *Vogue* that afternoon. She wasn't entirely sure what it meant, and the young editor laughed.

'Yes, he is.'

'What does that mean precisely?' Gaëlle looked at her intently.

'That he goes out with a lot of pretty women. Actresses, models, socialites. He's divorced, and considered a big catch. He's very successful. I don't think he'll be getting married again anytime soon. He's having too much fun.' He had been married to a well-known debutante from a family with an important name. She'd been half his age, the marriage had lasted for a few years, and they'd gotten divorced recently, in Reno. The papers had been full of it, and she got an enormous settlement from him, and their New York town-house. His ex-wife was already engaged to someone else. 'You need to be careful of men like him, Gaëlle,' she added wisely, although he had extremely good manners, women liked him, and he treated them well, and was very generous with them. But for a young country girl, Robert Bartlett was way out of her league, and Gaëlle knew it. And he was old enough to be her father. Gaëlle had never had a boyfriend, just a few harmless flirtations at school, and once the war started, she had had no

128

thought for romance, and had been careful to avoid German soldiers, and the local boys had gone elsewhere or were in the Resistance, and many got killed. Some girls had gotten involved in romances during the war, but she hadn't. And she was only twenty. She had time, and didn't need a man in her life at the moment. She had too much else to do, although her successful modeling career would change that. They had all seen girls like her who suddenly became the focus of every actor and playboy around the world. But Gaëlle was still an innocent, and it showed. Robert Bartlett had seen it too the night before and found it refreshing.

He called her at the hotel on the eve of her departure, while she was packing. He invited her to have a drink at the bar, but she didn't think her chaperones would like it, so she said no. Her recalcitrance was a new experience for him too. Most of the women he met chased him. He wished her a safe trip back to Paris, and told her he'd call her the next time he was in town, which she assumed wouldn't be soon.

She was busy with Dior's new collection in July, and several fashion shoots Madame Cécile arranged for her, with Monsieur Dior's direction. She was working so much she hardly saw her roommates. And in August the house closed for the month, and everyone left on vacation. Gaëlle was the only one who stayed in the apartment. She had nowhere else to go, and she didn't want to go home. Her departure had been too depressing and humiliating, and she didn't want to go back to the château. She had been planning to sell it, but didn't need the money for now, so she let her family home sit there, unused.

The war ended in August, with jubilation around the world. She enjoyed the quiet month in the city while everyone was away. She walked in the Bois de Boulogne and the Tuileries Gardens. She visited Versailles, where she had never been, Giverny, and Malmaison, Empress Josephine's home. She played tourist and loved it, and at the end of the month, the other girls returned and they all got busy again.

Her cover on *Vogue* created a sensation when it came out, and she was in constant demand after that. She barely had time to breathe. She turned twenty-one in November, and they told her the day after that that she was going to New York again for another *Vogue* shoot with Irving Penn and the cover of *Harper's Bazaar*, shot by a young photographer, Richard Avedon.

She thought about writing to Robert Bartlett to tell him she was coming, and then decided against it. It seemed too forward, and she'd probably be too busy to see him anyway. But she ran into him her first night there, at a party at Delmonico's. It was a big benefit event where *Vogue* wanted her seen and photographed. She wore a beautiful pale pink haute couture Dior gown, and she saw that Robert Bartlett was there with Ingrid Bergman, which caused a huge sensation. He managed to come over to say hello to Gaëlle, and danced with her later in the evening. And while they were dancing, Miss Bergman left with someone else, and he didn't seem to care.

'We're just friends. She asked me to bring her here tonight.' He'd had a hot romance with a young socialite over the previous summer, but Ingrid Bergman, although lovely, wasn't his style, and he was much more interested in Gaëlle. And to her amazement, she ran into Billy Jones, the recent POW she'd met in Paris before he went home. He was with a beautiful Texan girl and said he was engaged, and promised to call her if they came to Paris. They were in New York for the weekend.

Robert sent her flowers again the next day. The note was more intimate this time. 'So glad you're back in town. Robert.' And he called later to invite her to dinner at '21.' She hesitated and then accepted, and her chaperones didn't mind. It was good press for her to be seen with the dashing bachelor around town.

They had a wonderful evening, and went dancing afterward, and he brought her back to the hotel in his limousine at three A.M., and she didn't have a shoot the next day, so she could sleep in. He invited her out again for the following evening, but she was shooting for *Bazaar* and had to decline, since their shoots often went late. She stayed for a week, and they managed to have lunch before she left, and the conversation turned more serious than it had till then. He talked about his marriage and what a disappointment it had been. Gaëlle was impressed that he blamed himself as much as his ex-wife. He said she was a spoiled young woman, and expected a lifestyle from him that he thought excessive, and he had wanted a home life with her that she had no

131

interest in. She wanted to be out at parties every night.

'If that's what I wanted, I should have married someone else,' he said, recognizing his mistake. 'I knew what she was like before we got married. I'm old enough to know better. I expected her to turn into someone else.' And then he looked somber for a minute. 'And I rushed her into having a baby she didn't want. She wasn't ready for children, and the baby was born with a serious heart defect. She died in three months. I thought it was because my ex-wife partied too much when she was pregnant. That's probably not true, but I thought so at the time. It was tragic for both of us, and we never recovered from it. The baby died a year and a half after we were married, we separated six months later, and she went to Reno for the divorce. I'm just sorry I put her through it with a baby I wanted and she didn't. She wanted glamour, and I wanted children.' It was a side of him Gaëlle hadn't suspected, and she was touched that he had shared it with her. It gave her insight into him she didn't have before. 'It's awful to admit,' he added, 'but I'm sadder about the baby than I am about her. She was a beautiful little girl.' He touched Gaëlle's hand as he said it.

'You'll have other children one day,' she said gently. 'It sounds like it wasn't meant to be.'

'Maybe not. It's crazy, but my ex is already engaged to someone else. He's older than I am, and has kids her age. I don't think he wants children, and she won't try to have them again. The whole thing was too traumatic.' He changed the subject then, and he asked about her plans when she went back to Paris. She already had photo shoots lined up, and a trip to London for a cover shoot for British *Vogue*. She was amazed at how her career had taken off, and he could see how much she enjoyed it. And why not? She was young and beautiful and having fun, after the hard years of the war.

He looked genuinely sorry when he said goodbye, and she felt closer to him than she had before. He said he'd be in Paris soon, and she was beginning to feel like he was a friend. They'd had long conversations about art. He had traveled extensively in France. She still didn't share her war experiences with him, they were too personal and too intense, but she enjoyed his company, and he obviously liked spending time with her. He sent her a beautiful evening bag from Cartier before she left. It was black satin with an ivory and gold frame, and a little diamond clasp. It was a very impressive gift. Her chaperones thought so too, and she loved it and showed it off to her roommates when she got back to Paris and told them all about New York. They were jealous of the opportunities she was getting, but she was such a kind, decent, unassuming person that they liked her in spite of it. One of her roommates, Juana, had left and gone back to Brazil and was replaced by a very sweet Italian girl from Milan whom they all loved. The atmosphere at the apartment was more like a girls' boarding school than the home of five top models, and they were all young and happy to be there. Giovanna, the new Italian girl, told of terrible hardships during the war, which sounded even worse than what they'd experienced in France, and both of her brothers had been killed. She cried when she told them about it, and they all hugged her.

And two weeks before Christmas, Robert Bartlett called Gaëlle from the Ritz. He was in Paris on his way to London.

They had dinner at Le Pré Catelan, one of the best restaurants in Paris, in the Bois de Boulogne. And her life was slightly less frantic than in New York. They had no big events to go to, and enjoyed two quiet evenings and a very pleasant Saturday afternoon, walking along the Seine after lunch. And he took her to dinner that night at Le Voltaire, one of his favorite haunts in Paris, a small, elegant bistro. They had a delicious meal, although she ate sparingly. Monsieur Dior didn't like any of them gaining weight, he wanted his models rail thin, and Gaëlle complied with ease. After rationing during the war, she was used to existing on very little.

'What are you doing for Christmas?' he asked her casually after dinner, and Gaëlle looked out the window for a minute and decided to tell him the truth.

'Nothing. I'm staying here. All my family died during the war. Some of the girls are going home, but I like being alone in the apartment when Paris is quiet. It gives me time to think and do some reading, and go to museums. I never have time to do that when we're working.' It startled him to realize that she had no family left. She had never mentioned it to him before. He had no one to spend Christmas with either, since he had no children, both of his parents had died several years before, and he was an only child.

He hesitated for a moment before he asked her what he feared might be too forward.

'Would you like to go to St. Moritz with me?' he asked her cautiously. 'In separate rooms, of course,' he added quickly, since he had been very proper with her, and respected her conservative values. There was nothing racy about her, no matter how beautiful she was. 'I promise to behave,' he said, and she laughed and said she'd think about it, but she didn't feel comfortable going. He was a world-famous ladies' man. But he insisted this was different. He wanted to spend Christmas with her, and he'd loved St. Moritz since he was a child.

Gaëlle discussed it with the girls at the apartment the next morning. They all thought she should go, but Gaëlle wasn't sure Monsieur Dior would like it, or that she should. She was very taken with Robert, but she'd never gone anywhere with a man before, and it seemed like a big step. But she trusted him to be a gentleman about it. And he asked her again when he called her to say goodbye before he left for the airport en route to London. He sounded so sweet and sincere that in a burst of spontaneity she accepted his invitation, and then panicked as soon as she hung up. It seemed like a very bold thing to do. He was going to be in London for a week on business, and told her he'd meet her in Paris on December 23, and they could fly to Geneva together.

She was in a dither about it all week, deciding to call him and cancel one minute, and then excited and wanting to go the next. She loved being with him, but she didn't want to get in over her head. She liked the idea of the trip but was afraid the reality would prove awkward.

He arrived back in Paris, as promised, and picked her up at her apartment the afternoon of the twenty-third. And despite her hesitations and intermittent cold feet about the trip, she was packed and ready to go when he appeared with a chauffeured Rolls, which took them to the airport for the short flight to Geneva. He could see that she was nervous, and he was very kind to her, and very gentle. With Monsieur Dior's permission, she had borrowed a short sable coat from the collection for the trip, and another Rolls with a driver was waiting for them in Geneva, to drive them to St. Moritz, where he had reserved two suites for them at the Palace Hotel.

She told Robert she felt like Cinderella when she saw her room. He had had them fill it with white roses and orchids, and there was champagne chilling in a silver bucket, which he opened as soon as they arrived. Robert thought of everything.

They had dinner in the main dining room that night, and he seemed to know most of the guests at the hotel, who came to greet them at their table, in part to see who he was with.

'Do you come here often?' she asked anxiously, still feeling awkward to be traveling with him. She was sure her parents would have been shocked if they'd known, yet he was very circumspect with her, and she felt safe with him. And her life was so different now than when her parents were alive. She'd been a child then in a totally separate world. She led a very sophisticated life now, even if she was still innocent and a virgin. She was a good girl, and Robert knew it too. He kissed her lightly on the lips when he took her back to her room, and he left her without saying anything the moment she opened the door. He didn't want to pressure her to do something she wasn't ready for. He had arranged a ski lesson for her the next day, which she was looking forward to. She enjoyed his company, and felt increasingly at ease and close to him.

He was an expert skier himself, and met up with friends to ski with them, but he didn't leave Gaëlle's side until he was satisfied that she had a good instructor. He treated her like a doting father, and spoiled her whenever he could. It was the morning of Christmas Eve, and she had bought a cashmere scarf at Hermès for him, which had cost her a week's pay, but she wanted to give him something to thank him for the generous trip.

Gaëlle loved her ski lesson. Robert met up with her for lunch in the middle of the day, and then he went back to the slopes, and she took a walk around town and looked in the shops. There were beautiful jewelry stores, and elegant boutiques, and the crowd at the famous ski resort was incredibly elegant and wore black tie at night. She had borrowed several evening gowns from the house, and they didn't mind, but she had no jewelry of her own. Her mother had never worn any, it wasn't suited to their country life. She remembered that Mrs. Feldmann had had a very pretty diamond ring, and an emerald bracelet her husband had given her, but it was a small town, and no one wore anything showy, even if they had had money like the Feldmanns. By local standards, Mr. Feldmann was a rich man, and all of it had disappeared. Like all the Jewish families who had been deported, their bank accounts had been seized, and the money vanished. Gaëlle had heard that from others. She still thought of them all the time.

They had dinner in a very elegant restaurant that night, and when he took her back to the hotel, they exchanged Christmas gifts. He loved his scarf and put it on with his dinner jacket, and he handed her a long thin box, from Cartier again, and she was shocked when she saw that it was a narrow diamond bracelet. It wasn't vulgar, although she was sure it was expensive, and it looked suitable for a young girl her age, and went with the elegant clothes she had borrowed. She looked embarrassed when she saw it. It was much too important a gift to accept from a man she hardly knew, even if she was traveling with him, which was racy enough for her. Diamond bracelets were not in the plan. She felt awkward keeping it. In her mind it was the kind of gift a man gave his wife or his mistress, and she was neither. She still wanted to keep things light.

'Robert, I can't accept it. It's much too big a gift,' she objected, and he insisted she keep it. He told her it was her Christmas present, and he had had it made for her. He had wanted something delicate and beautiful but not showy, just like her. And he was so used to women expecting or wanting big gifts from him that it never occurred to him she might be embarrassed or think it was too much.

'I want you to have it,' he said as he kissed her cheek. 'It's from Santa Claus. He'll be very sad if you don't keep it, and so would I.' He smiled at her. One thing he was sure of, she was not a gold digger. She was just the reverse. She expected nothing from him, and he had to beg her to keep the gift. And she felt odd now having just given him a scarf. She was still wearing the bracelet when she went to bed that night, and called him in his room as she admired it on her arm. She loved it, after she got over the initial shock. But she still wasn't sure she should keep it.

'I feel very naughty accepting it,' she said guiltily, like a child who had opened someone else's gift but wanted to keep it now. He was happy she loved it. 'And I feel very strange,' she added.

'Why strange?' he asked, curious about what she meant.

'During the war, we had almost nothing to eat, and we were living in the maids' rooms in the attic, while the Germans lived in our old rooms. My mother refused to leave the room upstairs when they left. She felt the house had been tainted. And now I'm here with you, going to elegant restaurants, eating whatever I want, staying at this very grand hotel, and wearing a diamond bracelet. It's hard to connect the two

139

sometimes, that I'm the same person, and this is really my life now. I feel like it's all unreal and it's going to disappear, and I'll be standing next to a pumpkin, in rags with two white mice. I don't feel like this person, and you should be here with some famous movie star, not with me.'

'That's what I love about you, Gaëlle. You're real. I don't want to be with a movie star, especially not on Christmas. I want to be with you. I've never known anyone like you or felt this way. I don't have any family either, and maybe we were meant to find each other. I want to protect you and take care of you. I enjoy all the things I do, but they never feel real to me either. This does. And I wouldn't want to be here with anyone else.' She was touched by what he said, and she was developing feelings for him too. But the bracelet still seemed over the top to her, and her very conservative French parents would never have understood such a valuable gift unless they were married or engaged. And she didn't want anything from him, just to be with him, which was a new experience for him, and made her even more special.

He took her on a sleigh ride the next day, and they went to church, where she prayed for Rebekah. He saw her serious expression when she lit several candles and guessed that she was praying for the people she lost, and missed them. She didn't tell him about Rebekah, because talking about it would have been too painful, and Gaëlle felt very private about everything that had happened to her. Yet when they went for a walk that afternoon, she admitted to him that she had

140

been falsely accused of being a collaborator after the Occupation, but she assured him it wasn't true. She didn't want him to hear it from someone else, since some of the models knew too.

'The commandant who lived in our house gave me extra food for my mother, and the housekeeper thought I was doing something bad with him, but I wasn't. She denounced me at the end of the Occupation, and they paraded me through the streets after they shaved my head, and threw garbage at me. I never want to go back there again, and I have no reason to. Except that I still have a house there, but it's closed.' She didn't tell him it was a sixteenth-century château that was one of the largest in the region with extensive lands. She was a very modest person and hated to show off. And she had been betrayed by her village, which tainted everything there for her.

He cringed at the image of what they'd done to her. He couldn't bear thinking about it, and if she said she was accused falsely, he believed her. She was an honest woman, and had been brave to tell him about it, and he was deeply moved by her story. He wanted to erase all those memories for her. She said very little about her painful wartime experiences, but he could sense that it had been rough, and very grim at times. And she seemed to have come through it without bitterness, anger, or scars. He thought she was a remarkable girl. He could see the heartbreak in her eyes when she told him, and he pulled her into his arms and held her close, as a feeling of

141

peace and well-being came over her. Being with him almost made up for what had happened.

They spent a wonderful week together, and they both hated to leave when it was over. The diamond bracelet he gave her never left her arm, and she admired it constantly and finally decided to keep it and thanked him again and again, and he wore her Hermès scarf every day, and loved it and the gesture. It snowed on their last day in St. Moritz, and they stood outside with the snow on their hair and eyelashes. She was wearing a big fur hat she'd brought with her. She was the first woman he'd ever known who didn't try to get him to take her shopping. And before they went inside, he kissed her, more passionately than before. He had respected her totally for the entire time, and their behavior had been exemplary, which made her love him more.

'I'm falling in love with you, Gaëlle,' he said, as the snow fell around them, and he wanted to stop time. He didn't want to leave her the next day. And then he asked her something that had been worrying him. 'I'm forty-nine years old — twenty-eight years older than you are. Does that bother you?'

'Not at all,' she said seriously, and then she spoke in a whisper as he held her. 'I love you too.' They were not yet lovers, but their hearts were engaged now, and romance was heavy in the air, for both of them. And Gaëlle was so grateful they had waited to make love. This was more than just a physical attraction, it was something very powerful drawing them to each other, and becoming impossible to resist.

'I never thought I wanted to have a child again, after my baby girl died,' he said quietly, still holding her. 'But if I had one, I would want it to be with you.' What he said to her made her think instantly of the infants she had transported to safety during the war, but she didn't say that to him. She looked serious and sad as she remembered, and he wondered what she was thinking, but she didn't explain.

'If I had children, I would want them to be safe,' she said solemnly, 'and we don't live in a safe world.' The war had proved that to them, especially in Europe. What if it all happened again? She could never have given a child into strangers' hands to carry to safety, like the ones she had rescued. She had no idea how their mothers had parted with them, except to save their lives. They had had no other choice. And those children were alive now because of what their mothers had sacrificed for them.

'You would live in a safe world with me,' he said softly. He wanted to give her that now. She had been through so much during the war, more than he knew or could imagine. And she was far braver than he suspected. He put his arm around her then, and they walked inside.

The next day they went back to Paris, and he looked genuinely sad to leave her at the apartment. He was flying to New York that night, and had important meetings there the next day, or he would have stayed longer to be with her.

'I had a wonderful time,' she said as they kissed, and he smiled at her.

'To be continued.' She was going to New York

for another *Vogue* shoot at the end of January, and he could hardly wait. She was excited about it too. She had gotten used to seeing him every day on the trip, and being with him, but neither of them knew what the future held for them. Gaëlle knew only too well how uncertain life could be.

The porter took her bags upstairs, and the other girls shrieked as soon as they saw her arm. 'You got a diamond bracelet!' Ivy screamed in amazement, and Giovanna lapsed into Italian immediately.

'I tried to give it back, and he wouldn't take it,' Gaëlle explained shyly, embarrassed, and the others told her she was crazy. And all of them said they would have kept it. Now she was glad she had, it had real meaning to her after all she and Robert had said.

He called her from the airport before his plane left for New York, and she thanked him for the trip again. It had been magical and more than she felt she deserved. No one had a right to that kind of luxury, and all that he had lavished on her, but she had enjoyed every minute of it, and he couldn't wait to spoil her again.

'I'm going to miss you, Gaëlle,' he said seriously over the phone.

'Me too. I'll see you in New York in a few weeks,' she reminded him. And they would both be busy in the meantime. She had the January couture showings to do, constant fittings before that, and several photo shoots for Dior.

'Take good care of yourself,' he said gently.

'You too,' she said in a loving tone, and a

144

moment later they hung up, and she smiled as she noticed the diamond bracelet sparkling on her arm. And all she could think of, with immense gratitude, was how strange life was. It made her think of Rebekah again, and maybe she would have to live for both of them now. And if that was true, she certainly would.

And as the plane took off at Orly, Robert was painfully aware that he had left his heart in Paris, with a brave young French girl from Lyon.

9

Gaëlle felt like an experienced world traveler when she boarded the Pan Am flight in Paris for her third photo shoot for *Vogue* in New York. She had been constantly busy during the weeks before that, and Robert had sent her roses twice, saying he missed her, and several loving telegrams. She couldn't wait to see him, and flew into his arms when he was at the airport to meet her in New York. He drove her to the hotel, where he had filled the room with roses. Their romance was heating up considerably, and they had dinner in her suite that night. He had already made plans for dinner and dancing with her around town on the nights she was free. He couldn't wait to show her off. He was so proud of her.

They went to the Stork Club the next night, and the press went crazy over them when they walked in. They were the big new item, although it wasn't unusual to spot Robert Bartlett with a top model, but there was something endearing about Gaëlle that the press loved, and the camera ate her up. She looked spectacular in every photograph, and was friendly to everyone. She was pleasant to the people she worked with, and the editors of *Vogue* were crazy about her too.

Edna Woolman Chase, the legendary editor-in-chief, had a talk with her after the shoot.

Gaëlle had a way of wearing the clothes they chose for her that was easy and chic, and she was learning her new profession well. She added just a touch of spice and mischief to the looks, which kept them fun and youthful as well as high style. She had a distinct way of modeling all her own. She was a natural, and every photograph of her leaped off the page. She had never thought of modeling before, and it had already changed her life for the better in every way.

'I think you need to do some serious thinking about the next stage of your career,' the illustrious editor said to her after she'd called her into her office for a chat. 'Paris gave you a great start, but it's different there. The world of haute couture is very special, more elitist. And Monsieur Dior gave you a fabulous launch for your career. But New York is big business, and if you want a major modeling career, Gaëlle, the work is here. You'll have the whole fashion world at your feet, big designers, major magazines, important photographers, and the best opportunities for you are in New York. I think you should think about coming to live here for a few years. It will put you on the map forever. You have a reputation now, you should capitalize on it while you can. You know how it is in this business — you're young, you have ten years to be a big name, and after that you'll be in the hall of fame, and can pick and choose what you want to do occasionally. The time is now.' Her advice and her word were gold in the world of fashion. She urged Gaëlle to give it some thought.

She discussed it with Robert at dinner that

night at '21,' and it was music to his ears. He wanted her to move to New York too. Gaëlle wasn't sure how serious she was about modeling — it seemed like a frivolous short-term career — but it had been a fantastic experience so far, everyone had been kind to her in a usually cutthroat world, and she was starting to make the kind of money she had never dreamed she could earn. It gave her some sense of security and independence after the terrors of the war. She felt great loyalty to Christian Dior for what he'd done for her. And she was deeply attached to her country, and didn't want to leave France, although she loved Robert more every day, and it was getting harder to leave him when she went back.

'Everything moves so fast here,' Gaëlle said to Robert cautiously. She had been carefully nurtured and protected by Dior in Paris — she wouldn't have that if she moved her career to New York. There she would be thrown to the wolves of the fashion business, and she didn't feel ready for that, nor had the personality for it. She was wise enough to know it, and Robert was impressed that she had her feet on the ground, and even at her young age, she hadn't let her overnight success as a model turn her head.

'It depends what you want from your career,' he said thoughtfully.

'At first, I just needed to eat. I never expected it to turn into this.' And her main reasons for going to Paris had been getting away from the people who had condemned her, finding Rebekah through the Red Cross, and getting a

148

job so she could survive. She had too many bad memories now in Lyon, and didn't want to go back there to live. Or not for a long, long time. But she had no hunger to build a career based on her face and beauty, even though it had been good to her so far. But she knew it couldn't last forever. They had warned her to be careful with her money, because models didn't last long, and one day it would end as fast as it began. They were comets in a summer sky. But if she wanted to take advantage of the opportunity, the time was now. 'I think it would scare me to work here.'

'Why?' He was intrigued by what she said. She was a bright girl, with good common sense, and had used her wits and intelligence to get ahead.

'They protect me at the house in Paris. I have no protection here. They're very nice to me at *Vogue*, but it won't last. In a while, I'll be yesterday's face.' And she was right. She had already seen it happen to others, and there was turnover with the models who didn't catch on, or whose popularity began to wane, as hers would one day. She was already at the top at twenty-one, but for how long? And after the insecurity of the war years, she had visions of herself as a waitress somewhere at twenty-five, and said as much to Robert, which made him laugh.

'I don't think you need to worry about that yet.' But she was right to look ahead. 'And I'm always here to give you business advice, if you need it.' He was pleased that she didn't follow blindly what others said. She was a sensible and cautious girl for one so young.

'I appreciate that.' She smiled at him, and he knew she was sincere.

'And there's another element you haven't considered.'

'What's that?' Her eyes were wide and innocent. She had no ulterior motives with him, which made him trust her even more.

'I want to marry you, Gaëlle.' He said it in a voice filled with emotion. 'I want to be here forever to protect you, not just in your modeling career but in your life.' She didn't answer him for a minute. She felt the same way. But she didn't want to rush into anything. She didn't want to spoil what they had or expect too much. The world had fallen apart in Europe. What if it did again? And what if he tired of her? She would be far from home and her own country, engulfed by his power and life. In a way, she preferred a smaller life of her own that she could control. He existed in a very big world, and she wasn't used to it yet. At times it seemed overwhelming to her.

'I don't want to go too quickly,' she said softly. 'What if you change your mind later, or if you're unhappy with me, as you were with your ex-wife? I don't ever want to make you unhappy.' She spoke with tears in her eyes as he took her hand in his own. She looked frightened, and it touched his heart.

'I won't,' he said, holding her hand in his. 'You're an entirely different person than she was. You're the woman I've waited for all my life.' She nodded, as tears rolled down her cheeks, and she couldn't explain it to him. Everyone she had ever loved had died in the war. What if he died too? She'd be lost if she relied on him. He could see that she was trembling as he spoke to her calmly. 'Let's just give it a little time. This is a lot for you to get used to all at once.' He understood as he pulled her gently into his arms and held her, and he could feel her start to relax. She always felt safe with him. 'I won't let anything bad happen to you again,' he said in a deep, serious voice, and she knew he meant it.

But she had seen how easily the world could spin out of control, and terrible events took place that no one could have foreseen. It was hard to trust anything after that. Destiny could change everything in the blink of an eye. She knew that better than people in America, who had been relatively safe during the war, even though they had lost loved ones on foreign turf. But in France, the dangers had been right in her backyard and in her home. And for the Feldmanns and others like them, the whole world had turned upside down in their native land. Who could ever have predicted that? Robert could guess what was going through her mind. The war had left its mark, and not so long ago.

It was hard leaving him when she went back to Paris, and he called her every day to see how she was. He didn't pressure her about moving to New York or getting married, and she never brought it up, but she thought about it more than she wanted him to know.

In the end, she made the decision six weeks after she left New York. The farmer who was checking on the château for her told her that there was a problem, and she needed to come back to take a look. He wasn't specific about it, and with a heavy heart, she boarded a train to Lyon for the weekend, when she had some time off. And she saw instantly what he meant, when he drove her to the château. As soon as it came into view, she could see what they'd done. People had painted terrible things on the beautiful facade. 'Traitor . . . collaborator . . . whore . . . ' It tore her heart out as she read them. 'Go away . . . you are damned to hell, where you belong . . . ' Their hatred for what they believed was a collaborator was spelled out in words and awful slogans. She was glad her parents couldn't see it. Looking at the defaced walls, she knew it would never end. They had branded her forever, whether true or not. They would never forgive her for sins she hadn't committed. She felt sick as she read the words.

'I've tried to remove it,' the farmer said sadly. He felt bad for her, whatever she had done. She had been a frightened young girl with no father or brother to protect her for the last years of the war, and a half-mad invalid mother who had been destroyed by the Occupation. She was not the only woman to have sold herself for a loaf of bread, if that was what she had done. He was more tolerant than the others. And her memories of her home now were of her parents dying there, the Germans occupying it for three years, and what her fellow townsmen thought of her. It was too much to bear. 'Some of it won't come off. I've consulted a stonemason, and we may have to replace some of the stone, or paint it.' But there was only one thing to be done, and she knew it.

'Sell it,' she said in a low voice, and he didn't hear her at first.

'Sorry?'

'I want to sell the château.' She had heard that Parisians who still had money after the war, and some Americans, were buying up properties like hers in France, not for very large amounts, since those who were selling them were desperate for money and would take any small amount, whatever the property was worth. Nothing in France was worth much now. But she knew she couldn't ever live here again. It was too painful, too sad for her, and everything had gone too wrong. All she wanted from it were the memories of her peaceful childhood. Everything that had happened from the time she was fifteen had been a nightmare she would never forget, and nothing would erase it now, even if they got the ugly words off her home. This is what they thought of her here. They believed she was a whore who had betrayed her country and sold herself to the Germans, even if it wasn't true. None of them knew of her activities in the Resistance, and there was no reason to tell them, and they wouldn't believe her. Most of the other Resistance workers had faded into the mists and moved on. And the children she had saved were dispersed all over Europe, and some even abroad, with kind people who had taken them in.

She told him to put the property on the market, and sell it for whatever was offered. He looked shocked, but he understood, and then he made her an offer. He hadn't dared to before. He wanted to buy the farm his family had worked for generations, and the two farms adjoining it. The men on those two farms had died, and their widows moved away. It would give him a handsome piece of land, and she thought he deserved it for his loyalty to her father and kindness to her. They settled on a ridiculously small amount he promised to pay her within five years, and he was happy with the deal, although deeply sorry for her.

But he could see that her life was better in Paris. She had returned wearing simple but expensive clothes. She looked fashionable and like a sophisticated woman, even though he had known her as a child and young girl, and he could tell that the essence of her hadn't changed. He still believed she was an honorable person, of sound values, like her father, whatever they said of her now. He had been criticized for helping her by watching over the estate since she left in disgrace, but he didn't care what people said. And he was thrilled to own his own farm and the two others. She had been more than fair and sold it to him for a fraction of what it was worth even now. She didn't want much money from any of it. She just wanted to put the past behind her, if one ever could.

It was a sunny weekend, and she walked most of the property, gathering up memories like wildflowers in a field. She found an old bike that had been her brother's in the barn and rode out to the shed where she had hidden the children, and she remembered all those months of visiting Rebekah almost every day at the detention camp. She stopped at the stream where they had waded in the summer as children and were scolded for it when they disappeared for hours and forgot to say where they were going. And she remembered her parents in happier times when they were young and strong, and her mother of sound mind. And the mischief she had gotten into with her brother, and he would always blame her afterward. She thought of all of it, and smiled, and wiped tears from her cheeks.

And on Saturday afternoon at twilight, she made a final pilgrimage and rode to the Feldmanns' old home. She stood there for a long time, under the tree from where she had seen them taken away that awful morning. She watched two little girls run in and out of the house, with a young woman to keep an eye on them. The home had been freshly painted, and there were flowers in the front garden. It had a new life, and she saw the girls' mother drive up in a blue Delahaye, wearing a fur coat and a fashionable hat. They were obviously people with money, who had bought the beautiful home, probably for almost nothing. The houses of deported Jews could be bought all over Europe for pennies. Some speculators had even bought them and then sold them for what they were really worth and made a fortune since the end of the war, with no thought of who had lived there or what had happened to them, or the tragedies that had occurred. And the two little blond girls she had just seen reminded her of herself and

Rebekah as children. They weren't sisters but could have been, and now Rebekah was the sister of her heart forever. She cried all the way home, and walked up to the attic rooms where she and her parents had spent their final years at the château. She was anxious to sell it now, to be free of it and all that she remembered of the war years there.

Before she left on Sunday, she visited her parents' and brother's graves and said goodbye to them. 'I'm sorry,' she whispered, for not being able to save them, for leaving, for selling the château her family had owned for generations. But she knew she had to go to a better life and be free of her past in France.

When Gaëlle left, she closed the door behind her and hoped never to see any of it again. Everything she had loved there was going with her in her heart, and she wanted to leave the rest behind forever. She had told the farmer to take whatever he wanted from the house. She wanted none of it. He drove her to the train station, and he thanked her again for selling him the farms, and they shook hands.

'Good luck, Mademoiselle,' he said solemnly. He was going to contact a real estate agent and an attorney for her, and promised to call her when they had an offer on the château. And he was going to try again to get the slogans off the walls before they sold it, out of respect for her, if nothing else.

'Good luck to you too,' she said with sad eyes and a small, wintry smile.

He stood watching the train as it pulled out of

the station, remembering her father, her once-pretty mother, Gaëlle as a little girl, and her mischievous brother. He had children her age, and was proud to be a landowner now, with three farms. She had done a kind thing selling them to him. He silently wished her well as he got in his car after the train pulled out of the station, and he drove away. His last view of Gaëlle was of her looking out the window, at the home she had once loved and hoped never to see again.

She said nothing about the weekend to Robert, her visit to her home, or what she'd seen there. She couldn't find the words and didn't want him to know. She was too ashamed. She felt wounded to her soul, yet again.

She sent him a telegram instead: 'Moving to New York. I love you.' It was all that mattered. He was her future. Everything else was the past, and all she wanted now was to forget it.

10

Gaëlle moved ahead with determination once she made the decision to put the château on the market. When it sold, being free of it would make it easier for her. She would no longer have a home in France, which felt like sweeping away the past and a fresh start to her, and a little bit like throwing caution to the winds. If she hated living in New York, she could always come back.

She gave Madame Cécile notice the day after she returned from Lyon. She understood Gaëlle's decision to try working in New York and thought it was the right one for her. She asked her to stay for two months, which Gaëlle agreed to, and she called Robert and told him she would be there in May. He was ecstatic and hadn't pressured her about the decision. But he had been hoping she'd come to it on her own, for her own reasons, and she had. And once she decided to move, the rest was easy.

When it was time to leave in May, she said tearful goodbyes to her roommates at the models' apartment, and she made an appointment to say a proper goodbye to Monsieur Dior. He was as elegant and gracious as ever, wished her well, and said they would miss her. Madame Cécile cried when she left.

'You saved my life,' Gaëlle said in a choked voice as the two women hugged.

'Take care of yourself,' Cécile told her. 'Come

back to see us.' And Gaëlle promised she would.

The morning she left Paris, on the anniversary of victory in Europe on May 8, all the girls lined up to say goodbye to her. They had the day off from work, and they were all crying as she drove away, and so was Gaëlle. They had promised to stay in touch. And Gaëlle was quiet on the flight to New York. It was the first time she had taken the trip alone, and all she could think of now was Robert, waiting for her. She was determined to look forward now instead of back.

As soon as Gaëlle cleared customs in New York, and saw Robert, she felt joy and relief sweep over her like a tide of fresh water, and she felt washed clean of the past. He had found a small furnished apartment for her on Park Avenue temporarily, just so she could get her bearings and start work before they made plans. She already had appointments at *Vogue*, and several modeling agencies that wanted to sign her up. She had bookings for two shoots at *Vogue* and one at *Bazaar* in June. Her new life was off and running. And she talked excitedly to Robert about all of it on their way into the city. More than ever, this felt like the right decision to her. Another chapter of her life was unfolding, and he was pleased that she had had the courage to seize the moment. It was going to be the first time that she would have her own apartment without roommates. At twenty-one, she felt like she owned the world.

Robert waited for the early furor of her arrival to die down, knowing how frantic and preoccupied she would be. He was in no rush.

159

They went to his beach house in Southampton for the Memorial Day weekend, after three insanely busy weeks. They had lunch on the deck overlooking the ocean, as they relaxed, and Gaëlle thought about how lucky she was to be there with him, and he smiled at her, and got down on one knee in front of her. He had been waiting for this moment since the day they met.

'Gaëlle de Barbet, I know you're a very important person now, with a big career ahead of you,' he teased her, but it was also the truth, if she wanted it to be. 'But would you do me the honor of marrying me?' Her eyes filled with tears as she looked at him. It was the most important moment of her life, and what she wanted too. Her career as a model was exciting, but much more than that, she wanted to be his wife and share her life with him forever.

'I will . . . yes . . . ' she whispered, and he kissed her, and slipped a startlingly beautiful diamond ring on her finger. She still couldn't believe it as she looked at him. She had come from the horrors of war in France, and the heartbreak of losing everyone she loved, to this man who wanted to love and protect her, and have her as his wife. It was hard to understand how she deserved this, and why this hadn't happened to Rebekah too. But it was her destiny to be here and follow a new path with Robert. After so many losses, she felt blessed.

They talked about their plans all weekend, and since she had no family, and no real friends in New York other than him, they decided to have a small wedding in the city and spend their honeymoon at his old family home in Palm Beach. He came from a long-established aristocratic family, and the house had belonged to his grandparents and meant a great deal to him. He had happy childhood memories there, and wanted to share it with Gaëlle. They set their wedding date for the Fourth of July weekend, and had lots to do until then.

'Do you want me to stop working, Robert?' she asked him seriously. It was a sacrifice she was willing to make for him. She had enjoyed working as a model, but she wanted to devote herself to him too. He was her priority, not her career. She was an old-fashioned woman in many ways.

'It's entirely up to you,' he said breezily. 'Why don't you have fun with it for a while? You can retire whenever you want to.' It sounded reasonable to her, and she agreed.

News of their engagement was all over the press within a week. A great bachelor had been taken, the biggest catch in New York, and they were the instant king and future queen of the social set in the city. Everyone wanted to give parties for them. *Vogue* wanted to pick her wedding dress for her, and cover the wedding, which she assured them would be private, with only a few people present. Robert gave a cocktail party to introduce her to his closest friends, and she liked them. They were inviting only twenty of his most intimate to their wedding.

Her friends in Paris heard about it too. The girls she had modeled with at Dior sent her congratulations. And she got telegrams from both Monsieur Dior and Cécile, wishing her great happiness and the best of luck.

And then Gaëlle got busy working in New York in earnest. She worked until two days before the wedding. Robert had arranged for a judge to perform the ceremony at his Fifth Avenue penthouse, on the terrace overlooking Central Park, and after a small reception, they were leaving for their honeymoon in Palm Beach the next morning. They had thought of going to Europe, but it was still too disrupted in many places for an easy trip. And Gaëlle was happy to stay in the States, at his palatial home in Florida.

Their life together was a whirlwind, between her work and his, and their impending wedding. The big day sped by them, and before she knew it, they were on a plane to Miami, as Mr. and Mrs. Robert Bartlett. The wedding had been lovely, intimate and just what they wanted.

She was beaming, and Robert said he was the happiest man in the world. Neither of them cared about the twenty-eight-year age difference between them, and without even meaning to, or focusing on it, she had married one of the wealthiest men in New York, and he adored her. The fates had been kind to her at last, and given her beauty for ashes. The hard times during the war were fading slowly behind her, and her losses. And when they arrived, she was stunned by his home in Palm Beach, which was as big as their château near Lyon. She had told him about it, but didn't want to go there with him, and have him see the terrible things people had written about her on the walls. She was hoping it would

162

sell soon, so she could close that chapter too. She never wanted to live in France again, and she got a permanent resident's visa when she married Robert. Her life was in the States now, and she loved using his name, and practiced calling herself Gaëlle Bartlett at every opportunity.

He had a large staff at the Palm Beach house, and they were pampered for three weeks on their honeymoon. Since the fashion industry shut down in August, she had no commitments, so they returned to New York and spent the month at the house in Southampton, where she met more of his friends and they entertained lavishly. They returned to the city after the Labor Day weekend, and she hit the ground running with work after two lazy months. He was busy at the office, and she had given up her furnished apartment three days before they got married. And in the middle of September, she got a telegram from Louis Martin, their old tenant farmer, to tell her she had had an offer from a banker in Paris on the château and the rest of the farms that were part of the estate. It was a paltry offer given the size of the property and the history of the château, with all its contents, but all she wanted was to get rid of it. She sent back a telegram and accepted the offer, and said she wanted nothing from the house. She was selling it with the furniture, the family paintings, most of which weren't valuable, the silverware, the threadbare linens, and whatever else was there that had taken a beating by the Germans for four years.

'Are you sure you want to do that?' Robert

asked her when she told him about the offer. She was selling it for very little money, and he was afraid she'd regret it later, when her wounds after the war weren't as raw as they still were. But she was very determined that she never wanted to see the place again. And she lived in the States now with him. Keeping it made no sense, although he offered to help her with it, and told her they could hire a proper caretaker. It was a generous offer, and she thanked him, but refused. The sale went through very quickly, and she insisted she was relieved. The money was wired to her bank in New York as soon as escrow closed, and she felt that it had been the right thing to do. The Parisian banker had gotten a great deal, and he wrote to tell her how pleased he was too. She had no regrets about selling it to him.

By the end of September, Gaëlle was happy but exhausted. She had had half a dozen cover shoots scheduled for major magazines, had been photographed in ads, walked in fashion shows for three designers, among them Norman Norell and Charles James, though none as exciting as Dior. Her agency was working her hard, her career in New York was booming, and Robert was very proud of her. They were photographed everywhere they went, and the press referred to them as the Golden Couple. They went to parties at night, and she modeled by day. She had gotten even thinner than the magazine wanted her to be, and Robert sent her to his doctor. He thought she was working too hard, and wanted to be sure she was all right. She insisted that she was healthy, and she returned from the appointment looking sheepish.

'What did he say?' Robert asked her, sure that they had told her she was underweight, even for a model. He could see it himself and worried about her. And even Gaëlle realized that she was even thinner than she had been during the Occupation. 'You're too skinny, right?' Robert pressed her.

'A little,' she admitted, 'but he said I'm on a weight-gaining program that will really work.'

'And what's that?' Robert questioned her about it, and she giggled and put her arms around him and kissed him and whispered her big news to him. It was the best news she'd ever had.

'We're having a baby,' she said shyly, looking excited and happy, and he held her close and kissed her again.

'Oh my God, when? That's fantastic!'

'He says I'm about two months pregnant. I must have gotten pregnant right after we got married. I didn't notice because things aren't always regular,' especially when she got too thin, which she clearly was, even if it was fashionable and good for her career. 'The baby is due at the end of April, beginning of May.' They were both thrilled, although Robert said he would be an old man by the time their child was born. He was turning fifty. And she would be twenty-two when she gave birth.

'What did he say about your working?' Robert looked worried about it. She'd been working very hard, and the photo shoots were arduous days and long hours.

'He said I could do what I wanted, as long as I don't overdo it or do anything crazy, like ride horses, or ski. He said that it probably won't show till December, since I'm tall and underweight right now. I guess after that I'd have to tell the magazines and my agent.'

'Should you give them some warning? Do you want to work after the baby comes?' he asked her. 'You could take some time off, and then go back.' He was always very fair about her career.

'I don't know. They won't want me once it shows, so I probably won't be able to work after December. I'll see how I feel after that.' Her career was a lot to give up now, she had never expected it to take off as it had, but married to Robert she didn't need the money. It was an enviable position to be in, and she was grateful to him. She knew how lucky she was.

'Maybe you'd like to be a lady of leisure.' He smiled at her and kissed her again.

'I don't want to take advantage of you, Robert.' She didn't want him to think she was lazy or had married him for the money, but he knew better than that. And he liked the idea of her staying home with their child. But he left it up to her to decide. He didn't want her to feel stymied and bored, and cheated of her career as a model.

After the initial excitement, Gaëlle saw a shadow of worry in Robert's eyes, and suspected what it was, and he admitted to her that he was terrified that something would happen to their child, like the baby girl who had died at three

166

months in his first marriage. Gaëlle tried to reassure him, but she saw that his fears ran deep. He didn't want anything to happen to Gaëlle or their baby.

★   ★   ★

She told her agency about her pregnancy at the beginning of November, and no one had guessed so far. They were disappointed to hear it. She was the most successful model on their books, and in great demand. They agreed with Gaëlle that after January, they wouldn't be able to book her, once it showed, when she would be six months pregnant. She wouldn't be able to conceal it after that.

She worked hard until then. She felt fine and had no problems with the pregnancy, despite Robert's barely concealed worries. They were ecstatic about the baby, and she and Robert spent hours trying to decide on names. She preferred French names, and he liked them for a girl, although he favored family names from his side if they had a son.

Gaëlle did her last shoot, for *Vogue*, a few days before Christmas, and she was definitely starting to show. They spent a quiet holiday at home, cuddling and going to movies, and for the next three months, Gaëlle had lunch with some of her modeling friends, went to museums and art shows, read a lot, and got the nursery ready. She did it all in white since they didn't know if it would be a girl or a boy, and Robert confessed to her that he was hoping for a daughter. He couldn't imagine anything more wonderful than a little girl who looked like Gaëlle, and the one he had lost had left a void that nothing could fill. He was still worried about the health of this one and Gaëlle. He couldn't bear the idea of anything happening to either of them. It was his worst nightmare, although he tried to hide his fears from Gaëlle.

'You won't mind not having a boy to carry on your name?' They had talked about whether they wanted a second child, and given his age, Robert thought that one would be enough, and Gaëlle agreed.

'Not at all,' he answered her question about a son. He thought girls were easier, when he remembered how much trouble he had given his parents growing up. He wanted another daughter, after losing the last one.

Most of all, he was relieved that it had been an easy pregnancy for her. And despite her thin frame, it appeared to be a big baby, and they both laughed at how huge she got at the end. Perhaps because she was so thin, her belly looked enormous, but the doctor confirmed that the baby was large.

They reduced their social life dramatically in the final weeks of her pregnancy. Gaëlle was tired, and felt uncomfortable and awkward, and she really didn't want to go out, and Robert enjoyed their quiet evenings together, just talking. Gaëlle had loved not working for the past three months, and had taken some classes at the Metropolitan Museum about Renaissance art. The days of her pregnancy had passed quickly.

They went out to the house in the Hamptons on the weekend before her due date. They walked down the beach hand in hand, and were relaxed and tired when they got home to New York that night. They made dinner together in the kitchen, since the cook was off on Sundays. Gaëlle still felt guilty at times for the luxuries in their life, but Robert was used to living well. He wasn't pretentious or showy about it, but he was a very wealthy man, enjoyed the good life, and was happy to share it with her. She was slowly adjusting to it after nine months of marriage. She had adapted to his habits, and enjoyed the lifestyle he had had all his life. His family fortune had been established by his paternal great-grandfather, and his mother had been from an important family too, although more recently. Robert was very philanthropic and made large contributions to charity.

His financial structure was complicated and had been set up for generations. He was already planning a large trust for their baby, and had tried explaining it to Gaëlle, but the taxes and benefits and complex conditions were too convoluted for her. She left their finances to him, and had put the money from the château into a savings account, along with some of her earnings, which he had invested for her, although it was a small amount compared to what he had. She called it her dowry and made jokes about it, but she was grateful to have a little money of her own, and thanks to his generosity supporting her, she had saved most of the money she earned, except for what she spent on clothes and gifts for him, and minor extravagances, so she was pleased not to cost him money, or have to ask him for what she needed. She liked being an independent woman.

After they cooked dinner, they went to bed early that night. Gaëlle fell asleep with Robert rubbing her back. He was incredibly good to her, and excited about the baby, who kicked constantly. She awoke at four in the morning with sharp pains low in her belly. She waited a while to see what happened, and the contractions got stronger. She sat up in bed and turned the light on, and he woke up immediately.

'Are you okay?' he asked groggily, and she smiled at him.

'I think something's happening,' she said cautiously, as she had another contraction. Robert was wide awake in an instant.

'Call the doctor,' he said nervously.

'It's so early. Let's wait.' She didn't want to go to the hospital yet. She was more comfortable at home.

'No,' he said firmly, 'let's *not* wait.' He wanted her safely in the hospital in good hands, before anything major happened. He wasn't taking any chances, with her or the baby. They had made all the arrangements at Doctors Hospital, for the biggest private suite they had, which had its own living room to receive guests in, and she had the most prominent obstetrician. She was going to be there for a week. And Robert could stay with her. The hospital was so luxurious and catered to a high-end clientele, it was more like a five-star hotel than a medical facility, but the technical aspects were excellent too. He had checked it out. He didn't want his baby born in a second-rate hospital, particularly if there was a problem with this baby like the last one. He was very concerned, although Gaëlle was sure there was no need for him to worry. And she had been relaxed during the pregnancy.

Gaëlle went to take a shower, and promised to call the doctor if the contractions didn't stop. And as soon as she got out of the shower, her water broke, and she reported it to Robert, who had dressed by then, and had called the doctor while she was in the shower.

'I think it's for real,' she said meekly. And then she looked at him nervously with tears in her eyes. She was suddenly frightened for the first time. It was all so real. 'Robert, I'm scared. What if something happens, or there's something wrong with the baby? Or it dies . . . or I do . . .' Suddenly she was panicked, and he put his arms around her. She was wrapped in a towel, and he could feel her shaking. And with the daughter he had lost, he knew anything was possible but didn't say it to Gaëlle. She hadn't been nervous about it until then.

'It's going to be fine. I promise,' he said calmly, but he was worried too. He had put off having children until later, and now he was an anxious older father, and he had never loved anyone as he did Gaëlle. He didn't want anything to happen to her or the baby.

He kept her company while she dressed, and he timed her contractions. It was six in the morning by then, and the doctor told them to go to the hospital when Robert called him again. The doctor wanted them to check her, and he would come in if she was truly in labor. He had warned them that first babies usually took their time, and even if labor had started, he didn't expect her to deliver until late that night or even the next morning. Gaëlle had no idea what to expect, since no one close to her had ever been pregnant. She had no aunts or siblings, and her mother was gone. She had no experience with childbirth or babies, and Robert's only experience was a bad one. Gaëlle expected it to go well, with a competent physician in attendance, but she was afraid nonetheless. And Robert wanted the very best for his wife and child, and had paid handsomely for it. The hospital bill alone would be more expensive than the Ritz.

He would have liked to stay with her for the delivery, Gaëlle wanted that too, but the hospital didn't allow it. It was against the rules, and it was considered a shocking idea. Men weren't supposed to see the birth happen, and the doctor had assured her that she would be much happier with the nurses around her, and she could see Robert afterward, with her hair done and makeup on, he teased her. Gaëlle didn't agree, but no amount of insisting had convinced them. She had even suggested having it at home, which her doctor had thought a barbaric idea. Only poor people had babies at home, with their husband in the room. And he had told her that Robert might faint if he saw the delivery. He told her men weren't prepared for it, and he might feel differently about her afterward. He had a thousand arguments why Robert couldn't be in the room, and tried to make her feel uncomfortable for asking. She'd been stubborn about it, and convincing, but got nowhere. She wanted Robert with her when their baby was born.

The doorman had a taxi ready for them, and on the way to the hospital Gaëlle said to Robert again that she wanted him to stay with her, but they both knew it wasn't possible.

'He said you might faint.' Gaëlle smiled as another contraction started, and she gripped Robert's arm. They were getting stronger, and he was relieved they were on the way to the hospital. And as soon as they got there, they checked into her elegant suite. The bedroom had a decidedly sterile, medical feeling to it, but the living room was well decorated, for receiving guests and to show off the baby. The hospital supposedly had an excellent chef and kitchen. It was where all the wealthy New York socialites had their babies.

A nurse examined Gaëlle painfully as soon as she got settled. She assured her that the baby was hours away, would take a long time, and she had barely begun dilating. There was no need for the doctor to come yet, and he would be there later that morning. Gaëlle asked if she could go home then, and they said she couldn't. They told her that she might as well stay now that she was here, which seemed tedious and annoying to Gaëlle. She saw no reason to be there if the baby was hours away and in no hurry.

'I want to go home,' she complained to Robert

after she was examined. It made no sense to her to wait at the hospital for hours if nothing was happening, and their rules seemed absurdly rigid to her.

'For the sake of my nerves, let's stay,' he scolded her gently. 'I don't want to get stuck in traffic while you have the baby in a taxi.'

'People have babies in the field every day,' she reminded him, and he wagged a finger at her.

'Be a good girl!' And he could see that the contractions were getting painful. An hour later she was no longer asking to go home and couldn't talk through the contractions.

'Would you like your husband to leave now?' the nurse asked her after she checked her again. She was dilated to two centimeters. And the nurse said she had a long way to go, which disappointed her. The pains were strong enough that she thought she had made better progress, and Gaëlle was worried about how much worse it would get, and she was annoyed by the nurse's question about Robert leaving. They obviously didn't want him there, and thought he should go home and wait for news and they'd call him.

'No, I wouldn't like him to leave!' she barked at the nurse after her suggestion to have Robert go. 'He's not leaving until I'm in the delivery room. I want him with me. And I wish he could stay to see the baby born.' The nurse nodded and left the room, and reported to her supervisor that Mrs. Bartlett was French and had farm girl ideas about childbirth and wanted her husband with her. It was obvious that the nurse attending to Gaëlle on that shift strongly disapproved. She preferred patients who left their husbands at the door to the hospital, so she didn't have to deal with nervous fathers interfering, but he hadn't been a problem so far. He was concerned and attentive but let the nurse do her job.

'I've always thought that too,' the older nurse commented. 'Women should have their husbands with them, if they want them. It might go better and would be wonderful for both parents.' She was smiling, and the younger nurse looked horrified and left the room, as the older nurse laughed. She had less rigid ideas than the nurses she supervised. In her opinion, if they made the baby together, why not see it born together and let the husband help her through it, instead of strangers? But even the doctors, and hospital policy, strongly disagreed. She admired Gaëlle for at least asking, and stopped in to see her a few minutes later to check how she was doing. Gaëlle was shivering and pale and obviously in a lot of pain, but she said she didn't want drugs. She knew that once she had them, they would make Robert leave, so she was determined to be stoic.

'You're doing fine,' the nursing supervisor encouraged her in a gentle voice, and smiled at Robert, who was looking worried.

'Is this normal? For it to be so painful?' He hadn't been at the delivery of his first child, so he didn't know. This was worse than he'd anticipated.

'Yes, it is,' the supervisor reassured him, and didn't say it would get a lot worse before it was over. 'And you've got a big baby. Your wife is doing beautifully.' She smiled at Gaëlle, who was in the clutches of another contraction, and was in agony. Robert was still timing them, and they were two minutes apart now. They had been there for five hours, and the doctor wasn't due for at least another hour. Robert thought they should give Gaëlle something for the pain. But she was adamant about not wanting drugs.

'Are you okay?' he whispered to her after the nurse left the room. 'Why don't you let them give you something?' He hated to see her suffering.

'I want you here,' she said, clutching his hand. 'I need you.'

'I'm here, darling. I'm not leaving.' She wrestled with the contractions for another hour, while they waited for the doctor, and Robert couldn't bear watching what she was going through. It was inhumane. He didn't see why they couldn't just give her general anesthesia and put her out for the delivery, but the nurse said she would have to push eventually, and she needed to be awake for that. It sounded hideous to him, and as he watched her suffering, Robert knew that he would never put her through this again, no matter how healthy, young, and willing she was.

The contractions were so strong and so frequent that they were one long pain now, and Gaëlle was no longer talking to him, and she cried during the contractions. There was no relief. He wanted to send for the nurse and ask for the doctor to come sooner, but Gaëlle wouldn't let him.

'They'll send you away,' she pleaded with him.

'I don't care. They have to give you something.'

'I'd rather have you,' she said, and then looked suddenly wild-eyed with the next pain.

'What is it?' He could see from her face that something awful was happening, and he wanted the doctor *now*, but Gaëlle had a death grip on his hand and wouldn't let him leave her, nor ring for the nurse.

'I think the baby is coming,' she said desperately, and she could feel the forces of hell going through her. But he knew that wasn't true since the nurse who examined her said it was hours away. He was sure that something was wrong. 'It's pushing right through me,' she said, fighting to sit up and clutching him. She couldn't stop herself from pushing as Robert watched in panic, and the nurse assigned to them walked into the room and shouted at her.

'Stop immediately! The doctor's not here yet. You can't push, and you're not fully dilated. You'll injure yourself!' But Gaëlle wouldn't listen and kept pushing, as the nurse ordered Robert to leave the room. 'Your wife is not cooperating,' she said angrily. 'You'll have to go.'

'I'm not leaving!' he said just as firmly, watching Gaëlle's face as she clung to him for dear life, and let out a horrifying scream and fell back on the bed, as a loud wail came from between her legs under the covers, and the nurse pulled back the sheet, and their baby girl looked up at them and cried loudly, as Robert gazed at her, and tears poured down his cheeks. Gaëlle sat up to see her daughter and smiled through her own tears, and Robert kissed his wife. He had never loved anyone as much in his life as he did Gaëlle at that moment.

'You had the baby!' the nurse said accusingly, and Gaëlle laughed.

'Yes, she did,' Robert said proudly, and she had managed to have him with her after all.

The nurse called in an attending physician to cut the cord, and they had just put the baby, loosely wrapped in a pink blanket, into her arms as the doctor walked in.

'What happened here?' he asked, as though they had been drunk and disorderly and misbehaved, and Robert and Gaëlle laughed at the absurdity of it.

'I knew I was about to have her,' Gaëlle said to the doctor and Robert, 'and the nurse kept saying I wasn't, that I wasn't even dilated.'

'Sometimes things can change very quickly, but usually not with a first baby,' the doctor said gruffly, trying to cover the nurse's mistake.

'She told me not to push, but I couldn't stop, and I'm so happy Robert was here,' she said victoriously.

'So am I,' Robert said happily, looking at his daughter asleep in her mother's arms. Gaëlle was planning to nurse, which wasn't approved of either. Nursing had gone out of style among fashionable upper-class women. They used formula instead.

'Well, you two certainly managed to wreak havoc with hospital policy,' the doctor said tartly, trying to pretend he wasn't annoyed by it, but they could see that he was. He liked nice orderly deliveries, with the father in the waiting room or at home, and the mother as heavily sedated as they dared, not fathers at the delivery and wives who didn't want them to leave and refused all drugs.

Her nurse was just complaining about it to the supervisor, who smiled at the story. 'Well, good for her,' she said to the younger nurse. 'Maybe one of these days we'll change the rules,' she said, as the other nurse rolled her eyes and left the room to check on them again and take the baby to the nursery to be weighed.

Robert and Gaëlle hated to part with the baby when they took her away. The nurse cleaned Gaëlle up and helped brush her hair. She was shocked that she didn't want to put on makeup, and that Gaëlle didn't care. All of their patients insisted on looking as presentable for their husbands as possible after the delivery, and Gaëlle just wanted to be with him and kiss him. They assumed it was because she was French. And when they brought the baby back, they said she weighed exactly nine pounds. She was a beautiful baby, and had Robert's features and dark eyes and hair, not her mother's blond hair and light blue eyes.

They had agreed on naming her Dominique if it was a girl, and they thought it suited her once they saw her. Robert was pleased that she looked like him, and he thought Gaëlle was the most amazing woman in the world. She lay in bed and seemed as if nothing had happened. He had hated to see her suffer, but there was no sign of it now. She was peaceful and happy as their daughter slept in her arms. Dominique Davenport Bartlett had arrived. Davenport was Robert's mother's maiden name, and Gaëlle had agreed to it. She would have liked to use Rebekah as a middle name, but it was important to him. She didn't want to interfere with his family traditions, and Gaëlle wanted him to be happy since he was so good to her. She had it all now. She had a husband she loved, and a beautiful baby daughter. It really was a fairy-tale life.

11

Robert was nervous about the baby's health initially and brought in a pediatric cardiologist to check her for the defect his first daughter had died of, but Dominique was fine.

After her week's stay at the hospital, Gaëlle and Robert brought the baby home with the formally trained nanny they had hired to care for her. Gaëlle would have preferred taking care of the baby herself, but Robert still wanted to have time alone with her, and to travel with her, and having a nanny for the baby made more sense, but it left Gaëlle with time on her hands that she didn't know what to do with, and she needed to be around to nurse her on demand anyway.

She and Robert talked about her going back to work, but Gaëlle found she didn't want to once the baby arrived. It would be hard to limit how much she worked, with overzealous modeling agencies, magazines, and advertising clients, and she was afraid she'd never see Robert and the baby, or not enough, and she was more attached to the baby than she'd expected. So two months after Dominique was born, she told her agency that she had retired. She had enjoyed modeling, and it had been exciting and fun, and had been a godsend for her in Paris right after the war, but she had a husband and child and demanding home life now, and she was ready to give up her career. She was twenty-two years old but had moved into another phase of her life. She fully realized how fortunate she was and never took it for granted.

She missed her mother at times, and wished she could have seen the baby. It seemed sad that she had no grandparents and no other relatives, but Robert more than made up for it. He adored the baby, and although he worried about her health unduly because of his first bad experience, she became the joy of his life, and whenever he was home, he carried her everywhere, talked to her, read her books when she was old enough to understand them, put her to bed at night, and was frantic when she got sick. Gaëlle loved being with her too, and loved her deeply. But Dominique was Robert's passion, and greatest treasure. And as she got older, she could do no wrong in her father's eyes. He was blind to any misbehavior, and when her mother scolded her, or Nanny, she ran to her father to 'save' her, and he would cancel any punishment they had meted out, however slight. She was his little princess and ruled the house and everyone in it, which Gaëlle did not approve of. She had far more traditional European ideas about childrearing, and her parents had been quite strict. Robert forbade it.

'How can I ever make her behave if you spoil her all the time?' Gaëlle complained, but her pleas to him were futile. Robert didn't want Dominique punished, chastised, or disciplined, or even scolded. Gaëlle knew it was because he was terrified she might die like his first daughter, but she was a healthy, sturdy child. He couldn't get past his own terrors about her and didn't try. He was obsessed with her safety and happiness at all times. He hired a lifeguard just for her at their pool in Southampton, which Gaëlle thought was excessive. But Gaëlle loved her husband and didn't want him to worry, and he didn't want Dominique unhappy for an instant. His own parents had been hard on him when he was a child, and he didn't want her to experience that either. He was the quintessential over-indulgent, anxious older parent, while Gaëlle tried to provide balance, boundaries, and reason, without success. And Dominique's behavior and brattiness frequently caused arguments between them.

Gaëlle was painfully aware early on of how spoiled their daughter was becoming. Dominique was given to tantrums and screaming fits if she didn't get her way, and Gaëlle was unhappy about it, but anytime she tried to curb it, or get her to behave, Dominique would report it to her father, and Robert would intervene on her behalf and plead for leniency. His kind heart and love for his daughter didn't serve her well, but there was no convincing him of it, and Gaëlle was forced to mitigate her own ideas and say nothing in order to keep Robert happy. Dominique had a sharp tongue as she grew older, which often reminded Gaëlle of her mother, who had been a severe, joyless woman even before the war. Gaëlle was not at all sure that Robert's total indulgence would make Dominique a happy person later. There were no rules or boundaries in her life, and whenever her father was around, she was allowed to do whatever she wanted. She knew just how to charm and manipulate him to get her way. And she was often sullen and angry with her mother for no reason. She competed with her mother for Robert's affection, although she didn't need to, he loved them both. But Dominique wanted her father to herself, and seemed to see her mother as a rival. And no amount of reassurance changed that.

Robert criticized their nannies for being too harsh, and had fired several for that reason, after Dominique complained about them. It was a constant juggling act for Gaëlle to keep Robert happy and try to make Dominique behave. It was the only subject on which they disagreed, and she could never convince Robert to discipline their child. Their marriage was perfect otherwise, but Dominique created considerable tension between them. And she wasn't above lying to get her way, or blaming her mother falsely for something. Dominique toned down her behavior around her father but with no one else. And she was particularly vitriolic with her mother, which was disappointing for Gaëlle, who longed for a warm, close relationship with her daughter, and couldn't achieve it. She wanted a better rapport with her daughter than she'd had with her own mother. Dominique had been slightly cuddlier as a toddler, but not for long. Her father was the center of her world and her protector. And she treated her mother as an interloper, which made Gaëlle sad.

More than anything Dominique appeared to be jealous of her. She had a classic Electra complex, which Robert encouraged unwittingly, and he was duped by his daughter. She wanted all of her father's attention and affection, and considered her mother her archrival. When Gaëlle tried to suggest it to Robert, he disagreed vehemently, and insisted she loved them both equally, which wasn't the case.

And none of it improved with age. She was an extremely bright child, her passion was business, and she wanted to work on Wall Street like her father. She had intelligent conversations with him at an early age about business, investments, the rise and fall of the stock market, and he explained it to her. It was another way to exclude her mother.

In spite of their difficult daughter, Robert and Gaëlle had a solid relationship, and his bond with his daughter was strong too. What didn't work, and hadn't in years, was Gaëlle's relationship with her daughter. She had behaved like a bratty teenager almost since birth. And whatever the reason, Robert constantly indulged Dominique, and she took full advantage of it.

Robert was also a consummately responsible parent financially. When Dominique was three months old, Robert had sat down with Gaëlle and his attorney and explained in minute detail the financial plans he was making for their daughter. He established a huge trust fund that would essentially leave her his entire fortune, which was vast, and the ownership of all their homes, properties, and investments. The money was to be disbursed to her in increasing amounts over time, and he wanted Gaëlle to have the use of their homes for her lifetime, but Dominique would own them later on, for both tax and emotional reasons. Whatever he could leave to Dominique as a tax benefit he did, and he had planned a generous amount for Gaëlle, but with the bulk of his fortune being left to their daughter. He was leaving Gaëlle a sizable amount of money in his will, which would leave her set forever and able to do whatever she wanted, and enjoy their homes. It was a more than generous arrangement, for which Gaëlle was deeply grateful, but the lion's share would pass to their daughter, which seemed right to Gaëlle too. She had no desire to deprive or compete with their daughter, emotionally or financially.

Although they never explained the financial arrangements to Dominique in any detail, it was as though she knew or sensed it instinctively, and she acted like a spoiled heiress even as a very young child. And she once commented to her mother that she couldn't wait to be old enough to fire any of the servants she didn't like or who were mean to her. She had a shocking lack of empathy for others. It was an attitude and grandiosity that Gaëlle despised and ran counter to all that she believed in, about modesty and kindness, and was not the way that she or Robert behaved. He was exceptionally kind to all their employees, and so was Gaëlle. And Dominique was rude, entitled, and spoiled. She had a bitter quality to her, even as a child, not unlike Gaëlle's mother, who had been sour about life for years. She hadn't been a happy person, and Dominique wasn't either despite all the advantages she had, a father who worshipped her, and a mother who loved her and wished she'd behave, and be kinder to others. Dominique was very challenging at times, and rarely had the softness of her parents or that one expected in children. Dominique was like a nasty, small adult at an early age. She often hid that side of her from her father and showed him her sweet side. Gaëlle dreaded what she would be like to deal with once her father was gone and she inherited his money. And she fervently hoped it was a long time away.

★ ★ ★

Gaëlle never went back to modeling and didn't regret it. Instead she became fascinated by art history classes at Columbia University and NYU. She had no idea what she'd ever do with the degree, but she enjoyed the classes immensely, and adding to her knowledge about art, which was already extensive. She considered continuing for a doctorate, but that seemed redundant, and she was proud to have a BA in art history from Barnard and a master's from NYU.

When Dominique was six, Gaëlle and Robert took a trip to Paris. It was 1953, the scars of the war were less evident. It was an emotional homecoming for Gaëlle, and despite her initial reservations about the trip, they had a wonderful time. And on a free afternoon, they walked through the Louvre, and Gaëlle told him details about some of the paintings that he had never known about, although he was knowledgeable about art himself, and he was impressed. As they walked around the galleries, she stopped in front of one of the paintings and scrutinized it intently. She recognized it immediately. It was one of the first paintings she had been given to conceal by the commandant. It was like seeing a ghost from her past, and she looked wistful as she stared at it.

'Did that belong to your family?' Robert asked her, sensing that she had some kind of history with this beautiful small Degas ballerina, and she shook her head. She had never told him the whole story, but felt comfortable doing so now. She told him about how the commandant had asked her to hide the paintings he and his friend were spiriting away from officers who had stolen them and intended to keep them and send them back to Germany.

'I would go to his room after dinner, and he would give me a loaf of bread for my mother, with a painting rolled up in it. I had forty-nine hidden in a shed by the time he left, and I returned them to the Louvre as soon as I could get to Paris after the Liberation. They were quite shocked when I walked in with them.' She smiled at the memory. 'They thought they were forgeries or it was a scam of some kind, but they called in an expert who recognized them immediately as the real thing. I had three suitcases of them. Actually, the curator I returned them to gave me the address of Lelong, which was how I got my first job when I got here.' They were old memories now. It was eight years later, she was twenty-eight years old, and they had been married for seven years. And when she told him about hiding the paintings at the end of the war, to save them, he thought it was extraordinary. She was a national hero, to have concealed and returned forty-nine major pieces of France's art treasure that had been stolen from their rightful owners.

'Were you ever officially acknowledged for it, or thanked?' he asked, stunned by what she had told him so simply and modestly, which was so like her.

'No, why would I? I was just a young girl, a nobody from the provinces, doing my national duty.' She sighed then, remembering the rest of the story. 'On the contrary, it was why I was accused of collaborating with the enemy. When I went to the commandant's room after dinner almost every night in the last months of the war, our housekeeper thought I was sleeping with him in exchange for bread for my mother. She denounced me as soon as the Vichy government left. That was when they paraded me through the streets, shaved my head, and called me a traitor.' She had told him part of the story on their first trip to St. Moritz, so he would know she had been accused of collaborating. Now, years later, she told him all of it. It was still too painful to talk about the war years. But the story about the paintings just slipped out.

'Why didn't you explain it to them?' Robert looked devastated on her behalf. It pained him to think of what she'd gone through, and she never talked about it. She referred to the war even less in recent years than in the beginning. She didn't like to think about it, and never told him about her rescuing countless Jewish children. It was part of another life, and she felt like a different person now.

'They wouldn't have believed me,' she said simply. 'I just brought the paintings back, and that was the end of it. I never heard from them at the Louvre again. They had the paintings. We didn't need to speak about it. There were a lot of odd things that happened during and after the war.' She mentioned the names of the artists whose work she had hidden, and they spent the next two hours trying to locate more of them in the galleries of the Louvre. They found four of them, and she smiled when she saw each of them, it was like meeting old friends. It was an amazing story, and Robert realized that in some ways, Gaëlle was a mystery to him even now. She was such a discreet woman that she never mentioned her achievements or her past.

'What other stories about the war haven't you told me?' he asked as they left the Louvre, and stopped for a glass of wine at a café nearby. She didn't answer him. There was much she hadn't told him, most of it, and still didn't feel ready to now, and then after a sip of the wine, she told him about Rebekah.

'My best friend for all the years of my childhood was a girl called Rebekah. We were the same age, and her family was Jewish. She had two younger brothers and a little sister, and her father was the most important banker in our village. They had money, more than we did, and a beautiful house. I loved her like a sister. I went to her house every morning, and we rode our bicycles to school together. I came to pick her up one day, right after the Occupation started, and they were rounding up her family at gunpoint. They put them in a truck and drove away. They took them to a detention camp two hours away, and it was awful. Thousands of people, many women and children, families, in terrible conditions, living in tents and an old barn. They took everything away from them, as they did with all the Jews in France, their homes, their money, their businesses. They kept them at the camp for almost sixteen months. I rode out to see her every day. I never got caught, and my parents never knew. I never told anyone. I got sick then, and couldn't go for a week, and when I came back, the camp was empty. They were all gone, they had been deported on trains to Germany and the east. I always believed that she was alive and we'd meet again. And as soon as I came to Paris, I went to the Red Cross and asked them to help me find her. They'd been gone for three years by then. It took months for them to find out what happened. They were all sent to Auschwitz, and had died two years before. I never saw Rebekah again . . . I still have a piece of a hair ribbon I once gave her. It got caught on the fence at the camp.' Her voice drifted off as the story ended, and Robert felt a lump in his throat the size of a fist. He didn't know what to say to her to make it better, and he took Gaëlle in his arms and held her as she cried at the

191

memory. It had been more than eleven years since she'd last seen her, and it still felt like yesterday. She didn't have the courage to tell him about the children she had transported later, because of her. She just couldn't say any more. It was enough. Some things were part of a past he didn't need to know. And it had taken her seven years of marriage to tell him about the paintings and Rebekah.

They were silent as they walked back to the hotel, but one thing was certain. She was an extraordinary woman of immense fortitude, and he loved her more than ever. He was grateful every day that he had married her. She was a wonderful wife to him, and she had given him his greatest treasure, their beloved child whom he adored.

12

Dominique's character didn't get easier as she got older. As she entered her teens, she was more jealous than ever of her mother, and worshipped her father. Robert said that all teenage girls were difficult with their mothers, but Dominique carried it to an extreme degree. She demonized Gaëlle and argued with her constantly. It was discouraging, but Gaëlle couldn't get along with her, no matter how hard she tried. She tried to talk to Robert about it, hoping he would intercede for her, but he always had some excuse for Dominique's behavior. She'd had a bad day or had a nasty teacher or a cold or a headache, or someone had upset her or treated her unfairly. Gaëlle eventually realized it was hopeless to make him see reality about their child. Dominique could do no wrong in his eyes.

And as the nastiness that seemed natural to her increased from thirteen to fourteen, it reached a crescendo at fifteen, which the literature about teenage girls said was normal. Gaëlle read everything she could lay her hands on, to learn new theories about how to deal with her constructively, but nothing she tried ever worked. Dominique was consumed with jealousy, hated her mother, and wanted her father to herself. Nothing had changed, but her weapons were more powerful and hurt more, and her knife-edged tongue got sharper as she got older.

She even hated the idea that she was half French, which was another way of rejecting her mother. When anyone mentioned it, she immediately said that she was American, not French. And although she understood when her mother spoke to her in French, she would respond only in English. She wanted to be only her father's daughter and disapproved of her mother. Gaëlle had almost given up hope of having a decent relationship with her. Dominique didn't want to. Maybe when she was older, Gaëlle thought, but not at fifteen.

It was a hard year dealing with her as she got more independent and seemed meaner at the same time. She was a sophomore in high school, and said she couldn't wait to leave for college, and she was a good student. She wanted to go to business school one day, and work on Wall Street with her father. She had no interest in anything that Gaëlle was passionate about, like art, history, or fashion. She dismissed Gaëlle's career as a famous model. Only her father's career counted.

They went to Europe that summer, to France and Italy, and ended the trip in London. And Dominique insisted that she had hated France, although she'd had fun while she was there, but wouldn't admit it. She made it clear that she disliked anything related to her mother.

They had just gotten back from Europe, and were staying at the house in Southampton until school started. Gaëlle was on the phone talking to the caterer about a dinner they wanted to give in September. She and Robert loved giving elegant dinner parties and hadn't given one since June. Dominique was at the pool, reading, with her radio blaring next to her, and Robert had gone to play tennis with a friend. He was due back at one for lunch, and the table was already set for the three of them by the pool. Gaëlle had just hung up when the friend Robert was playing tennis with walked into the house. He looked ashen, and the moment Gaëlle saw him, she knew something terrible had happened.

'Matthew, what's wrong?' She ran to him immediately.

'Robert . . . ' he said, choking on a sob. 'We were playing . . . he was laughing about something . . . he was beating me . . . and he just dropped on the court. I tried to revive him, I gave him mouth-to-mouth. Louise called the paramedics . . . they were there in under five minutes. They worked on him for half an hour, but he was gone.' He cried like a child as he told her, and she put her arms around him and cried too. It wasn't possible. This couldn't happen. But it had. She had loved him from the first moment they met. And now he was gone, and so much too soon.

They sat down at the kitchen table and held hands, and then she went to get them both a glass of water. Louise called her husband at Gaëlle's house to make sure he was all right. He had been badly shaken by his friend's sudden death, but he wanted to tell Gaëlle in person. Louise asked if she could do anything. She was a younger wife too. At thirty-seven, Gaëlle was the youngest of their group, and she suddenly realized she was a widow. And how was she going to tell Dominique? The thought of it was terrifying. How would she survive losing the father she adored? He was the center of her world, and Dominique his.

Matthew left a few minutes later, and promised to come back that afternoon. Robert's body had been taken to the morgue of the nearest hospital. And she had to deal with that too. But first she had to tell her daughter that she had lost the father she worshipped and loved more than anyone on earth. Gaëlle had no idea how to do it, and Robert wasn't there to help her, for the first time in seventeen years. The years had flown by, sixteen of them in a marriage that everyone envied. And now the fairy tale had ended, and they weren't going to live happily ever after. It was over, in a matter of seconds on a tennis court. Just like that.

She went out to the pool to find Dominique, and sat down on the chair next to her, as Dominique looked annoyed. A new English group was singing a song, and she put down her book and stared at her mother.

'What?'

'I have something terrible to tell you,' Gaëlle said, and reached out to hug her. Dominique was stiff in her arms, which didn't help.

'What now?' She assumed that her mother was going to cancel some cherished plan. But this was far, far bigger, almost too big to understand.

Gaëlle looked at her intently, as her lips trembled, and she tried to be strong for her daughter.

'It's Daddy,' she said, as she fought back tears. 'He was playing tennis with Matthew, and — ' Dominique jumped to her feet and stared at her mother and stopped her.

'No! No! Don't tell me! I don't want to hear it . . . ' She was crying too and wanted to run away. But they couldn't, neither of them. They had no choice but to face the truth, no matter how awful it was.

'He had a heart attack,' Gaëlle said, feeling weak and dizzy. She didn't know what else to say.

'Is he okay?' There was desperation in Dominique's eyes, as her mother shook her head.

'No, baby, he's gone.'

'No, he's not!' Dominique shouted at her, wanting to kill the messenger, and wanting it not to be true, but it was.

Gaëlle pulled her into her arms then, and Dominique fought her way out by force and ran into the house crying. Gaëlle heard the door slam, and followed her in, and a few minutes later went to her room. Dominique was lying on her bed, sobbing. She was incoherent with grief, and Gaëlle sat on the bed next to her for an hour, trying to console her, until she told her mother to get out of her room. It was almost too much for Dominique to bear. Nothing had prepared her for this. And they hadn't expected it. He hadn't been sick. He had been healthy and vital and full of life, and wonderful to both of them. And now he was gone. It was an unimaginable blow, especially to Dominique.

Gaëlle went to her own room and called the hospital where they'd taken him, the funeral home in New York, and Robert's lawyer to tell him, and then she called his assistant to ask for her help. She was in shock too. He had been a wonderful man and everyone loved him. And now they had a funeral to plan.

And then Gaëlle went back to Dominique's room. She wanted to handle this perfectly for her daughter, but had no idea how, and she was the last person Dominique wanted now. Dominique told her mother to leave the room. She had called two of her closest friends, and they came over that afternoon and sat with her while she cried.

There was an unreality to all of it. Gaëlle felt as though she were swimming under water for days. Scenes went in and out of her mind, things she had to do, the terrible funeral arrangements, people she talked to at the service, the music and flowers, and dealing with Dominique, who had the shell-shocked appearance of an abandoned child in a war zone next to her mother in church, and looked daggers at her mother whenever she tried to hold her or comfort her. Somehow she blamed Gaëlle for surviving instead of Robert. Gaëlle had never felt so devastated and heartbroken and disconnected herself since the war. He had lulled her into believing their life would be perfect forever, and now he was gone, after sixteen extraordinary years of marriage. She felt frightened and abandoned too, but had to be strong for her daughter.

She met with the lawyers the week after the

funeral, and the trust for Dominique and the bequest for Gaëlle were as he had described. There were no surprises, and Gaëlle had a very large amount of money at her disposal now, more than she'd ever need, and all their houses for her lifetime, although they belonged to Dominique as part of what her father had left her. Gaëlle didn't want money and houses, she wanted him. And so did Dominique. She was inconsolable and refused to go to school. Gaëlle didn't insist, and the school gave her a month off, with the promise to catch up later. Dominique was too upset to function, and her school was allowing her to start late, and extended their condolences to her and Gaëlle.

At the beginning of October, Dominique finally went back to school, but she came home every day looking ravaged, and Gaëlle felt no better. Suddenly everything they had and did, the people they knew, the places they went, the houses they lived in had no meaning. And much to her own amazement, for the first time since she'd moved to New York, Gaëlle was homesick for France. She missed her country, the food and the people, speaking her own language, and everything familiar. She couldn't even explain it. It made no sense, even to her. But New York had been all about Robert for her, and the life they had together. She had married him months after she arrived. She had left France hating it, in the aftermath of war, but all she wanted now was to go back, at least for a while. She didn't say it to Dominique, but almost as much as she missed Robert, she missed France. She had turned her back on her country after it had betrayed her, but now she longed to go home, at least for a visit or maybe a summer.

And by Christmas, she was sure. Dominique was miserable and hating school. If she could have, she would have skipped straight to college, but she couldn't, she had two more years of high school to finish. She had been just about to start her junior year when her father died.

Gaëlle broached the subject with her one night after Christmas, which had been a nightmare without him. They had gone to Palm Beach and been depressed there. Gaëlle didn't want to see their friends now, she felt strange and alienated from them. They were all couples, and she was alone. They made her miss him even more. She felt like a broken bird with one wing, and she couldn't stand the pity in their eyes.

'I've been thinking,' Gaëlle said after she and Dominique finished dinner one night, and sat lifelessly at the kitchen table. They were like two people who had been shipwrecked and dragged up on shore. Life without him was awful, for both of them. His death had been shocking, and every day without him was an agony ever since. She was doing no better than Dominique, whose grades had plummeted. Three months after his death, neither of them had started to recover from the blow. And she wondered if they ever would. 'Maybe we need to do something different,' she began cautiously. His death had driven them farther apart, and she felt like she couldn't reach Dominique at all, but she knew she had to try, even if Dominique rebuffed her again and again. Gaëlle refused to give up trying to bridge the gap between them. She hoped that maybe a change of scene would help them both.

'What do you mean, we need to do something different?' Dominique eyed her suspiciously. 'Like what?' Her mother was the enemy now. She was alive. Her hero was dead. And she was trapped with the parent she didn't want.

'I don't know,' Gaëlle answered vaguely. 'I don't have the answers either. But it's ghastly sitting here like this. It's like we're waiting for him to come home.' And he wasn't going to. Dominique felt the same way.

'I don't want you to sell the apartment,' she said angrily, to cover her fear. Fear and jealousy ruled Dominique's world now, much as before, only worse.

'I'm not going to sell the apartment,' Gaëlle said quietly. 'It will belong to you one day. But maybe we should go somewhere else for a while, a few months, a summer.'

'Like where?'

'I've been thinking about France.'

'I hate France!' Dominique spat at her, which was like saying 'I hate you!' since she associated her mother with France and all things French. She hated having a French mother, and criticized her accent, although Gaëlle's English was nearly perfect after so many years.

'Well, we're not having fun here. This isn't working, for either of us.' Every one of their homes felt like a tomb now without him, New York, Southampton, Palm Beach. Gaëlle didn't want to make any major long-term changes, but she wondered if maybe a short-term one would get them both back on track. 'Maybe I could look for a house in France for the summer. Or maybe they'd let you do spring semester in Paris. There's a good American school there.' Friends of theirs had spent a year in Paris and loved it. She also realized now that whatever she suggested, Dominique would hate. She wanted her father back, and so did Gaëlle, but it was the one thing they couldn't have. They had the money to do whatever they wanted, thanks to Robert, but they couldn't have him. It was a hard adjustment for mother and daughter. He was so much to lose, and the bridge between them.

'Why don't you think about it,' Gaëlle said gently. Dominique didn't answer her, got up from the table, and slammed the door to her room. 'So much for that,' Gaëlle said to herself and put their plates in the dishwasher.

She spoke to a psychiatrist about it a week later. She predicted that it was going to take Dominique time to mourn her father, probably a long time, wherever she was, and that she wouldn't approve of any plan her mother came up with. Gaëlle would have to make the decision herself, based on what she thought best. Dominique couldn't.

'Right now, you have to do what makes sense to you. If it will help you to spend a few months in France, then do it. You can always come back if it's not working. How bad can it be? I gather money isn't a problem, so try it. The worst that can happen is you come home. Or maybe it will make this interim period easier, for both of you. Unfortunately, right now Dominique needs a place or a person to vent her anger, and you're it.'

'She's always been an angry person, particularly with me. She was very possessive of her father, and jealous of me. He was her hero. And now he's gone, and she's stuck with me. As far as she's concerned, that's as bad as it can get.'

'You may wind up closer than ever at the end of her grieving period,' the psychiatrist said hopefully. What she said was encouraging, but Gaëlle didn't believe it. Their relationship had never been good, and now Dominique was an angry teenager, and she had lost the father she loved so much. She felt as if she'd been robbed. Gaëlle knew how hard it was for her, and wished she could find some way to help her. But nothing she tried made it better, which only made it harder for Gaëlle too. She was the scapegoat and recipient of all Dominique's sadness and rage over losing him.

She thought about it for a month, as they dragged around the apartment, and Dominique's grades continued to drop, which the school psychiatrist said was normal.

Gaëlle was reading a travel magazine one weekend in January when she saw an ad for a house rental agency in Paris. It specialized in high-end furnished rentals of beautiful homes and apartments in good neighborhoods, mostly the seventh and the sixteenth arrondissements, the two best residential areas in Paris. She stared at the ad for a long time, and then put it on her

203

desk. She had to do something, and the weather had been particularly bad that year. It was freezing cold, and had snowed three times since New Year's. The city looked as bleak as their spirits.

And more out of curiosity, she called the agency in Paris the next morning and asked if they had a six-month rental of the kind they described in the ad.

'We have several,' the realtor said haughtily, and asked what Gaëlle had in mind. She said she wanted something bright and sunny, big enough for her and her daughter, in one of the neighborhoods mentioned in the ad. 'I might have something,' the woman said thoughtfully. 'It might be too big for you. It's a duplex on the sunny side of Avenue Foch, two blocks from the Arc de Triomphe.' Gaëlle knew the street. They were beautiful old Haussmannian buildings from Napoleonic days, with big rooms and high ceilings, beautiful moldings, and marble fireplaces. She had gone to parties there when she modeled for Dior. Most of the apartments were owned by diplomats, embassies, and foreigners. 'It's owned by an American couple, who might want to sell it. They want to rent it furnished while they decide. They never use it. It comes with a housekeeper and a maid. It has four bedrooms and a garage.' She quoted the rent, which was high, but given what she described, it came as no surprise. And they could afford it. Money wasn't the issue. Recovering from Robert's death was.

'I think I'd like to see it.' Gaëlle surprised

204

herself when she said it. She promised to call back the next day. And then she called the American School in Paris and made an appointment for the following week. She felt better as soon as she did. She had decided to go to Paris to look at the apartment and the school, without saying anything to Dominique. There was no point worrying her yet. She could decide what to do after she'd seen them. It sounded like a crazy idea, even to her, but it might be just what they needed. She wasn't sure. And there were worse things than spending six months in Paris.

The following Sunday night she left her housekeeper with Dominique and took a flight to Paris. She stayed at the Ritz and saw the apartment and the school and loved them both. She thought Dominique would be furious at her for dragging her to Paris, but as the psychiatrist had said, they weren't joining the Foreign Legion and could always come home if it didn't work out. And the decision had to be hers, not an angry fifteen-year-old's.

She wired the money for the apartment and the school when she got back to New York, had Dominique's transcript sent over, and spoke to her counselor, who thought it might do her good. The school in Paris had agreed to follow her curriculum from New York, so she didn't get too far off track. It was a big, friendly American-style school, with lots of extracurricular activities and sports, from kindergarten through twelfth grade. Gaëlle had loved the upbeat atmosphere when she visited.

She told Dominique her decision the day after she got home. They were leaving in two weeks. She felt slightly insane herself when she told her. It was a big leap for them both, but it felt right to at least try it, and she said as much to Dominique.

'So now Daddy's dead, and you want to move back to France?' she said accusingly.

'We're not moving, we're going for six months, for a change of scene. We're both miserable here. Why not give it a try? If we hate it, we'll come back sooner.'

'I don't want to get stuck in Paris with you,' she said rudely. 'What about my friends?'

'They can come to visit for spring break, or we can come back here. This isn't a prison sentence. It might be fun. And it's only four months till summer vacation by the time we get there. It's not a lifetime.' But it felt like it to Dominique. Gaëlle was doing it anyway. It was what she needed, and she hoped it would be good for Dominique too. And it was a chance to broaden their world and make new friends.

When they left for Paris, Dominique looked and acted as if she were being taken to jail, or Siberia. But Gaëlle heard her on the phone, telling her friends she'd be back in March for spring break, and she admitted that the school there sounded cool. It was bigger than her school in New York, and had lots of activities and clubs. And the students were mostly American kids living in Paris, and others from a number of other countries. It had a very international flavor with an American base. Dominique was more excited than she let on, which gave Gaëlle hope that it really might work.

When they arrived, the apartment was filled with sunlight, and the housekeeper had flowers everywhere. Dominique had a beautiful room, all done in pink silk and antiques, with a big canopied bed. Gaëlle's had one too and looked as if Marie Antoinette had lived there. Both the maid and the housekeeper were nice women, and there was a stuffed zebra in the living room. As promised, the apartment had style, was bright and cheerful, and was well decorated in a lovely building in a good neighborhood. They couldn't ask for more. The next day Gaëlle dropped Dominique off at school with the car and driver she'd hired. And when she picked her up at the end of the day, Dominique looked happier than she wanted to admit to her mother.

For better or worse, they had done it. They had six months in Paris, a school, and an apartment. And Gaëlle was determined to make the best of it, and get the most out of it, whether Dominique wanted to enjoy it or not. That was up to her. And much to her own surprise, Gaëlle was happy to be back, and it felt like home. It felt better than she'd expected to be back in France.

13

By the end of their first week in Paris, Gaëlle knew she had done the right thing. Dominique still sulked whenever she saw her, and was sullen, but she heard her on the phone with new friends at school, and she sounded better than she had in New York. She had joined a film club, a ski club, and a tennis club. And once she saw the apartment, she invited her best friend from New York to come to Paris for spring break. She wouldn't admit it to her mother, but she was having fun. She went to parties on the weekends, had friends from school over to study together, and went to American movies on the Champs Élysées. Gaëlle knew she still missed her father, and always would, but it was the change they had both needed in order to recover from the shock of his sudden death. And it was a big adjustment for Gaëlle too. She hadn't lived in France in seventeen years, and was surprised how much she liked it, how at home she felt, and how French.

Being there brought her back to her early modeling days. She thought of visiting Dior but didn't know anyone there anymore. Madame Cécile had retired years before, and Gaëlle had finally lost touch with all the models she'd lived with. She had come to Paris more than eighteen years before. It had been a lifetime, and a very full one, since then.

She walked all over Paris, went to her favorite museums, and signed up for a course at the Louvre. She was insatiable about art history classes. She bought French food she hadn't had in years, like boudin noir and kidneys, and her favorite childhood pastries, and enjoyed them thoroughly. And just hearing French spoken around her everywhere felt right again. She had had an entirely different life with Robert, and he had given her security and stability she would never have had otherwise, if she'd stayed in France. But now she longed to come back to her roots, not to return to where she'd grown up and suffered so many losses, or to see the château she had sold years before, but just to be back in Paris. She thought Robert would have understood. He had always been very respectful of her being French. She was grateful for the country she had adopted to be with him, but France was still home. It was in her genes, and her soul, and her heart, like a long-forgotten friend she had rediscovered. It was part of her. And she had needed to come home to familiar turf to get over losing him. She was finding herself again, and the person she had once been. There had always been an unreality to her life with him, and an awareness that other people didn't live that way. She was fortunate in what she had shared with him, and what he had left her, but she had always known that the world they lived in was his, and not hers, even their friends. She had never deluded herself that she was the Golden Princess. She had married the Golden Prince. Her own family had been country aristocrats, and far simpler than his.

She and Robert had often discussed how much to tell Dominique, and when, about what she would inherit one day. And the time had come sooner than anticipated, but his attorney and Gaëlle decided not to explain too much to her yet. She was turning sixteen and didn't need to know the extent of the vast fortune she had inherited. She would know soon enough. But oddly, even without being told the details, she had always had a sense of entitlement. Robert had somehow conveyed to her, without words, that she was special and different and privileged. Gaëlle didn't think it was a good thing, and hoped that she would enjoy simple pleasures in Paris, with ordinary kids. Her fortune, and all that went with it, could prove to be a great burden one day, and could isolate her from a more normal world. This seemed like a great opportunity to be a kid in a remarkable city.

Gaëlle loved her classes at the Louvre once she started them, and remembered when she and Robert had combed the galleries, looking for the paintings she had saved and returned to them. That was all part of another lifetime now. She liked the people in her class, and one of them mentioned an interesting museum to her, which she visited on a free afternoon, when Dominique was playing soccer after school. She had joined a girls' team and discovered she was good at it. She had her mother's long legs, even if she had her father's looks. She was the image of him.

The small museum her classmate had referred Gaëlle to was the Musée Nissim de Camondo, on the rue de Monceau in the eighth arrondissement. It was a small, elegant house that had belonged to a family of extremely wealthy Jewish Turks who were philanthropists and bankers, and it was filled with exquisite antiques, in a magnificent jewel of a home. The house had been restored, and the furniture replaced in 1935 by a relative of the original owners, a group of concerned Parisians, and friends of the family to honor Nissim de Camondo, who had died in World War I. And the rest of the family was later deported and died in concentration camps in World War II. It reminded Gaëlle instantly of Rebekah and the Feldmanns, and the beautiful home they had lost, although this one was even finer and grander. And instead of being buried and forgotten, the family that had lived in the house she visited was honored and remembered. Gaëlle wished that she could restore a home like that, and honor her friends, with the money Robert had left her. There were so many like them that had disappeared. There was a quiet sadness, as she toured the home, admiring the art and antiques. They had died in Auschwitz like Rebekah and her family. And even all these years later, they had left an indelible footprint on the history of France that still lingered. Gaëlle was quiet and thoughtful when she left and went back to the apartment on Avenue Foch.

She told Dominique about it that night, and for the first time she told her about Rebekah, and Dominique was quiet as she listened. Her mother had never shared it with her before. And she didn't tell Dominique about the ribbon she had brought with her. She took it everywhere, and it was back in Paris now, in a drawer in the desk she was using.

'I don't understand,' Dominique said at the end of the story. 'Why didn't someone stop the Germans? Or why didn't people like the Feldmanns refuse to go?' It was hard to explain to someone so young, who had lived in freedom all her life, without persecution, how an entire race of people could be hunted and killed by their own countrymen in what they considered their home.

'They had no choice. Soldiers or police would show up at their door and kill them if they wouldn't go. They could have tried to escape before, but they had nowhere to go, and they didn't think it would touch them.'

'Even little kids were sent to the camps?' Gaëlle nodded, thinking of Lotte, and the children she had hidden in the shed and the basket of her bicycle, as she took them to safe houses in other villages. But it was more than Gaëlle felt ready to share with her. And Dominique went off to do her homework and call her friends, with new insight into her mother. Gaëlle wondered if it would make a difference. Dominique already seemed happier since they'd been in Paris, and less angry at her mother, at least some of the time.

They both started making new friends a short time after they arrived. Gaëlle liked a number of parents from the school. She wasn't ready to go to big social events yet, and didn't know if she ever would again, but a number of times she spent enjoyable evenings at other parents' homes, or invited them to the apartment. They found it interesting that she had lived in New York for seventeen years, and come home. And one of the women remembered that she'd been an important model a long time ago, and was impressed. Gaëlle was still beautiful at thirty-eight, and looked very young.

It was a beautiful spring in Paris, and little by little they both began to heal.

Dominique's best friend from New York came over for spring break and loved her new school. Gaëlle chaperoned a dance there, and although they were very different and never as close as Gaëlle hoped, Dominique slowly began to forgive her for her father's death. It had been a terrible loss for both of them. And Dominique was very young to lose her father. Gaëlle had been only two years older when she lost hers, and had never been close to her mother either. In a strange way, history repeated itself.

★   ★   ★

Their lease on the Paris apartment was up at the beginning of August, and in June, the owners offered to extend it to the end of the year. They weren't ready to make a decision about selling the apartment yet, and Gaëlle wasn't sure she was prepared to decide what to do either. She had promised Dominique to spend the summer in Southampton, with her friends, although she had qualms about what it would be like being

213

there after Robert had died there the summer before, but Dominique wanted to go anyway. And Gaëlle had to decide where to enroll her in school for her senior year, Paris or New York.

She took a long walk through the streets of Paris, thinking about it, and by the time she got back to the apartment, she knew what she wanted to do. She wasn't sure if it was fair to her daughter, but she knew she wanted to keep the apartment and come back after the summer for another school trimester, or even the entire school year. And Dominique would be leaving for college in a year anyway. If she was willing, why not spend it in Paris? She had just completed her junior year, and would have to apply to college in the fall. They were going on a college tour at the end of August, even though she had her heart set on Radcliffe. And Harvard Business School afterward, since they had recently started accepting women. So now she could follow in her father's footsteps perfectly, as she'd always hoped. Her dream of becoming an investment banker like her father hadn't changed. She was even more determined now than she had been before his death.

Gaëlle waited for her to come home from school that afternoon, and told her that she wanted to come back after the summer, and to have her finish high school in Paris. She waited for the explosion she expected, but it didn't come.

'Why bother asking me?' she said stiffly. 'You make all the decisions anyway.' It was a typical teenage comment, and had the hard edge Gaëlle had come to expect from her, but she was relieved that she hadn't objected strenuously. And she overheard her talking to a friend on the phone, excited to be coming back to the American School in Paris in the fall, but she would never have given her mother the satisfaction of admitting she was pleased.

They were packed and ready to leave for the States in time to spend the Fourth of July weekend in Southampton, when Gaëlle got an interesting call. She had spent a long time talking to the curator of the Nissim de Camondo Museum when they first moved to Paris, and he wanted to let Gaëlle know that there was another small museum like it being set up on the Left Bank, by a family who wanted to honor their lost relatives, and they were looking for a curator. And he knew she had a master's in art history from NYU and wondered if she was interested. And now that they would be back in September, she loved the idea of taking a job, particularly that one. He told her who to speak to, she called the next morning, and set up an appointment with the executor of the project for that afternoon. She was leaving the next day.

When she got there, the house was beautiful, although it needed some work. It had passed into other hands for twenty years, a family who had bought the house for nothing when the original family was deported. And now American relatives had bought it and wanted to restore it, and turn it into a memorial for their lost family members. They needed someone to oversee the work, and to purchase and furnish it with

215

antiques and art similar to those that had been in the house originally. There had been five children, and there were albums of photographs of the interiors for her to work from. The original residents had had an important art collection, which would be expensive to replicate, but the family had the money to do so. It sounded like a wonderful project to Gaëlle. She left her CV with them and advised them she'd be back in early September, and how to reach her in the States.

She told Dominique about it that night, and Gaëlle was excited about it. Dominique didn't look pleased.

'That means you're staying here, Mom, if you're looking for a job here. You'll never come back to live in the States.' She was angry again.

'I don't know what I'm going to do,' her mother said honestly. 'You're going to college in a year, and I'd be alone in the apartment in New York.' It was already too lonely there now without Robert. And Gaëlle had always felt a little bit like a guest in their homes. He had owned all of them before he married her. Some had belonged to his family, although he'd bought the penthouse on Fifth Avenue himself. But she had moved into his world, and now that he was gone, she felt like an interloper. She needed to find her own world, which felt like it belonged to her. And all their homes would be Dominique's one day. Nothing was hers. She felt homeless. She had been thinking about it since Robert died.

'But why get a job? You don't need to work.' Dominique looked at her critically, as she always did, although less so lately.

'I won't have anything to do once you leave for school,' she reminded her. 'I need something to keep me busy. I can't take classes forever, I'm too old to model, and I wouldn't want to anyway. That was fun when I was a kid, before I married Daddy, but it's not a job for me today. This could be an interesting project for me, and a way to honor families like the one I told you about. People should never forget, especially here, where they let it happen.' Persecution and betrayal like that happening in the States was unthinkable. And Dominique hadn't lived through it, so she didn't understand.

'Why don't you just do charity work?'

'It wouldn't be as interesting as this museum. They probably won't hire me anyway. I'm not a curator, which is really what they need.' Dominique nodded and lost interest in the subject, and went to finish packing. And Gaëlle went to complete hers. But Gaëlle was still thinking about it on the plane the next day, and knew she'd love it if they hired her. It was something that would keep her occupied, it was a noble project, and a way of honoring those who were lost.

And when they got to New York, she was busy and forgot about it. Dominique filled the apartment in New York with her friends visiting her night and day. There were sixteen-year-old girls everywhere, and a number of boys showed up too. And by that weekend, they were in Southampton, and it felt like one of their normal summers, except Robert wasn't there. They gave

217

their annual Fourth of July party, and it was strange without him, but it felt good now to see her friends too. They all said they had missed her. And everyone was surprised to hear that they were going back to Paris in September, and Dominique would be finishing high school there. Slowly but surely in the last year, life had changed. And they all said she looked more French again, which made her laugh, but she wondered if they were right. She felt more French again too.

At the end of August, Gaëlle took Dominique on the college tour they had planned carefully that spring in Paris. They had a lot of schools to see, and it was intense. They saw Radcliffe, Boston University, Vassar, Wellesley, Smith, and Barnard, although Dominique said she didn't want to go to college in New York. She had considered a few schools in California, but decided that she'd rather stay in the East, which Gaëlle thought was a better idea too. California was just too far from home. And even farther from Europe.

'We can look at the American University in Paris too, if you want, when we go back,' she reminded her, and Dominique vetoed it immediately.

'I'm going to college in the States, Mom, whatever you decide to do. I'm coming home, and this is home to me.' Just like Paris was home to her mother again now, Gaëlle thought, but didn't say it.

Dominique had liked many of the colleges she'd seen, but Radcliffe was still her first choice,

218

and she was applying for early admission, since she had excellent grades. They'd picked up again in Paris, after her slump when her father died. And she had nearly perfect SAT scores. Robert had been a generous donor to Harvard, his alma mater, and her grandfather had earlier attended Harvard as well, which Gaëlle suspected wouldn't hurt. Dominique was hoping to hear by December, and was already working on her application.

They got back to Paris two days before school started, which gave Dominique a chance to catch up with her friends, after the summer. Many of them had gone back to the States, but some had gone to Brittany and the South of France, Spain, Portugal, and Italy. Their life experience was broader and more interesting than her friends in the States, which Gaëlle thought was good for her daughter.

She signed up for another class at the Louvre for the fall semester, and was two weeks into it, when the executor of the museum she'd interviewed with called her and asked if she was still interested in the curating position. They had been away for the summer too. Everything in France came to a screeching halt in July and August and got moving again in September.

'Yes, I am,' she said enthusiastically. 'I thought you'd forgotten me, or hired someone else.'

'Not at all. We're very keen on you. How about coming to the house tomorrow?' She agreed to be there after her class ended, and when she arrived at the house, the architect, the contractor, a patron, and two family members were there. They explained their mission for the museum more specifically. She was surprised by their asking if she had been living in the States during the war.

'No, I was here,' she said calmly, and she wondered if her reputation as a collaborator had followed her, but they didn't know her maiden name, or what region she was from, so she realized it couldn't. 'I worked for the OSE from 1943 till the end of the Occupation.' It was the first time that she had said it openly, and it felt good to do so. When she did, she noticed that the patron smiled at her. She was a warm, lively woman younger than Gaëlle, with bright engaging eyes.

'Rescuing Jewish children?' the executor asked her. The family looked surprised and pleased. She was obviously sympathetic to what they were doing, if so.

'Transporting them to safe houses,' she explained.

'How old were you?'

'Eighteen when I started. I had a close friend who was deported with her family. They were at Chambaran detention camp in Vienne for fifteen months, and I discovered later that they died in Auschwitz.'

'Our family died in Buchenwald.' The museum was going to be named after their relatives. The Strauss Museum. She could tell they were impressed by the interview, and they called her the next day and offered her the position. She was thrilled and agreed to start the following week. She would have to drop her class at the Louvre, but she didn't mind, she had just signed up for it as a time filler. And the salary they offered her was a pittance, but she didn't care. Thanks to Robert, she could do jobs she loved, without worrying about supporting herself.

Half an hour later the patron at the interview called her too and invited her to lunch the following week. Gaëlle had a good feeling about her and liked her at the interview. Her name was Louise, and as they agreed to meet at Fouquet's for lunch, a lasting friendship was born.

She told Dominique about it that night, and she barely commented on it. It didn't sound very intriguing to her.

They were both busy after that. Gaëlle went to the house every day, and worked with the contractor on the restoration plans, and she spent hours combing antique shops and auctions in order to find furniture similar to what they had in the photographs. They had had some very handsome pieces and important art. And it was exciting each time she found another piece. It was like putting a puzzle together, while they restored the house.

She was just leaving the auction rooms at the Hôtel Drouot with a small painting under her arm, which was almost identical to one in their living room, and she felt victorious, although she'd paid a handsome price for it. When she left the building, she noticed people talking animatedly on the street. She had the sense that something major had happened, but didn't know what. She turned the radio on in the small

221

Peugeot she had bought so she could drive herself now, and she heard the news of John Kennedy's assassination, and sat in her car without moving, in a state of shock. It seemed impossible that it could have happened. She drove straight to Dominique's school to pick her up. She knew she would just be finishing a soccer game and would have heard the news by now.

When she got to the school, there were clusters of students outside with arms around each other sobbing, and she got out to go and find her daughter. She found her with a group of crying students, watching television in an assembly room. They were showing the film clips from Dallas that morning, and Gaëlle went to put her arms around her, as Dominique sobbed. She was a big Kennedy fan, and Jackie was her idol. They were showing her in her blood-stained suit, and Gaëlle cried too as they watched her. It was all so poignant and tragic, especially seeing his children. It was an unthinkable event. Gaëlle knew she was watching history, like the day Paris fell. There were some moments and events that you remembered in every detail — what you were doing and wearing, who was with you, how you felt when you first heard the news. She and Rebekah had been together when they heard that France had surrendered to the Germans.

Several of the students came home with them, and crowded into her small car, or followed on bicycles. She fed them dinner, and they continued to watch the news there, late into the night. Some stayed, and slept in their guest rooms, one on the couch in their TV room, and

222

several on the floor. They wanted to be together. And the ensuing days were raw with emotion. The school closed to honor the late president, and the coverage on television was heartbreaking and seen around the world. And it seemed irrelevant even to her that in the days afterward Gaëlle turned thirty-nine, and she didn't care about her birthday. She cried every time she saw the First Lady with her children. They all felt as though they had lost someone close to them when it was over, and it was hard going back to school and work on Monday.

They had Thanksgiving in Paris after that. Gaëlle invited two families from Dominique's school for a traditional turkey dinner, and Louise from the museum. And she cooked the meal herself, with Dominique's grudging help. But the atmosphere around the table was lively and friendly, and Gaëlle was happy she'd done it. And she liked Louise even more. She had brought her son and daughter to dinner with her, who were younger than Dominique, and she was also a young widow. They had much in common. She had lost close friends in the war as well, and was helping to fund the museum. She stayed after dinner to help Gaëlle clean up as they chatted.

And they went back to the States for Christmas. They were planning to spend two weeks in New York, and a week at their home in Palm Beach, which seemed particularly depressing. It was their second Christmas without Robert, but still very hard. And when they returned to Paris after Palm Beach, the letter

Dominique had been waiting for so desperately was there. She opened it with trembling hands, and they both wished that her father were with them. Gaëlle watched her face intently as she read it, and then Dominique let out a bloodcurdling scream.

'I got in! I got in!' She had been accepted early admission by Radcliffe, and her degree four years later would be issued by Harvard. She ran to her room to call her friends, and as Gaëlle watched her run down the hall, tears slid down her cheeks, knowing another era of her life was about to end when she left for college. Their life was a constantly changing landscape, and it made her feel better knowing she had decided to stay in Paris. The apartment in New York would have been intolerably lonely without her. And Gaëlle had a life and a job now in Paris. Dominique would be going to Radcliffe and have a Harvard degree like her father. Gaëlle was happy and excited for her. Good things were starting to happen, for both of them. At last.

14

After the excitement over Dominique's early acceptance to Radcliffe, they settled into their Paris routine of school and work. Dominique had her last semester to finish, and Gaëlle was busy at the museum. She was combing art galleries and auctions, to complete furnishing the house. And the contractor and architect were pushing the construction schedule as hard as they could. They were hoping it would all come together by the end of the new year, which seemed feasible though a challenge. Keeping workmen on track in France wasn't easy. And Gaëlle brought home copious notes with her every night, about things to do and buy for the house, and marketing ideas to make locals, tourists, and guidebooks aware of the new museum. She and Louise talked often to discuss it, and it was a good excuse to have lunch together as they got to know each other. Gaëlle was working on rugs now, and the children's bedrooms, which was heart-wrenching for her. She had known too many children like the five Strauss children, whom she felt as though she knew now after poring over photographs of them and their rooms for months. There were four sons and a daughter, all under twelve. She knew their names and their personalities, what books and toys they liked best, and had learned all of it from letters relatives had kept from their mother.

And Naomi Strauss, the children's mother, sounded like a lively, fun-loving, intelligent, well-educated woman, who adored her husband and children and was devoted to them. They were part of Gaëlle's life now, which in some ways was very painful, and at the same time healing. They always reminded her of Rebekah.

She had been back from New York for three weeks when André Chevalier, the architect, invited her to dinner. He and his wife Geneviève lived in a walk-up apartment in Montmartre. She liked him and accepted the invitation. Dominique was home studying the night she went to dinner, so she didn't mind going out and leaving her, and promised to be home at a decent hour, since she had early appointments at the museum with vintage toy dealers the next day. The children's bedrooms were proving to be harder to reconstitute than their parents'.

'Have fun,' Dominique muttered over her shoulder, and didn't look up from her books.

Gaëlle drove to Montmartre, looking forward to dinner. She had brought a bottle of red wine with her, and she was wearing slacks and a sweater, since André had told her it would be casual.

She arrived at the apartment out of breath, after climbing six flights of very slippery stairs in an ancient building with no elevator. André apologized as soon as he opened the door and saw how winded she was, which was no more than the other guests when they had made the climb.

'Just be glad we didn't ask you to carry the groceries up the stairs,' he said as she handed him the bottle of wine, and he thanked her, and led her into the living room, where seven other guests had arrived before she did. They were smoking and talking and drinking, and already engaged in lively conversations, which continued as they sat down to dinner. She was seated between a female architect who was André's business partner, whom Gaëlle had already met at the museum and liked, and a violinist who was a friend of Geneviève's, since she taught piano and singing at the conservatory.

André said that the man seated across from her was a composer. His name was Christophe Pasquier, and André said he wrote music for television and movies, and had had some successes. He seemed interesting and serious, and got into a conversation with Gaëlle and the violinist, talking about politics. Gaëlle hadn't realized until she got back to France how much she had missed French dinner conversation, intellectual discussions, and political arguments. People stayed forever after dinner just to talk. And the meal was as good as André had promised. Geneviève was a superb cook and had made a delicious *hachis Parmentier*, and *confit de canard*, and there had been crab salad first.

'How did you get talked into André's big project?' Christophe asked her with interest.

'She's a brilliant woman, and has a good heart,' André answered for her, and she laughed.

'I think it's very exciting. I went to the Musée Camondo de Nissim last year and was very moved by it. They recommended me for the project, after I'd talked to their curator. These small individual museums are so intimate and personal, and the message is so important.' She said it with passion. They talked about other things then, and he asked if she was half-American, and she said she had been married to one, hence the name Bartlett.

'And very sensibly, you divorced him and came back?' he teased her, and she smiled politely when she answered.

'No, I'm a widow.' He looked instantly mortified and said he was a disaster at social situations, which was why no one except André invited him anywhere. They had gone to school together, so he usually forgave him. He said most of the time he forgot invitations entirely and remembered them the day after, when the hosts called, furious with him. André had called to remind him. She laughed at what he said. He seemed genuinely repentant for the comment, and he had electric blue eyes and very blond hair, was very tall and in his early forties. To break the ice, she asked if he had children, and he said he didn't, and had never been married.

'No one will have me,' he said matter-of-factly.

'That's right,' André added. 'He's a workaholic. That's why he's successful.'

'I'm not successful,' Christophe corrected him. 'I'm still working at it.' They went on talking then, and he asked Gaëlle what she had done before the museum, and she said that she hadn't worked while she was married, but she had been a model as a young girl after the war, which didn't entirely surprise him. She still had that look, and managed to be chic even in slacks and sweater, with a big gold bracelet on her arm, and

228

he noticed she was still wearing her wedding band. He had completely missed seeing it until now, and she hadn't taken it off yet, despite being widowed. 'And modeling qualifies you as a curator?' he asked, curious about her.

'I have a degree in art history.'

'And she's damn good at what she does,' André vouched for her.

'I don't doubt it,' Christophe said, smiling at her, as Geneviève brought out a *tarte tatin*, an apple tart she had baked herself, and offered coffee. 'And you have children?' Christophe asked her. She had mentioned her daughter, but he wondered if she had more.

'One daughter. She's leaving for college in the fall.'

'In the States?' She nodded. 'Is that a good thing? Going away to college, I mean?' Most French students stayed home, attended university in their own cities, and lived with their parents. She was familiar with the system, although her brother had studied in Paris.

'It's good for her. It will be lonely for me, though. But she doesn't want to stay here. I kind of forced her into moving to Paris when her father died, for a change of scene. And I wanted to come home. I lived in New York for seventeen years, and I didn't realize it, but I missed Paris. And after my husband died, I was homesick.'

'I couldn't live anywhere else,' he said with fervor, as he dug into Geneviève's apple tart, after serving Gaëlle a slice. 'Are you originally from Paris?'

'No, near Lyon. I lived here for a year, when I

worked for Christian Dior after the Liberation.' Dior had opened his own fashion house shortly after she left, and had died six years ago. His young assistant, Yves St. Laurent, was designing for the house now.

'Sounds very glamorous,' he said. 'Paris, New York, modeling.' She wasn't pretentious about it, and he liked that. She seemed very simple and unassuming. 'And your daughter doesn't want to go to college here? What a pity.'

'She's totally American, and she just got into the school she wanted, so she's on her way.'

'And what does she want to be when she grows up?'

'A banker like her father.' She smiled as she said it, and he raised an eyebrow in surprise. It seemed like an odd career choice for a girl to Gaëlle too, but Dominique was very determined about her passion for business. 'And I'm sure she'll be good at it. She loves business, economics, and math. None of the things I'm good at.' She smiled at Christophe again.

'How old is she?' Gaëlle looked around thirty to him but had to be older if her daughter was going to university.

'Almost seventeen. She'll be young for her class.'

'So she's obviously bright like her mother,' he said, complimenting her, and then she got involved in another conversation at the other side of the table, and she didn't talk with Christophe again until they were both leaving at the same time. It was after one o'clock, but the conversations around the table had been lively and engaging, and she'd enjoyed the evening.

'May I escort you down André's perilous stairs? I usually fall down at least a flight of them after I drink enough wine at dinner. I'll go first, so if you fall, you can land on me,' he said, and she laughed but was grateful for the buffer. They were nasty stairs and they scared her, and her shoes were flat but slippery. She made her way down them gingerly as Christophe walked carefully in front of her, and she almost slipped twice. The timer for the lights kept turning them off, and she was glad he was with her as they groped for the light switch in the dark every few minutes. They were both relieved when they got to the bottom without falling. 'I hope he makes some decent money one of these days, so he can move into a building with an elevator and proper lights. His stairs are suicidal,' Christophe commented, and she laughed. He walked her to her car and told her he had enjoyed meeting her, and wished her good luck with the museum. She thanked him and said good night, and drove back to her apartment, where she found Dominique tucked into bed and sound asleep.

The next day when she saw André, he told her that Christophe had been very impressed by her and had asked for her number. 'Should I give it to him, or tell him to get lost?' She laughed at the question and wasn't sure what to say.

'I thought he was nice, but I haven't gone out with anyone since my husband. I don't think I'm dating.' It was the impression André had but didn't want to ask.

'I'll tell him to forget it. He's a pain in the ass

anyway. All he does is work.' But she thought that sounded interesting too. He seemed like a pleasant person, and his long-standing friendship with André was a good reference.

'I guess you can give it to him. It never hurts to meet new friends,' she said casually.

'You won't hear from him anyway. He'll forget your name by tomorrow and be back at his piano composing. I think he's working on a movie score right now. I was surprised that he came. He probably needed a decent meal, and he loves my wife's food.'

'It was fabulous. I had two helpings of the *hachis Parmentier* and a huge piece of the tart.'

'You need it,' he said, and rolled his eyes at how thin she was.

Despite André's predictions Christophe called her that night, as soon as he got her number from André.

Dominique answered the phone, told her mother about the call, and then disappeared back into her room after Gaëlle picked it up.

'I really enjoyed meeting you last night,' he told her warmly. 'And André is right, I usually work at night and don't go out, but I hadn't had a decent meal in a week and Geneviève's cooking is so damn good.' She laughed.

'That's why André said you came. He told me you're working on a movie.'

'Trying to. I'm on a tight deadline and only halfway through the score.' He sounded worried about it.

'It must be interesting.'

'Sometimes it is. I like what I do. I'm very

232

passionate about it.'

'Me too. I'm having fun with the museum. I'm running a little behind on it too.' But she had done well that day with the children's toys, and got all the ones she wanted and had been looking for. It was all taking shape.

'It's a touching project,' he said thoughtfully. 'Do you have a personal interest in it?' He didn't know why, but he suspected that she did. And he was sure her salary was small. She wasn't doing it for the money.

'Yes, I do,' she said softly. 'A family I knew got deported. My best friend.'

'We all know someone,' he said in a serious tone. 'It was a terrible time we should all be ashamed of.'

'I agree, which is why the museum is important, even if it's small.' But she was hoping to make it a must-see in Paris of social, cultural, and historic importance, although she hadn't figured out how to do it yet and bring it to people's attention.

'I look forward to seeing it when it's finished,' and even more so now that he'd met her. André had mentioned her and said she was a very bright, attractive woman and terrific to work with, but it hadn't clicked for him till he saw her at André's. 'Could I take you to dinner sometime?' He tried to sound nonchalant about it, and wasn't sure what she'd say, remembering the wedding ring on her finger, but she said she was a widow. It was apparently fairly recent, since André had said she wasn't dating, just to warn him.

'That would be nice,' she said blandly, but didn't pursue it, so he decided not to push and suggest a date.

'I'll call you when I get a little more work done,' he said, not wanting to pressure her or seem too anxious.

She thanked him for the call and hung up, as Dominique came back into the room.

'Who was that?' she asked brusquely with a frown.

'A friend of the architect I'm working with at the museum.'

'He didn't ask you out, did he?' she asked her, and sounded like the Inquisition.

'No, he didn't. I met him at dinner last night.'

'You wouldn't date anyone, would you?'

'Not at the moment. I haven't thought about it. I don't really want to. Why?'

'You're too old, you don't need another husband, and Daddy wouldn't like it.' She swept the board, and her mother laughed.

'Well, that certainly wraps it up. Thanks for making it so clear, especially the part about being too old.'

'You are, and you don't need to get married again. Daddy left you enough money.'

'How do you know?' Gaëlle frowned at her.

'He told me he would. He said he'd leave you enough to live well on, and I'd get the rest.'

'He took very good care of both of us,' she said, to end the discussion about money. 'And you're right, I don't need another husband. But I wouldn't marry someone for money anyway.'

Robert and Dominique had talked about money

more than she liked. And Dominique was obsessed with it. Who had what, how to make more, and what were good investments. She was headed for the right profession as an investment banker.

'You got lucky with Dad,' she said bluntly, and Gaëlle was shocked.

'I got lucky because he was a good man and we loved each other very much,' she corrected her.

'And a rich one.' Gaëlle didn't like the comment or her attitude. It made her sound so venal.

'People should marry for love, not money,' Gaëlle said firmly.

'Money helps. I would hate to be poor,' she said matter-of-factly, and her mother didn't like that comment either.

'I was poor after the war,' Gaëlle said honestly, 'and if you're poor, you work hard, which is a good thing.' But admittedly poverty wasn't fun and had been stressful.

'I want to work hard and do even better than Dad,' Dominique said with a look in her eyes Gaëlle had never seen before. There was cold ambition there and iron determination.

'Life isn't all about money. Or it shouldn't be. You can be happy without it, or very unhappy with it, if you're with the wrong person,' Gaëlle said gently.

'Like Daddy and his first wife. She was after money,' Dominique said blithely. 'I don't want to get married anyway,' she added, and then left the room, as Gaëlle mused about the conversation.

She hated hearing her so focused on money, and it didn't bode well for when she found out exactly what her father had left her, although the global amount of his worth had been mentioned in the press. She was going to get the first installment at eighteen, which Gaëlle thought was too soon. She didn't need it as a young student, but Robert had had his own ideas about money, and hadn't agreed with her. At least the first of what she'd receive was a year away. He had wanted Dominique to learn how to manage and invest her fortune, and be responsible at an early age. Too early, in Gaëlle's opinion. It would set her apart from her peers, and she might spend it frivolously. Robert didn't think she would, Dominique wasn't generous by nature, unlike her father.

Christophe called Gaëlle again a few days later, and invited her to lunch. He thought it might be a gentler way to get to know her, and suggested they meet at an old bistro that she liked.

When they met, she arrived on time after a busy morning. She'd gone to an exhibit of furniture, and was going to an auction the next day for the Strauss Museum. She had been to the preview for the auction, and showed him the catalog at lunch and what she would be bidding on. He liked her choices, and then they talked about his music. His eyes lit up when he talked about it. He had taken a trip to Prague recently, with special permission, to hear a symphony composed by a friend. And he mentioned that he had taught at a well-known music school in Boston for a year, the Berklee School of Music, and had enjoyed it a great deal, although he couldn't see himself living there forever.

He was an interesting, intelligent man, and from everything he said, it was easy to see that music in all forms was his life. The time they spent together sped by, and as they stood outside the restaurant after an excellent meal, he asked if he could see her again. She hesitated for a moment before she answered, remembering her conversation with Dominique.

'I'd like that,' she said honestly. He was good company, and had been fun at lunch, 'but I had a recent talk with my daughter about dating. She says I'm too old, and I don't need a man in my life. So I've been warned.' She laughed as she said it, and he frowned.

'And do you agree with her?' he asked with a piercing glance.

'Sometimes,' she said, looking out at the Seine, and then back at him. 'It's been eighteen years since I had a date. I'm a little out of practice.' But this wasn't dating in her mind — it was lunch with a new friend.

'And you're definitely not too old, by the way. Children are cruel. That's why I never had any. My ego is too fragile — they'd hurt my feelings.' She laughed again at what he said.

'They definitely hurt one's feelings, every chance they get. But to answer your question, yes, I'd like to see you again.' She liked him, as a friend, as a man, as something, she didn't know what. But he wasn't proposing marriage, just a meal. And she didn't have to tell Dominique and didn't plan to.

'That's good news. I'll call you.' He kissed her on both cheeks, and she got into her car and drove off a minute later with a wave, after thanking him for lunch. He walked back to his own car then, and looked very pleased. He thought she was terrific, and her daughter sounded like a pain in the ass, a typical teenage girl.

★　★　★

Gaëlle didn't hear from Christophe for two weeks after that, and she wondered if she'd offended him. But she was busy, and it didn't really matter. If he never called her again, that was all right too. It had been a nice lunch, and didn't have to be more.

And then he surfaced again and invited her to dinner. He offered to pick her up, and she said it would be easier to meet him at the restaurant. She didn't want to have to explain him to Dominique. She hardly knew him, and it was probably nothing, and not worth getting in a fight about. Her daughter apparently expected her to remain chaste and faithful to Robert for the rest of her life. And it might happen that way anyway. She herself wasn't ready to move on, but dinner was fine.

He suggested a small, cozy restaurant on the Left Bank that she'd never been to. And they had a very long dinner with great food and talked for hours. He had told her during the meal that he had lived with a woman for seven years, and it ended because he didn't want to get married and have children, so she had left him, and he said he had no regrets, she had done the right thing, and had married someone else and had three children.

'Most men don't want to marry at a certain age,' she had said, and told him that Robert had been forty-nine when they married, and was divorced after a brief, bad previous marriage. He had been gun-shy afterward, and it all changed when they fell in love. It intrigued him that she had married someone so much older — it seemed unfortunate to him, since she was alone now. She was a lovely woman.

'I've always been afraid that a serious relationship and children could interfere with my work,' he admitted. 'I'm married to my music. I've never wanted to sacrifice that for anyone. You have to give children an enormous part of yourself, and love can be so distracting.' She smiled at what he said.

'Yes, it can.'

He had brought her a recording of some of his music, and she promised to listen to it. And she told him about her latest acquisitions for the museum. Like their lunch, the evening flew by, and they left the restaurant at two A.M. She was shocked at how late it had gotten.

'Will you get home all right on your own?' he asked, concerned.

'Do I look drunk?' she teased him.

'No, but it's late, and I don't like you driving around alone at this hour, or walking into your building. Where do you live, by the way?' He didn't know, and she hadn't said.

'Avenue Foch.'

'Very fancy. I love those old Haussmann buildings. You must have fabulously high ceilings.' Haussmann had designed beautiful buildings throughout Paris, hers among them, during the Second Empire.

'I do have high ceilings,' she confirmed, and he smiled at her.

'Drive carefully.' For a man who cared only about his music, he was very chivalrous with her.

'I always do,' she assured him. He kissed her on both cheeks again, and promised to call her soon, and she suspected he would. They had both had a good time, and he looked sorry to see her leave. She thought about him as she drove home, and passed the Arc de Triomphe. He was very appealing, and handsome in a rugged way. He was very intellectual and well read, had a nice sense of humor, and seemed like a gentle person. She liked him, and at the same time, it felt odd going out with a man again. She really didn't know him, and there was so much to learn about each other. It was much easier being married, and it made her miss Robert. They knew each other so well, and had been a perfect match. The world was full of strangers now, and it was unnerving getting to know them, but exciting too. She had no idea what this would lead to, probably nothing, and Dominique would see to it that it didn't. But that didn't seem right either. She was going to leave soon, and have her own life, and Gaëlle needed to have a life too, or she should. But Dominique was correct in a way. Gaëlle had the freedom to do what she wanted, and didn't have to get tied down to anyone again.

She put his recording on in her bedroom, it was beautiful and tender, and she could tell how talented he was. And whatever it did or didn't turn out to be, Christophe Pasquier was a very appealing man. She fell asleep listening to his music, and dreamed about Robert. She remembered it in the morning and felt utterly confused.

'Who were you out with last night?' Dominique asked her over breakfast, with a look of suspicion. She had radar for whatever her mother did, and an early warning system that was uncanny.

'The architect I work with,' she lied to her, and poured herself a cup of coffee.

'Are you falling in love with him?'

'Of course not! He's married.'

'French people don't care about that. They all cheat on each other,' Dominique pronounced as she stood up to leave.

'No, they don't.' Gaëlle looked shocked and came to the defense of her countrymen, but she knew that what Dominique said was true, in many cases. They didn't all cheat, but many did, both husbands and wives. Infidelity did seem to be more frequent in France and was often tolerated, since divorce was so difficult to obtain.

'Have a nice day,' Dominique said over her shoulder, and left for school, as Gaëlle sat alone in her kitchen, thinking about Christophe and hoping he'd call her soon.

15

Christophe Pasquier surprised both his friend André and Gaëlle by dropping by the museum one afternoon, when he said he was in the neighborhood to go to a sound studio to work on his current movie. He had an overstuffed briefcase with him, filled with sheet music, notebooks, and extensive notes.

The Strauss house was under heavy construction, and there were workmen everywhere, but he was impressed by the progress they'd made. It was starting to look like a real home that people could live in. They had even reconstructed the kitchen exactly as it had been thirty years before. Gaëlle had found the identical stove at an auction and bought it for almost nothing and had it refurbished.

'I think you'll have the place ready before the end of the year,' Christophe predicted after looking around.

'We hope so, but we still have a lot to do,' André said, with the plans in his hands to show a carpenter a change. Christophe wandered through the rooms, and Gaëlle explained which rooms were which. The five children's rooms were on the top floor. And they were going to put in the secret room in the basement where they had hidden the children for months, but they'd been found anyway, tragically. A suspicious neighbor had denounced them.

As he was leaving after the tour, Christophe said to Gaëlle in a soft voice, 'I had fun at our dinner last week. Do you want to go out tonight?' It was short notice, but he had the feeling that casual was better with her, and offhand. That way she didn't have too much time to think about it, and she didn't need a babysitter for her daughter at her age anyway. She could just go out, if she was free.

She nodded assent, and he was pleased, and then she had an idea. It was Friday, and Dominique was going away for the weekend with friends. They were leaving that afternoon for Normandy. Her friend's family had a house there, and she was frequently invited to stay with friends on the weekend, which left Gaëlle alone and free.

'Would you like to come to my place? I'm not much of a cook, but I can pick something up on the way home,' she suggested. He liked the idea and smiled at her.

'I'll bring the wine. What time?'

'Eight-thirty?' It would give her time to finish work with André, shop for food, and change for dinner.

'Perfect.' She gave him the door code of her building, which was standard in Paris. There was a guardian but no doorman, unlike similar apartments in the States, and after he left, André didn't comment. He was rooting for his friend and didn't want to make Gaëlle anxious. He could tell that she was skittish and shy with men, and 'out of practice,' as she said. She still hadn't decided to start dating, but was continuing to tell herself he was just a potential friend, as she had after lunch.

She stopped at Lenôtre on Avenue Victor Hugo on the way home, bought a roast chicken and some vegetables, sliced salmon for the first course, and a beautiful strawberry tart for the two of them. By the time she buzzed him in on the intercom, she was wearing jeans and a white sweater. There was an elevator, but he bounded up the stairs when she told him on the intercom that it was on the second floor, French style, and he handed her a bottle of excellent Bordeaux when he walked in. He had splurged on the wine to impress her, and succeeded. It was a very good year of Château Margaux.

He admired the high ceilings in the hall immediately, and loved the zebra in the living room. The apartment was elegantly furnished and she told him that it all came decorated as he saw it. It was an interesting mishmash of chic and eclectic with a touch of crazy, like the zebra standing next to the couch.

'Am I going to meet your daughter?' he asked nervously as they sat down.

'She's away for the weekend,' Gaëlle said breezily, and laughed at how relieved he looked.

'I'm sorry, girls that age scare me, especially when they're defending their mothers. They can be quite fierce.'

'She's really defending her father more than me,' Gaëlle said quietly. 'They adored each other, and I'm afraid he spoiled her. She's not anxious to have me meet someone else, to protect his memory.'

'I understand.' But he was happy to be alone with her anyway, and not have to deal with Dominique, who sounded like a dragon to him. Most girls her age were. He had dealt with similar situations before, usually with divorced women whose children didn't want a new man on the scene. It was a tough position to be in as a man. And with a deceased father, undoubtedly elevated to sainthood in her mind, it would be worse. Gaëlle offered him champagne then, Cristal, which he accepted, and followed her into the kitchen. She had set the table for dinner there, with flowers in the center. The apartment was huge, but the kitchen was warm and friendly, and she had put photographs and personal things around to make it feel like home. He noticed a photograph of Gaëlle with Robert. He was a very handsome older man, and they looked very happy. He was suddenly sorry for her, to find herself widowed so young.

He opened the champagne for them and the Bordeaux to let it breathe. He liked the fact that she had invited him for a relaxed dinner in the kitchen and didn't appear to be a woman who wanted to show off, although she obviously lived well. He was more attracted to her each time he saw her. And like Gaëlle, he had no idea where this was going, but he was shocked to realize that he had feelings for her. No woman had ever affected him so quickly. He hoped it didn't show. He didn't want to scare her off, and sensed it might if she knew. It unnerved him a little too, since he usually kept his distance and remained aloof, and had no trouble doing so, but he felt

245

open and vulnerable when he was with her, like a flower in summer. And he wanted to compose music for her.

'Tell me about modeling for Dior after the Occupation,' he said to keep it light, and she laughed.

'I was so green I had no idea what I was doing. They put us in models' apartments then, and chaperoned us. It was like living in a girls' school, we loved it and had fun, and couldn't believe our good luck to be there. I would have starved if they hadn't given me a job. The work got more serious when I moved to New York, but I modeled there only for a year. The fashion business is very intense. But Robert and I got married very quickly, and then Dominique came along. I worked till I was five months pregnant, and then I retired and never went back to it. It would have interfered with our family life. So I stayed home with my husband and baby, took some classes, and the years flew by. Too quickly,' she said wistfully, and instinctively he reached out and touched her hand.

'I'm sorry,' he said in a gentle voice, 'it must be hard now.' He could sense that she'd been happily married and loved her husband a great deal.

She smiled to cover the depth of her emotions and how much she missed Robert. 'It's a big adjustment. He was a wonderful man. Our life was very full, and very complete. I still can't believe he's gone. And it's been very hard on my daughter. Her father adored her, and she worshipped him. I used to feel left out

246

sometimes — they had a very special bond. But he was good to both of us — he was a very kind person.'

'And will you be all right when she leaves for university?' He looked concerned. She sighed before she answered and shrugged philosophically.

'I'll have to be. It happens to all parents eventually. They move on, and you become obsolete. I can't hang on to her, I wouldn't do that to her. She can't wait to get started with real life. And although she's half French, she feels no ties to France. She wants to live in New York after college. And I'm happy here.'

'And this isn't real?' He raised an eyebrow in reaction to her comment about Dominique wanting a real life. 'It looks very real to me. A beautiful apartment, a loving mother, a comfortable life, a year or two in Paris, and I'm sure you spoil her too, not just her father.' He smiled at her, and she laughed. 'And probably lots of other advantages I can't even guess at. She's a lucky girl, even if she doesn't know it.'

'No child feels lucky. They think their parents are brutes, or unreasonable, or stupid, or mean. They only discover our virtues later, if we have any. But usually by the time they realize it, we're long gone or they've moved on.' It was the nature of parenthood and seemed like an ungrateful task to him.

'Were your parents stupid or mean, or brutes?' He wanted to know more about her. He sensed that she kept a lot to herself.

'Not really. My mother was a very withdrawn,

247

frightened person, and the war made it much worse. She was terrified all the time. She lost my father in the Resistance, my brother in a foolish accident a month before that. The Germans had taken over our home, and they killed my father. She never recovered from it.' And she didn't tell him that her being falsely accused of being a collaborator was the final blow that had killed her mother in the end, just as Apolline said. 'We all paid a high price for what happened during the war,' she said seriously.

'I was with De Gaulle in North Africa,' he said. She hadn't wanted to ask. Sometimes people had done things they didn't want to talk about now. 'I was very young, eighteen, and it was an amazing experience, though I wouldn't want to go through it again. None of us would.' She nodded agreement, and then asked him about his music for the movie he was working on, and she told him how much she had enjoyed the recording he'd given her. 'Did it put you to sleep?' he asked her. 'It does most people. I should sell it specifically for that.'

'Actually, it did.' She laughed in embarrassment. 'But it was late and I was tired, but I loved it before I passed out.' They both laughed at what she said.

'See what I mean? Better than sleeping pills!'

They sat down to dinner when they finished the champagne, and the food wasn't exciting, but it was simple and good and greatly enhanced by the bottle of Château Margaux.

He lit a fire for them in the living room after dinner, and they talked for a long time, about his dedication to work, her plans for the museum, and ideas she had to publicize it tastefully, all of which sounded good to him. She was a bright woman, and he was sure she would do a good job. It was after one again when he stood up, and thought it was time to leave.

'Can I interest you in lunch tomorrow?' he asked as they walked into the hall, and she shook her head with regret.

'I have to go to an auction, for the house. Do you want to come?' she suddenly asked him, and he smiled. He was delighted she'd invited him to join her.

'I'd love it.' They agreed to meet at the Hôtel Drouot, the auction house, the following afternoon at two. They had the best auctions in Paris, and she'd found great things there, from fine paintings to clothes, toys, gardening equipment, rare books, wine, antique military uniforms, fabrics, rugs, and vintage kitchen appliances. The variety was astounding. There were several paintings she wanted to bid on the next day. And she was actually thinking of buying and donating one of them to the museum herself, but she was too discreet to say that to him.

He thanked her for dinner and walked down the stairs with a wave, and she sat alone in front of the fire for a while, thinking about him and the evening. She finally went to bed, and put his music on again, and just as he had said, she was asleep in two minutes, and woke up the next morning with sunlight streaming into the room. It was a beautiful day.

★ ★ ★

Gaëlle arrived at the auction house right on time, and saved a seat for him next to her, despite several raunchy-looking antique dealers' protests at her keeping an empty seat in the crowded auction room. The people who frequented Drouot always looked unsavory and disreputable, with the occasional aristocrat thrown in, usually on weekends. She had worn jeans and an old fur coat, with Hermès black leather riding boots. A few minutes after she'd arrived, Christophe sat down next to her, in weekend country clothes, with very elegant brown suede shoes. It was just the right look and matched hers. She was concentrating on the auction, and the first lot she wanted came up very quickly. She was successful and thrilled, and he grinned with her. He loved seeing her pleasure and excitement. And she got her second choice too. In the end, they left the auction with four paintings, and they took them back to her apartment. They were very handsome pieces and were almost exact duplicates of what was in the Strauss photos of their living room.

'It's strange re-creating their life and home now. I almost feel as though I'm working for them,' she said, and offered him champagne, and this time he declined. She was tempted to invite him to stay for dinner but wasn't sure if two evenings in a row would seem like too much, and she didn't want to give him the wrong message and encourage him. But he was starting to feel like an old friend. She threw caution to the winds

250

then and invited him to forage in the fridge with her and eat leftovers from the night before.

'I'd love to,' he said sincerely when she asked him, 'but I'm having dinner with my sister and her husband, and her two badly behaved children. She never says no to them.' Robert had been guilty of the same thing with Dominique, and it had had unpleasant results that Gaëlle still felt the effects of now.

'How old are they?'

'Five and seven. Two very naughty little boys, although they can be endearing at times.' She was sure they were, and boys that age weren't easy to control. She suspected they weren't as bad as he said.

'What does your sister do?'

'She's an artist by passion, and a nurse by profession. Her husband is a lawyer. He does all my contracts for me.'

'That's useful,' Gaëlle said practically, intrigued that he had a normal-sounding, traditional family. He seemed more bohemian than that. 'Do you have other siblings?'

'Just the two of us. We're very close. We lived together until she got married. We lost our parents when we were very young. I'd invite you to join us, but she's a terrible cook, and I love my brother-in-law, but he falls asleep at the table and snores after two glasses of wine, and the boys would drive you nuts while she lets them run around until they wear themselves out. She says they sleep better that way. And you can't have a decent conversation while they throw things and scream.'

251

Gaëlle laughed at his description of his family scene. 'They sound like typical boys.'

'I'm hoping Amandine sends her kids to boarding school so I can have a decent conversation with her again. We haven't talked properly in years, they're always around and very noisy. So enjoy your dinner tonight in peace,' he said, and eventually he left and congratulated her on the four paintings she'd bought. He liked them too, and thought they were good choices for the museum.

She didn't hear from him the next day and was surprised that she missed him, which seemed ridiculous even to her, since she hardly knew him. She liked talking to him, and it had been fun having company at the auction, as the tension mounted while she was bidding, and to share the excitement with him when she got what she'd come for.

She went for a walk, and came back to the apartment to read a book. She put his recording on and fell asleep again, on the couch, and laughed when she woke up. Maybe he was right and there was something sleep-inducing about his music. When Dominique came home in the late afternoon, she asked her mother what she'd done all weekend. Gaëlle showed her the paintings, said she had gone for a walk, and told her all the little things she'd done in the apartment. But she didn't mention a word about Christophe. She had no idea what to say to her, except that she had had a lunch, two dinners, and spent an afternoon with a man she liked a lot, whose music put her to sleep. What else was

252

there to say? And however she described it, she knew Dominique wouldn't approve, and Gaëlle concluded that she owed her no explanations and kept her lovely weekend to herself.

16

Gaëlle planned to take Dominique and one of her school friends skiing in Val d'Isère over spring break. She had seen Christophe a few times for lunch and dinner, mostly when Dominique was busy or out and had her own plans. Gaëlle didn't want to steal time from her, and she was trying to keep them from meeting, which Christophe had figured out.

'So are you going to hide me from your daughter forever?' he asked her with a wry grin the day before they left to go skiing.

'Of course not,' she said, looking embarrassed, but he was right. She was in no rush to organize a meeting. Dominique was too unpredictable and had made her position clear. She didn't want her mother to date. Gaëlle wasn't sure if they were dating, but it would look that way to Dominique.

'I can behave very properly around people's children,' he assured her, which she was sure was true. He had been very proper with her too, and after two months of meeting for meals regularly, he hadn't even tried to kiss her, which was a relief. She wasn't ready for more, and he had accurately sensed that. But he was curious about Dominique and how difficult she really was. From little things he had gleaned from her mother, without actually saying so, she sounded like a spoiled brat to him, and he wanted to see the truth, in the flesh, which Gaëlle had done everything to prevent happening. She didn't want to give her ammunition for more battles or a tirade and accusations on her father's behalf.

'Maybe when we get back,' Gaëlle said vaguely.

'Or when she graduates from college?' he teased her.

'Yes, absolutely. I think that would be the perfect time,' she said, laughing. 'I'm just nervous about how she'll react, Christophe. She's so devoted to her father, even now. She thinks he was a god.'

'Oh dear, that's worse than a saint. Maybe I'll wait till she gets married and has a couple of kids.'

'She says she'll never marry,' Gaëlle said seriously. 'She's hellbent on a Wall Street career, and I really think she'll do it, and be good at it. She's a lot like her father, with a much sharper edge. My mother was a lot like her too, although she was an unhappy person.'

'That sounds tough,' he commented, 'from what you've said about her.'

'It is. She's a strong-minded girl, with a will of iron, and she's never been as close to me as she was to her father, or as forgiving as he was. She has his brain but not his warmth or compassion.'

'Even now that you're all she has?' Gaëlle nodded, and he felt sorry for her. At least if they were close, it would have been solace for both of them, but clearly it wasn't. 'Well, I'll leave the timing up to you, but I'd like to meet her. I'm ready. Are you?'

255

'I'm not sure,' Gaëlle said honestly. 'Let's see how it goes.'

But the week in Val d'Isère turned out to be difficult. Dominique hurt her knee on the first day, and was on crutches for the rest of the week, and in her room, while her friend skied and was gone all day, and she came back to Paris in a terrible mood. It was clearly not the right time to introduce her to Christophe. And for the next several weeks, until her knee healed, she was a demon to deal with, and angry at everyone. Gaëlle postponed a meeting between them as a result.

Dominique was off crutches and going to a movie with friends on the Champs Élysées on an evening in May. And Gaëlle made plans for Christophe to pick her up and take her out to dinner after Dominique left with her friends, who were meeting at her place. Gaëlle was going to call him when the coast was clear, and somehow they got their signals crossed. She had said Dominique was going out at seven, and at seven-thirty he buzzed the intercom, and Dominique let him in thinking it was one of her friends who was late, and she pulled their front door open and said, 'Where the hell were you?' And instead of her friend, she found herself gazing up into the bright blue eyes of a tall stranger. It was Christophe, who was just as surprised to see her. 'Oh. Sorry,' she said awkwardly. 'Can I help you?' She had no idea who he was, since Gaëlle had never told her about him, or when they went out together.

'Hello, Dominique,' he said politely, extending

a hand to shake hers. 'I'm Christophe Pasquier. I'm here to see your mother.' She didn't dare ask him why, but she clearly wanted to slam the door in his face, and for a minute, he thought she might. She was a beautiful girl, with dark eyes and long straight dark hair, and looked nothing like her mother, except for her tall slim figure. He would never have guessed that they were mother and daughter, as Dominique stepped aside to let him in, reluctantly. And since Gaëlle wasn't expecting him yet and thought the doorbell was for Dominique, she was nowhere to be seen.

'It's nice to meet you,' he said with a warm smile. And it was visibly not reciprocal. He seemed too much at ease for Dominique to take his unexpected presence lightly, and even his good looks were a threat. And he sounded like he knew her mother. He waited in the front hall for Dominique to tell her mother he was there, which she ran to do immediately. She marched into her mother's bedroom and glared at her.

'What the hell is some tall, good-looking guy named Christophe doing here? He says he's here to see you, and he acts like he knows you.'

'He's a friend of André's,' Gaëlle said, trying to make it seem innocent, and so far it was.

'And you've gone out with him?' Dominique looked shocked.

'We've had a meal a couple of times, to talk about the museum.' She felt like a traitor lying about him as she followed Dominique out of the room to the front hall where Christophe was waiting patiently and Dominique watched them like a hawk as he kissed her on both cheeks and greeted her.

'I just met Dominique,' he said pleasantly, and smiled at her, as Dominique stared him into the floor and looked like a furious four-year-old. It was not a proud moment for her mother, and Dominique's worst behavior was in evidence. She made it clear that he wasn't welcome in their home.

'You can go join your friends now,' Gaëlle told her gently. They were waiting for her in her room. Dominique stomped off and slammed two doors on the way.

'Well, that was fun,' Gaëlle whispered to him as she led him into the living room, and they sat down.

'It's about what I expected,' he said in a low voice, 'so don't worry about it.' But actually, it was worse. At seventeen she was too old to be that rude to a guest, no matter what she thought of him, and she didn't even know him. But he made light of it to her mother. And he could see what he was up against now, and why Gaëlle had postponed their meeting for as long as she could. But they couldn't put it off forever, and he was glad it had happened. More so than her mother, who knew she'd be facing the forces of hell later, when Dominique came home.

She left with her friends a little while later, never said goodbye to her mother and Christophe, and slammed the front door as hard as she could on the way out. Gaëlle was mortified, but clearly Dominique was in one of her rages, and no one could control her when

258

she was. They were the adolescent version of her tantrums as a child, when she was angry about something, or didn't get her way.

Gaëlle was nervous all evening, and distracted at dinner, and she decided to go home early so she'd be there when Dominique came home.

'You can't let her control you.' Christophe tried to reason with her over the dinner she hadn't eaten. She was too upset to eat, think, or talk. She didn't want a full-on war with her about Christophe. She had been enjoying his company for four months by then, and she didn't want to stop seeing him. But she also knew that Dominique could make her life miserable when she wanted to. And if she alienated her daughter, she would have no one. She wasn't ready to face that. 'You're her mother, you're an adult. You have a right to do what you want. You're not whoring around. You haven't even kissed me' — much to his chagrin, but he didn't say it — 'and her father has been gone for almost two years. She has to be reasonable.'

'That's a message no one has ever given her, particularly her father. She was a tyrant at home when she was little, and she's always quick to criticize me.' And Robert had always let her do it. For a strong man, he had exhibited nothing but weakness with their daughter, in the guise of love, which had been a huge mistake.

'Don't let her! Put your foot down!' They were the right theories, but hard to implement at seventeen with a girl who had been indulged all her life, and supported in her every whim by a doting father who was now dead. Gaëlle was always careful with her. She wished she could have been firmer with her when she was younger, but Robert hadn't let her, and it was late in the day now. And having no children, Christophe didn't understand the compromises you had to make at times to keep the peace. She didn't argue the point with him, but she wasn't looking forward to the inevitable battle she knew she'd have with Dominique when she got home. Maybe one of their worst, if she thought her mother was being unfaithful to her father. She tolerated no betrayals of him and was fierce about it.

He took Gaëlle home early and hugged her on her doorstep, and then promised to call her in the morning, while she apologized for what a mess the evening had been. He told her not to worry about it and went home, thinking about them, and wondering how Gaëlle was going to deal with her in the future. Dominique was almost a woman, acting like a very spoiled child. And she wasn't even embarrassed about it. She had been allowed to do whatever she wanted all her life, and this was the result. He was relieved yet again that he had no children of his own — he couldn't have managed one like this.

Dominique came home after midnight, and Gaëlle went to find her in her room. 'You were very rude to my guest,' she said in a stern voice, feeling that she owed Christophe at least that, and herself. Dominique had shown no respect for either of them, which didn't seem to bother her at all. She had no remorse, no matter how badly she behaved.

'Don't give me that, Mom,' she said harshly with her eyes blazing. She had been upset all evening too, and left before the end of the movie and was mad about that as well. 'He's not your 'guest,' he's your boyfriend. Do you think I'm stupid?' *No, a brat*, her mother wanted to say, but didn't.

'He's not my boyfriend, but even if he were, you can't treat my friends like that. I don't treat yours that way.'

'How long have you been sleeping with him?' she accused her mother, and Gaëlle started to get angry with her, at last.

'I'm not sleeping with him, but it's none of your business if I am. I haven't even kissed him. And you have no right to talk to me this way. As long as you live under my roof, Dominique, I expect you to respect me, and anyone who comes here to see me.'

'Don't worry about it. We're going home in six weeks, and then I'm leaving for college after the summer, and you can do anything you want with him after that. I don't give a damn what you do.' Her tone was furious bordering on vicious, and pure venom. Gaëlle had seen it before.

'Yes, you do give a damn,' Gaëlle said quietly, 'or you wouldn't be this upset.' It was true. Just as she had been possessive of her father, she was equally so of her mother now too.

'I expect you to respect my father!' Dominique screamed at her. 'He's your husband, and he made you what you are. How dare you drag men into our home and disrespect his memory!' What she said broke Gaëlle's heart as she listened.

261

Both of them were crying by then.

'I would never disrespect your father, and I never have. Nor will I. I loved him, and I still do. But he's gone, and I have to figure out how to live my life now. You're not going to be here. And what do you mean 'he made me what I am'? I've been who I am all my life, and I have principles, whether you believe it or not.' It felt like being called a collaborator again, by her own daughter. And what she said next shocked Gaëlle even more.

'I meant that you wouldn't be who you are now without his money. You wouldn't have all this without him.' She waved her arms at the apartment, and Gaëlle understood.

'I didn't marry him for his money, Dominique. The money isn't important. It's a lovely gift, but it's not why we were together. And he didn't 'make' me anything, except a happy woman because we loved each other. And don't you *ever* say something like that to me again.' And this time it was Gaëlle who slammed the door of her daughter's room. But she realized now that her husband's money had poisoned their daughter. She thought the world revolved around money, and it didn't. Far from it. It made Gaëlle sad just thinking about it, and she cried more. She felt sorry for her daughter and the rage inside her. Dominique was full of bitterness, and she didn't want her mother to be happy.

Dominique didn't come in to apologize to her — she never did, even when she should. Dominique always said whatever she wanted to, no matter how hurtful. And she had no remorse about it. She wanted to hurt her mother, and she had. If anything, she was pleased. Gaëlle could see it.

Christophe called her in the morning and seemed worried. He was afraid that Gaëlle wouldn't see him again. He didn't want to lose her, especially not to satisfy her tyrannical daughter who'd been indulged all her life and led to believe she could rule the world. She couldn't. Not his anyway. But she could convince her mother to stop seeing him. For now, it was his worst fear.

'How was it when she came home last night?' he asked Gaëlle, with genuine concern.

'As bad as I thought it would be. Actually, worse. She thinks you're my boyfriend, and accused me of all sorts of things, none of them true. She implies that I married her father for his money, and would have been nothing without him, and am disrespecting him now. She's still angry about his death.' But Gaëlle couldn't pretend that her rages were new. She just played with bigger weapons now, and what she said about money was terribly upsetting, so wrong, and not true.

'She has no right saying that to you.' He hadn't known Gaëlle for long, but he could tell that she hadn't married her husband for money. She had married for love. She was an honorable, upstanding woman. He was sorry he couldn't tell Dominique off himself — she needed that desperately and to be reined in — but he knew it would only make things worse for Gaëlle if he confronted Dominique, and he was in no position to do it. 'Did she tell you to stop seeing me?' he asked in terror.

'Of course. But I'm not going to.' He exhaled gratefully when she said it. 'But I want us to keep out of her face for a while, until we leave for the summer. There's no point making it worse.' He agreed, although in theory, he thought they should have stood their ground, but they had no official relationship. Her daughter was a nightmare. And Gaëlle also hadn't felt ready for a deeper involvement. She was loyal to Robert too. 'We just have to be discreet,' she said. And for Christophe, it was like dating a married woman, which he'd never done either. Instead he'd be hiding from her jealous, crazed daughter, which seemed entirely wrong, and unfair to Gaëlle and him. He had said as much to André, who agreed. He thought Gaëlle was a remarkable woman and well worth it, if he could get through the barbed wire and high walls that surrounded her, which was no easy feat.

In spite of her difficult daughter, they continued to meet each other for lunch, and for a few evenings when Dominique was busy. Gaëlle refused to discuss Christophe with her, and Dominique stopped asking, convinced that she had scared her mother off him, which Dominique felt she owed her father. And she saw no evidence of Gaëlle seeing Christophe, since they were being careful, and smarter than Dominique. And finally after two weeks of their clandestine meetings, Christophe pulled Gaëlle into a doorway one night as they left a restaurant, and he kissed her, passionately, the way he had wanted to since he met her. And it felt wonderful to both of them.

'If we're going to be punished, we might as well make it worthwhile,' he said, taking charge of the situation, and kissed her again. 'Want to come back to my place?' he asked her, only half teasing as she caught her breath. She could just imagine what the rest would be like, after the intensity of his kisses.

'I'd love to, but I'm not going to,' she said regretfully. 'I don't want to sneak around with you. I want to have a real relationship with you,' she said, and he smiled broadly at her. 'And I want to figure out if we can have one. I don't know if I can love another man. And then there's Dominique.' He didn't like what she was saying, but the prospect of a relationship with her warmed his heart.

'You can't let her rob you of a normal life,' he insisted.

'Maybe she'll be more understanding when she's older. But right now I need to think about it too. If it's right for both of us, we'll figure it out. Let's think about it over the summer. I'll be gone for two months, and I'll be alone when I come back.'

'I will be here,' he said, and meant it with every fiber of his being, especially after kissing her. But this was more than just a woman he wanted physically. He had fallen in love with her and didn't want to give her up now to satisfy Dominique.

'Tell me that at the end of August when I

come back,' she said solemnly.

'Are you telling me you won't see me again until then?' He wanted to know what the ground rules were now.

'Of course not. I couldn't do that. We can see each other till I leave, as long as we're careful. I'm just telling you what I'm thinking.'

'I'm thinking that I love you, Gaëlle,' he said, and kissed her again.

'I think I love you too. I just need time to adjust to all this.' Robert had been gone for two years, and she had loved him deeply, but now she felt she was in love with Christophe. And if it was right, Dominique couldn't stop them. Gaëlle wouldn't let her. But she wanted time to decide over the summer if it was worth the risk of alienating her daughter forever, unless she forgave them for what she saw as betraying her father, however unreasonable that might be.

★ ★ ★

For the next month, it was difficult, but not impossible. They spent time together, went for walks, kissed, held hands, but didn't sleep together. Gaëlle didn't want to confuse herself further, and she had old-fashioned values. The sexual revolution that was happening had bypassed her completely, and he loved her more for it. They promised to talk by phone over the summer and come to some conclusion at the end of August when she returned. He was terrified that Gaëlle would decide it was too complicated, but he had to trust her and believe that she meant what she said, that if she thought it was right, she'd stand by him, and come back to him with open arms. It was going to be a long, tough summer, and he was glad he'd be busy working on a movie score that was all consuming.

He saw her the night before she left Paris for the next few months. They sat on a bench under the trees on Avenue Foch near her apartment and kissed like two teenage kids.

'Take care of yourself,' he told her. 'Don't let her beat you up.'

'Don't worry, and don't work too hard,' she said, and kissed him, and he watched her walk back to her house alone and prayed she'd come back to him in August. All he knew for sure was that he loved her. The rest was in her hands, and her daughter's.

17

The summer wasn't easy for either of them. Christophe and Gaëlle missed each other intensely. It was hard to believe that they had met in January and now he felt as though he couldn't live without her. They spoke several times a week on the phone.

She and Dominique spent July and August in Southampton. And she kept occupied looking for things for the museum in New York and antique shops in Connecticut and on Long Island, and she found some great items.

Dominique had friends over constantly, all of whom were leaving for college, as she was. There was a party atmosphere at the house every day, as they went from home to home in a large group of her old friends. She had gone to school in Paris, but her real friends and her life were here. She told her mother she would never live in Paris again, although she'd enjoyed it, and Gaëlle believed her. Dominique would be in Cambridge, at Radcliffe, and she was going to friends' for Thanksgiving, but promised to come to Paris for spring break. Gaëlle would be in New York to spend Christmas with her, and New Year in Palm Beach.

All their plans were made, and the rest of the time, it was up to Gaëlle to fill her own life. If Robert had been alive, it wouldn't have been easy either, when Dominique left. It was a big change, but without him, Dominique flying from the nest was much more dramatic. And there was a constant reserve between Dominique and Gaëlle now after their battle over Christophe. Gaëlle had neither forgotten nor forgiven the ugly things she had said about him and her father's money. Even worse, she knew Dominique had meant them. She expected her mother to stay alone forever, and thought that the money Robert had left her should be enough to make her willing to do so. In so many words, she had called her mother a gold digger, which apparently was what she thought. And Gaëlle was deeply hurt by it. Dominique did nothing to heal the wounds she had inflicted, had no regrets, and kept her distance, which made their final days together even sadder for Gaëlle.

They drove to Boston in a van toward the end of August, with her bags and boxes, her record player, a new bicycle, and the new clothes she'd bought for college. Gaëlle had been helping her get ready for the entire month, and the big day finally came. They took a driver they hired to help them carry it all and set it up. And she got her assignment to Cabot House at the Radcliffe Quadrangle. She would live on the Radcliffe campus, but she would be taking some classes with the men at Harvard. She was going to be an econ major, and was planning to work in her father's investment banking firm every summer, if they accepted her, in order to qualify early for business school, right after she got her bachelor's degree. She wanted a Harvard MBA, without having to work for several years before graduate school. She had her goals and her future all set.

Gaëlle was sad as she hung her clothes in the closet, and put all her belongings away, while Dominique explored the campus with a girl from her dorm. She had brought a lot of short skirts with her, and had her hair styled in a pixie cut before she started school. She looked adorable and innocent when Gaëlle hugged her before she left. She knew that Dominique wasn't as guileless as she seemed, she had no qualms about punishing her mother or trying to deprive her of a real life. Dominique was a lot tougher than she appeared and a lot less forgiving. But Gaëlle held her for a long moment, left the dorm with a heavy heart, and got into the van to go back to New York. She was crying as they drove away. Dominique was all she had now, and they wouldn't see each other for four months, until Christmas.

It had been a hard summer of decisions and goodbyes. And Dominique leaving for college was a hard transition for her mother, and more painful than she expected. Gaëlle had seen some of their old friends, but it was different now without Robert. They were all much older, she was living in Paris, and she no longer felt close to them. She and Christophe had spoken often, but they hadn't come to any conclusions. She didn't want to talk about it on the phone, and preferred to see him face to face. She felt lonely when she closed the apartment in New York and left for the airport.

Christophe was waiting for her when she cleared customs in Paris. She hadn't seen him in more than two months and didn't know what to expect. He took her in his arms and held her without saying a word. He had missed her more than he had imagined possible, and was afraid he'd never see her again. He had written several pieces of music for Gaëlle, which he promised would put her to sleep instantly. And then he looked down into her face, and kissed her. Everything they both needed to know was in their embrace.

'I thought I'd lost you,' he said in a voice raw with emotion. And maybe he had. He didn't know yet. Maybe she was going to say goodbye. He was trying to brace himself for that and afraid he might cry if she did.

He put her bags on a cart, and they went to find his car, and then she got in and gazed at him with a long, slow smile.

'How was Radcliffe?' he asked her.

'Hard. But she's off and running now. Her father was so attached to her, it would have killed him to leave her there. She couldn't wait for me to go.'

'What about us?' He couldn't stop himself from asking anymore. He had to know, whatever she answered. And she seemed different to him somehow, calmer and more at peace. The two months in the Hamptons had done her good, and given her time to think.

'I'm here,' she said simply. That much was easy to see. She hadn't avoided him or refused to see him when she got back.

'What does that mean?' he asked anxiously.

'I came back to you. Dominique has her life

now. I have mine. Ours, if you still want that.' He stared at her, unable to believe what he was hearing for a minute. 'I love you, Christophe.'

'I love you too,' he said, and then kissed her. He started the car and drove back to Paris. They went to his apartment first. She had been there only once, when he had to pick something up. She had been uncomfortable being there then, but she wasn't now. He had a small, charming apartment in an old building on the Left Bank. Their clothes started to come off in the front hall, and he pulled her toward his bedroom, grateful that his cleaning woman had been there that morning, changed the sheets, and made the bed. But neither of them cared, they were a tangle of bodies and sheets, as they lay on his bed a minute later. She had come back to him. A new life had begun for them, a fresh start together, whatever it turned out to be. They couldn't get enough of each other, as he felt the silk of her long blond hair on his face when he kissed her. He had been dreaming of this moment since January, and without knowing it at first, so had she. The world belonged to them now. Their time had come, and she was his. He had never been happier in his life, as she nestled in his arms after they made love, and fell asleep.

★ ★ ★

Two weeks after Gaëlle got back, they gave a dinner party at her apartment, and invited André and Geneviève, and she brought one of her fabulous apple tarts, and a chocolate cake she

272

had baked. They entertained a few friends of Christophe from the music world, a well-known composer, Louise, and some other people Gaëlle had dealt with for the museum. There were a dozen guests at her kitchen table, and it felt like a celebration of their new life. André was particularly happy for them — he knew how madly in love Christophe was with her, and Gaëlle looked just as elated. And they had both noticed that Gaëlle was no longer wearing her wedding band when she got back from New York. She was free.

They all talked a lot about the museum opening in December. They had so much to look forward to, and Christophe had finished his latest movie score while she was gone. He would have gone crazy without that to focus on. And he had just signed contracts for two more films, and an album. His career was going exceptionally well, and he was becoming increasingly success-ful. Gaëlle was proud of him.

They were staying in her apartment most of the time. It was larger and more comfortable than his, and he made occasional jokes about being a kept man, which he wasn't, since he was generous with her, paid his own way for everything, and shared expenses with her. And by October, he was essentially living with her openly, which worked since they had their own little world, and day by day they felt more at home living together.

She turned forty in November, and com-plained about how old she was. He was three years older and told her she still looked like a kid. They made a handsome couple, both of them tall and blond. His movie opened right before her birthday, and the score was brilliantly received. The world was smiling at them. And she had a month before the Strauss Museum opened. Each room was now almost complete, and the family was thrilled with what she and André had done. And she had given several guidebooks and magazines tours of the house to draw attention to it. There was going to be a big article about it in *Le Figaro*. The curator of the Camondo de Nissim museum had called to congratulate her. And a television network wanted to do a show about the Strauss Museum.

Every day was better than the last one, and they had so much to look forward to. They gave a Thanksgiving feast in her dining room, and Christophe was a gracious host. Gaëlle missed Dominique, but they had spoken that morning. She was spending the Thanksgiving weekend at the home of one of her Radcliffe friends.

'You look happy, my friend,' André said to Christophe, looking pleased, as they decanted the wine together.

'I am.' Christophe smiled at him. He had never been happier in his life. And a new plan had been gnawing at him for days. He wanted to take André into his confidence, but thought better of it. He wanted Gaëlle to hear it first.

They were lying in bed on Saturday morning, recovering from a busy week for both of them, when Christophe rolled over in her Marie-Antoinette canopied bed and looked at her with a smile.

274

'I have a possibly crazy idea,' he whispered to her, wondering what she would think. But life was short in some instances. They had both survived a war when they were young, her only child had left home, and losing Robert had made her more aware of how fleeting time was too. He didn't say anything for a minute, and she glanced at him quizzically.

'What's the idea?' she prodded him, running her long slender fingers across his chest. Their sex life was wonderful too.

'Will you marry me?' He said it without preamble, and she hadn't expected that from him.

'Are you serious?' she asked, her eyes enormous in her face. 'What about Dominique?' Her brow furrowed as she thought of it.

'That's up to you.' She wouldn't be happy about it, but she could get used to it, if she had no other choice. She was critical of her mother anyway, no matter what she did. He didn't think Gaëlle should give up her own happiness for that, just to humor her, and give her control over her life. 'I'll do whatever you want.' She wanted him to love her forever and promise never to die, which was a promise she knew he couldn't keep.

'You don't think I'm too old to get married?' She propped herself up on one elbow, smiling at him. 'You make me feel young again.'

'You are young. And why shouldn't we get married if that's what we both want?'

'Is it?' she asked him shyly. 'Is that what you want, Christophe?'

'Yes, it is.' He was sure of it — he had never

275

wanted anything more in his life. He wanted to spend the rest of his life with her, and make it official. He knew now that he had been waiting for the right woman for all these years. And then he surprised her again. 'Do you want to have more kids?' She was utterly amazed by the question. She knew he didn't want children, and never had. He had told her several times.

'I never thought about it.'

'Could you?'

'I don't know,' she said honestly. 'Women my age do. But not for much longer.' She knew that at forty it started to get dicey, and for some women it was no longer possible.

'I wouldn't want to do anything extreme or heroic, like medications or the new artificial insemination techniques. I don't want to put you through that. But maybe we could see what happens, after we get married.' She smiled at the tenderness in his eyes. He looked like a new person, or an even better version of the one she'd met ten months before at André's dinner party in Montmartre.

'I haven't said yes to your proposal yet,' she reminded him with mischief in her eye.

'Oh, no? What are you waiting for, woman? I want to marry you!' Now that he had decided, he wanted to do it right away.

'When?' She thought about it for a minute. 'I'll have to tell Dominique first. I don't want to tell her after the fact.' It would have been hurtful and make her feel left out, which Gaëlle didn't want. 'Do you want a big wedding?'

'No, I don't. Just a few friends.' That sounded

right to her too. 'And my sister and her family of course.'

'Dominique is coming for spring break,' she said thoughtfully. 'We could do it then, in March.' It was four months away, and seemed like a reasonable amount of time for everyone to adjust to the idea. No one would be a problem, except Dominique. 'I can tell her when I see her at Christmas. She could be my maid of honor.' She smiled, and liked the idea. Marriage hadn't been on her agenda, but she loved him, and now she was excited about becoming his wife, with a lifetime together ahead of them.

'So we almost have a date, we have a maid of honor, we know how many people . . . do we have a groom?' he asked her expectantly, and she laughed.

'I almost forgot . . . I think we do . . . would you like to be the groom, Mr. Pasquier?' She held her arms out to him.

'I thought you'd never ask,' he said as he folded her into his and held her tight.

'We'll get married in March,' she said dreamily as he started to make love to her, and she thought about how much she loved the idea of being married to him.

'I wish we could do it sooner,' he said, as passion overwhelmed them both.

'So do I,' she whispered, and forgot about the wedding and Dominique and all the details. He didn't mention a baby again. All they thought about was each other, and how sweet life was going to be from then on. It already was.

★ ★ ★

They told their closest friends their plans. André and Amandine, Christophe's sister, were going to be their witnesses. Louise was coming to the wedding and was excited for them.

The museum opened to rave reviews and excellent press the week before Gaëlle flew to New York for the holidays with her daughter. Gaëlle was going to tell Dominique the news the day after Christmas, so they wouldn't have any drama on the actual holiday, and she expected some reaction, but not the one she got.

Gaëlle shared with her as simply as she could that she and Christophe were getting married, and they were going to wait until March, when she could come. It sounded like a perfect plan to them, and Gaëlle expected Dominique to make a fuss but reluctantly accept what they'd decided. The decision was made.

'You're joking, right?' Dominique stared at her mother in disbelief. 'You can't be serious, Mom. I don't even know him. I just passed him once in the front hall. You can't marry someone I've barely met.'

'You told me you didn't want to see him again,' Gaëlle said calmly.

'You told me he wasn't your boyfriend,' she accused her mother. 'You lied to me.'

'I didn't. He wasn't then,' Gaëlle said quietly. She knew it was important not to lose her temper in order for it to go smoothly with her daughter, and not take the bait.

'So what did you do? Jump right into bed the

minute you went back, after I left for school? That's revolting, Mom. And why does he want to marry you? For the money my father left you? Isn't he some kind of starving musician? I'll bet he's excited about having you subsidize his career. That's not why my father left it to you.'

Gaëlle was appalled that it was always about money with her. And that she was so outrageously rude to the point of cruelty.

'He wants to marry me because we love each other. And he's a composer, not a starving musician. He doesn't want your father's money, or mine. And he doesn't need me to subsidize anything. The whole world is not after money. I'm sad you feel that way. And what you're saying is disgusting.'

'I'm sad that you didn't love my father enough to stay faithful to him now. I see that you took off your wedding ring. What did you do, throw it away?' She was so hurtful.

'It's in my jewelry box, and I waited two years to take it off,' Gaëlle said in a choked voice. All Dominique wanted to do was wound her now, as revenge for getting married and loving another man. Gaëlle wasn't abandoning her daughter, or even Robert. She would always love him deeply. And she was adding a wonderful man to their family.

'You can do whatever you want, but I'm not going to the wedding. I'll go to Palm Beach for spring break with a friend. I think you're pathetic to do what you're doing.'

'I'm forty years old, not a hundred. I have a right to a life after your dad. I loved him, but he's gone. I don't have to stay alone for the rest of my life to prove that I loved him. And there's room in our life for you. You're my daughter. I'm not abandoning you for him, Dominique.' She said it in case that was part of the issue.

'Maybe you do need to stay alone to prove you loved Dad,' Dominique said in an icy tone. 'Marrying someone else certainly doesn't show any loyalty to him, or gratitude for what he left you.' And Gaëlle had the sense that she was never going to forgive her for marrying Christophe, no matter how she explained it to her, or what she did. She was determined to damn her mother and Christophe for wanting a life now, even though they wanted to include her. And if she had died instead of Robert, who knew if he wouldn't have remarried too? He probably would have. He was a healthy, normal man, who liked sharing his life with a partner. So did she. But she didn't discuss that with her daughter, and stayed focused on the immediate future.

'I'd really like you to come to the wedding.' Her mother tried to reach out to her again, but Dominique's eyes were cold and remote, and her face was hard.

'I would die first. I owe it to Dad not to be there. I don't know how you can live with yourself. You got a hell of a lot of my father's money, now you just want to play around.' She was calling her mother a whore without actually saying it, but her message was clear.

'I'm sorry you feel that way,' Gaëlle said tensely, using all her self-control not to lose her temper at Dominique. But she wasn't going to

280

let her continue to insult her and Christophe. She was loyal to him now too. 'We really want you there, but it's up to you.' She wasn't going to grovel and beg if Dominique refused to be at their wedding. She had done all she could. And all Dominique wanted to do was to reject her. She always had.

Two days later Dominique announced that she had decided not to go to Palm Beach for New Year's with her mother, as they always did. She was going skiing in New Hampshire with friends from school, and going straight back to Cambridge afterward. Gaëlle had been dismissed. She was being punished severely, and Dominique added more cruel words and insults when she told her mother. 'Don't think I'm going to forgive you for betraying my father,' she said venomously, 'or that deadbeat you're marrying. Dad left almost everything he had to me. I'm his flesh and blood. You're not. I'm the head of the family now. I'll have all the power when I inherit the rest of it. You can't tell me what to do anymore. I'm a Bartlett, you're not. I own everything. And you'll be nothing and no one when you marry Christophe.' Her words cut through Gaëlle like a sword.

'I will *always* be your mother,' she said in a glacial tone. 'Money doesn't change that. Your father would be ashamed of what you just said.'

'My father would be appalled by what you're doing. So am I.' Gaëlle turned on her heel and walked out of the room after that.

The morning Dominique left, she hugged her mother coolly and told her to have a safe trip back. Gaëlle was still deeply injured by everything Dominique had said. The money she knew she would inherit had ruined her.

'And just so we're clear, I'm not coming to your wedding. I'm sure Dad wouldn't want me to.' Gaëlle refused to discuss the subject with her again. And however twisted, Dominique was still her child. Her refusal to attend the wedding was a huge disappointment to Gaëlle.

'I'll come over for your birthday in April, then,' Gaëlle said with a look of determination, refusing to be as severely injured as Dominique intended, although her daughter was turning into someone she didn't know.

'Don't bother. I'm sure Dad left me plenty to celebrate with.' She knew she was getting the first installment of her trust at eighteen. 'I'd rather spend my birthday with my friends.' What she'd implied about the trust money was offensive and vulgar. And her words to her mother had been an outrage.

'We can talk about your birthday later,' Gaëlle said, not letting her see how much she was hurting her. There were tears bright in her eyes, which Dominique pretended not to notice.

'I'll see you next summer when you come back, but don't bring him,' she told her mother harshly.

'He'll be my husband,' Gaëlle said clearly. 'And the house is mine,' she reminded her.

'For now. You only have the use of it. It'll be mine one day, and I don't want him there. I won't come out if he is.'

'You don't need to be rude or cruel,

Dominique,' Gaëlle said sadly, 'to either of us. I love you. I'm not trying to hurt you by marrying him. But I have a right to a life too.' She tried to reason with her, but for now she could see it was pointless to try and stop her from damaging or even destroying their relationship as mother and child. That was all Dominique wanted to do. It was her primary goal.

'Tell that to someone else,' Dominique said, and walked out of the room without saying goodbye. Gaëlle heard the apartment door close a few minutes later when Dominique slammed it. And an hour later, as she wandered around the apartment unhappily, still in shock over Dominique's brutal words and reaction to her mother's remarriage, she found that Dominique had put all her Christmas presents from her mother back in Gaëlle's room, with a note that said she didn't want them. She was a purist till the end. Gaëlle put them back on her bed, and waited a few days to see if she'd come back, but Dominique didn't call her or relent. Gaëlle didn't know where to call her. She left a message for her at the dorm, wishing her a happy new year, to find when she got back.

She felt as though she had lost her daughter, but she knew she couldn't give in to her. If she did, she would never have a life again, and she loved Christophe. He was the future now.

She called him and told him she was coming home the next day, the day before New Year's Eve. She hadn't called him in two days, hoping she'd have something better to report, but she didn't, and might not for a long time. She didn't

want to tell him how shockingly nasty Dominique had been, and how hurtful.

'How did it go?' he asked, but he could hear in
Gaëlle's voice how disappointing it had been,
and how sad she was, far more than he could
imagine.

'Not well,' she said, sounding tired. It had
been a depressing trip, and a hard one, and had
ruined the holidays for her. And he wasn't
surprised to hear what she said. He had a lot less
faith in Dominique than her mother did. She
was a twisted, bitter person, who tried to take all
her grievances out on her mother. She wanted to
hurt others. There was something missing in her,
even at her young age, a heart. The only person
she had ever loved was her father. She had no
room for anyone else, and she was severely
damaged and furious now over his death. It
wasn't a normal reaction, and Christophe
doubted she'd ever recover, despite Gaëlle's
hope that she would.

'Come home,' he said gently. 'I miss you.' He
wanted to put his arms around her and comfort
her.

'I miss you too.' She smiled and told him she
loved him before she hung up. She changed her
reservation then, and she flew home to Paris that
night. And when she walked into the apartment
the next day, he was thrilled to see her, and she
climbed into bed with him. He held her in his
arms and told her everything would be all right.
She didn't believe it, but it was so good to hear,
and she wanted it to be true. She tried not to
think of Dominique and the terrible things she

had said. She focused on Christophe and how much they loved each other, and how lucky she was to have met a good man. She had had two great loves in her life with two wonderful men. Maybe having a daughter who loved her too was too much to expect. She hoped she would come around and accept Christophe one day, but maybe she never would. Gaëlle was starting to see that. And for now it felt as if she and Christophe were alone in the world. And if it had to be that way, it was enough. She couldn't let Dominique ruin their life, or wound her anymore.

She had survived terrible losses and a war — she couldn't allow herself to be destroyed now by her child. It wasn't right.

18

Since Dominique insisted she wouldn't come to their wedding in March during spring break, they decided to get married in February. Why wait? Louise was going to take Dominique's place as witness beside Gaëlle. Dominique still had time to change her mind about coming. Gaëlle sent her a letter about the new wedding plan, and she didn't respond. Gaëlle heard nothing from her, and the plans for the wedding went forward.

She and Christophe had a quiet New Year's Eve together, and with the new date they'd chosen, their wedding was six weeks away. It was going to be simple, and André's wife Geneviève had agreed to cook a wedding lunch at the apartment for twenty people, after the brief ceremony at the town hall of the sixteenth arrondissement where Gaëlle lived. She was still considered French by the authorities, although she had dual nationality, and Robert had gotten her an American passport after Dominique was born. He liked the idea of their all having the same nationality in case there was ever another war, which made sense to Gaëlle too. But there was no problem with her getting married in France.

She went to the museum every day, and was very busy. They had hired a young woman as an intern to do their paperwork and escort visitors through the museum, and she reported excellent reactions. She said most people cried, particularly when they saw the children's rooms. It brought what had happened in France during the war into sharp focus for everyone. And they got a photograph of the family at the end of the tour. Their relatives wanted them and others like them never to be forgotten.

Gaëlle was still meeting with members of the press and editors of guidebooks and magazines. The World Center for Holocaust Research in Jerusalem filmed it for their archives, and thanked Gaëlle for her contribution to an important piece of history. And RTF did a show on the museum for the news on television.

The week before the wedding, she went to the Faubourg St. Honoré and bought a beautiful white silk suit with a matching hat. It looked very Jackie Kennedy and suited her, and the morning of the wedding she carried small white *Phalaenopsis* orchids, and wore white silk shoes. She called Dominique the night before and couldn't reach her, as usual, so Gaëlle sent her an emotional telegram and said that she wished that she were there. She knew their new wedding date but hadn't acknowledged it. Gaëlle had a fantasy that she would show up at the last minute, but she knew she wouldn't. Dominique couldn't let her anger and resentment go. It consumed her.

André and Geneviève drove her to the town hall on the day with Louise. And Amandine and her family brought Christophe. Out of superstition, Gaëlle hadn't wanted him to see her before the wedding. He was nervous and handsome, and Gaëlle had attached a small white face veil to the pillbox hat before the ceremony. She looked exquisite.

They pronounced their vows. The mayor of the sixteenth arrondissement declared them man and wife, and an hour later they walked into her apartment and he addressed her as Madame Pasquier, and kissed her. Their friends and family were waiting for them, and Geneviève had left the cooked lunch in the oven, and just had to warm it up, after André and Christophe and a waiter Gaëlle had hired served the champagne. They had decided to keep it simple. But her apartment looked beautiful, filled with sunlight and flowers. They had Christophe's music playing in the background, including three songs he had written for her. It was a perfect day.

★   ★   ★

'Well, Madame Pasquier,' Christophe said, smiling at her as they lay in bed that night. He loved the sound of it and so did she. 'It was a nice day, wasn't it?' He looked so pleased and happy with their life, and she was too. The only sadness for her was that she hadn't heard from Dominique at all. Not a gesture or a word. Or a flower. But she hadn't really expected to, after all the hideous things Dominique had said the last time Gaëlle saw her. But she had hoped anyway.

'It was beautiful,' she said, and kissed him, still amazed that they were married. It had all happened so quickly. They had known each other for thirteen months and it felt right.

It was all different from her life with Robert. They were more on an equal footing, closer in age, and had the same goals, and similar lifestyles. Robert's world had been so much grander, and she had been enveloped in it, like a warm blanket, his homes, the apartment where they lived, everything belonged to him, and the money. She had entered his ready-made existing life. And he had been generous with her when he died, as he had been in their years together, but she didn't want an extravagant existence with Christophe. They were going to build a new life together of their own. She wanted a far simpler one and possibly a baby, although she wasn't counting on it. She had consulted with her doctor, who had said that it might or might not happen, but it wasn't a certainty at her age, or even likely. They had agreed to be philosophical about it, and see what came of not using birth control, and started for the first time on their wedding night. They were both relaxed and happy, and tired after a wonderful day. They were going to spend a few days in the South of France in May after the Cannes Film Festival as a belated honeymoon. One of his movies was opening the festival, and he had just started working on pre-production of his new film with some very big-name actors in it. He was consumed by the project, loving it as always, and had taken Gaëlle to the studio with him several times, so she could hear what he'd done so far and tell him what she thought. He valued her opinion about everything in his life, his work as well. She was fascinated by his creative process and the intensity with which he dove into everything he did. He was very talented and dedicated.

Gaëlle went to visit him at his studio again the following week. She loved watching him work with all his synthesizers, and play his music on a keyboard for her. He wanted her to hear a piece he had just finished, and he loved having the latest equipment to experiment with.

She finally managed to speak to Dominique a week after the wedding. She didn't ask her mother how it had been, or congratulate her. All she said was, 'Are you married?' And when Gaëlle answered affirmatively, she made no further comment and changed the subject. Gaëlle felt as though she had slammed a door in her face. It was a familiar feeling now, and almost as effective as her words. Gaëlle could still hear the echo of their last exchange.

In March, Gaëlle reiterated her invitation to Dominique to come over for spring break, and she declined sharply, and said she was still planning to go to Palm Beach with a friend.

The museum was running smoothly by then, and had had numerous visitors. And in April, Gaëlle called Dominique on her eighteenth birthday, and she could hear that she sounded different. She had wanted to visit her in school for her birthday, and Dominique said she had exams and wouldn't have time to see her so not to come.

'Is something wrong?' She worried about her, and hated the distance her daughter had imposed between them, in protest against her marriage.

'Not exactly.' There was a long pause before

she explained. 'I just got notified of the first amount from the trust today.' She sounded shocked, with good reason, since Gaëlle knew how much it was. The first installment at eighteen was five million dollars, which was more than Dominique had expected on her birthday. She had thought the first installment would only be one million, not five times that. It made what she would inherit that much more real and lent weight and credence to the ugly things she had said to her mother before the wedding. Overnight she had become a rich woman in her own right, and could do whatever she wanted. It wasn't a distant eventuality, it was her reality now. She was an extraordinarily lucky girl. And the trustees had told her she was going to receive ten at twenty-one, the same at twenty-five, twenty-five million at thirty, and a hundred million each at thirty-five and forty, and the final two hundred and fifty million at fifty years of age. By the time she was fifty years old, she would be worth half a billion dollars, even without new investments that would increase it. The amount Robert had left Gaëlle was extremely generous, and she was very grateful, but he had left Dominique an enormous fortune, far more than Dominique had ever imagined, or could even conceive of. It was huge. Gaëlle had always worried about Dominique having that much money, even with advisers, and if they invested it wisely for her, she would be worth even more over time. There was no way to change that, nor any reason to. But it was a lot for an eighteen-year-old girl to understand and absorb, even if she was financially wise for her age and always knew she would inherit a large fortune. But this was so much more than she had thought, and the press had guessed, which surprised her too. For the rest of her life she would have to carry the burden and responsibility that went with it. 'I never thought it would be so much,' she said to her mother in a stunned voice.

'You have to learn how to manage it with Daddy's advisers, and use it kindly.' Her fondest hope for her daughter was that she would develop compassion. She was a long way from it now. Dominique wouldn't be deprived of anything in her lifetime, but Gaëlle worried that having so much would affect her thinking, twist her irrevocably, and make her feel entitled to treat others badly, as she did now.

She was already on that path, and it would be a lonely life if she stayed on it, wielding her power to hurt people, as she had with her mother. Dominique sounded lost and dazed, and got off the phone after a few minutes to meet her friends. It was the first birthday Gaëlle hadn't spent with her, and she felt terrible about it, but Dominique had refused to let her come and didn't seem to care, and Gaëlle couldn't force her to be with her if she didn't want to. She would see her in July when she and Christophe went to Southampton, if Dominique was willing to visit them. Gaëlle was sure she would be, Christophe less so. Dominique was on a mission of revenge to hurt her mother, and knew just how to do it because Gaëlle loved her. It pained Christophe to see it. Both Gaëlle's vulnerability, as her mother, and Dominique's lack of heart.

Gaëlle had the flu in May and missed a week of work at the museum. She used the time in bed to catch up on her reading, but she still felt woozy when she went back to her office, and went to see her doctor the day after. Christophe was busier than ever in his studio, so she didn't want to bother him and complain, and he worried about her. After a long talk, the doctor gave her vitamins and told her to gain weight, and she was smiling mysteriously as she left his office. When Christophe came home late that night, she was half asleep but woke up when she heard him come in. He slipped into bed a few minutes later, naked as usual, and tucked himself in behind her and kissed her neck. He could tell she was awake.

'Did you miss me today?' he whispered, and she turned to him.

'Desperately.' She kissed him. 'We had a change of plans today for Christmas.'

'Dominique won't be there?' They were planning to go to New York to be with her, although it was still months away.

'No, she'll have to come here, whether she likes it or not.'

'That won't sit well with her,' he warned Gaëlle, but she knew it anyway.

'Maybe not, but we won't be able to travel then.' She sounded definite about it.

'Something happening at the museum?' His movie was opening in November, but by the beginning of December he'd be free. They had planned it carefully, to go to New York, and now her plans had changed.

293

'No, we have an appointment we can't shift,' she said firmly.

'What's that?'

'We're having a baby on December first.' She grinned at him and watched it sink in, as he stared at her incredulously and sat up in bed.

'What? Say that again.' She did, and he reached down and hugged her and looked as though a miracle had just taken place.

'I'm two and a half months pregnant.' And it had happened just the way they wanted, with no medical intervention or heroic efforts.

'Are you okay?'

'Very much so.' She'd had no problems with it and felt fine, and hadn't even suspected she was pregnant since she had always been irregular because of her meager diet. 'Except that I'll be ancient when the baby's born. I'll be forty-one.'

'When will you tell Dominique?' He was worried about that, and could just imagine her reaction when she heard that a baby was on the way. And he didn't want her upsetting Gaëlle now. Dominique's impact on her mother the last time had just been too upsetting, even though Gaëlle never told him the details and insisted that she was weathering it. But he knew that Dominique had wounded her deeply, even beyond what he could see, or Gaëlle let on. She felt as though she were losing her daughter, or already had.

'We can tell her this summer, I'll be four months pregnant by then, and it will show, so we'll have no choice. She'll have to come here for Christmas now.' Dominique hadn't been back since she'd started college, but she had friends here as well. And Gaëlle wouldn't be able to travel a few weeks after she delivered.

They settled into bed after that and talked about the baby. Gaëlle wanted a boy for him, and he said he didn't care as long as she and the baby were both healthy, and then he looked at her apologetically, and asked her a question that was worrying him.

'Does the doctor think it will be more dangerous for you at your age?' He was embarrassed to ask her.

'Thanks a lot. No, it will be fine.' She fell asleep smiling in his arms that night, thinking about the baby. She could hardly wait. She hadn't suspected that any of this would happen to her. Life was so unexpected, both the good and the bad.

They told André and Geneviève about it the next day. And Gaëlle called Louise to tell her, and she was delighted. Christophe called his sister, and Amandine was thrilled for them.

'Now you can stop complaining about my boys. You'll have a little monster of your own,' Amandine said, and Christophe laughed. He was ecstatic. December couldn't come soon enough for him, and Gaëlle was happy too. She just hoped that Dominique wouldn't be too upset about the news. And she silently prayed that her second child would be easier and more loving than her first.

★   ★   ★

They went straight to the apartment when they landed in New York at the beginning of July. Everything looked meticulously neat. They had hired a new housekeeper she hadn't met, who seemed very efficient. And she was happy to be there for the first time in six months. Dominique had finished her classes two weeks before, but she was still in Boston, and planning to meet them in Southampton for the Fourth of July weekend. It gave Christophe and Gaëlle time to spend a few days in New York together.

The baby had started to show earlier this time. She was older, but she was healthy, and felt great, and the baby had started to move a few days before. She had put Christophe's hand on her belly, and he felt it, and had never shared anything so miraculous in his life. She just hoped that Dominique would be happy for them, and accept their marriage now.

When they got to the Southampton house, they settled into Gaëlle's usual room, the master bedroom, and he was impressed by how beautiful it was. He put some of his records on and looked out at the beach. They were holding hands on the deck when Dominique walked in and put down her things. And Gaëlle turned with pleasure to greet her daughter, came back into the house, and walked toward her, as Dominique stepped backward and stared at her with revulsion. They hadn't seen each other since Christmas and their disastrous explosive meeting then over Gaëlle marrying Christophe. Gaëlle was wearing a loose shirt over pink cotton slacks, with gold sandals.

'OhmyGod, you're pregnant. Why didn't you tell me?' Dominique said, with an expression of disbelief and horror.

'I wanted to tell you in person,' Gaëlle said gently, and gave her a hug, which Dominique didn't return. She was wearing diamond earrings that her mother had never seen before, that were very pretty and looked very expensive. They were from Van Cleef and Arpels. She hadn't wasted any time using her money any way she chose to. Dominique looked appalled at her pregnancy but said nothing.

'Was it planned or an accident?' she asked brusquely, as though that made a difference. But it was there now, undeniably.

'A little of both,' her mother admitted. 'We decided to see what happened.' She patted her stomach as she said it and felt the baby move again. Gaëlle was beautiful, and Christophe thought she had never looked better, but Dominique made no comment and didn't mention the pregnancy again. For the next four weeks in Southampton, she ignored it, as they occupied the house together. Dominique was out a lot and avoided her mother, but at least she had come. And once in a while, though rarely, Dominique set aside her anger and laughed with her mother. And when she couldn't avoid it, she said a few words to Christophe, but she wasn't warm with either of them. She had grown haughty and full of herself in the year she'd been at Radcliffe, or Gaëlle wondered if it was the money. She was different and more grown-up, but not warmer.

She was stiff and cold with her mother whenever anyone noticed the baby she was carrying and mentioned it. It was a sore subject with Dominique, and Christophe commented to Gaëlle in private that Dominique was intensely jealous, of her mother and the baby. She didn't get along with her mother, but she clearly didn't want her to have another child. She had been her parents' only child for eighteen years, and now there would be an intruder in her life, to share her mother's affection and attention. She said she hoped it would be a boy, which made it more obvious too. So not only was Christophe unwelcome, but so was the baby he had caused her to have.

But despite her shock over their announcement, the month passed uneventfully, with no major explosions, just an underlying tension, and a marked chill between them, and the occasional snide remark from Dominique, which Gaëlle and Christophe ignored, to keep the peace.

Christophe and Gaëlle left at the end of the month. Dominique was planning to stay for August, and to have friends at the house on weekends, and work in her father's office in the city during the week. It sounded very grown-up to her mother, and was for a girl of eighteen. But she trusted Dominique alone in the house with the staff. She and Christophe were going to the South of France for August. He had earned a peaceful vacation, after a month with Dominique.

Gaëlle had gotten much bigger while she was in New York, and had gotten a good tan, and so had he. They looked relaxed and happy as they boarded the plane to Paris. Dominique had even promised to come for Christmas. She had made her big protest move over the marriage and not coming to the wedding. She didn't want to miss Christmas with her mother, despite her objections to Christophe, and annoyance about the baby. And it was obvious they couldn't come to New York with a newborn. 'My due date is December first. I want you to see it as soon as it's born,' Gaëlle had told her warmly.

★ ★ ★

They spent a week in the apartment in Paris, catching up on mail and work, and then they went to visit friends in St. Tropez for three weeks, which was a lot more relaxing than Southampton with Dominique. By the end of the summer, Gaëlle's belly had grown exponentially, she was six months pregnant and complained that she felt huge. She said she was much bigger than the day Dominique was born, and she still had three months to go. They were sure the size indicated that it was a boy, although the doctor said that some girls were big babies too. Dominique had been nine pounds, which proved the point.

Christophe pampered Gaëlle constantly for the last three months of the pregnancy, even more than before. Having waited so long to have children, now he was terrified that something would go wrong. Gaëlle was more relaxed, and they spent hours in bed every night feeling the baby kick and talking to her belly. It thrilled him every time it moved, and he was impatient for the baby to come. Gaëlle was excited about it too, and more in love with Christophe than ever. And she heard very little from Dominique after the summer. Gaëlle called her at school, as she always had, and left messages for her at her dorm. Dominique often waited days to return the calls and was chilly on the phone when her mother finally reached her. She never asked about the baby, which she viewed as another betrayal by her mother.

They turned one of the guest rooms into a nursery. And Gaëlle decided not to hire a nanny. She was planning to stay home from work in December and January, to nurse the baby, and she was going to take care of it herself, at least in the beginning. Christophe had promised to help. They were already doting parents, even before their child arrived.

By November, and the premiere of Christophe's latest movie he'd written the score to, Gaëlle felt as if she could barely move. She was excited for him, and the reviews particularly for the score had been fabulous. They were playing his big hit theme song on the radio constantly. And that weekend she turned forty-one.

'I'm ugly, fat, and ancient,' she said miserably as she lay in bed that morning, upset that she had gained so much weight this time, far more than with Dominique. Someone at the museum had even asked if she was having twins, and she cried afterward, but the baby just kept getting bigger, and that night she felt like she was going to explode. She didn't even want to go to dinner, and she insisted that she'd prefer to stay home. Christophe was disappointed. He had promised to take her to a nice restaurant to celebrate her birthday, but she said the last thing she wanted to do was eat, so they went to a movie on the Champs Élysées and then to bed early. Every night she lay in bed next to him feeling like a whale, and she had warm-up contractions that hurt more than she remembered. Her body was responding very differently than it had nineteen years earlier at twenty-two. She was more tired this time and more uncomfortable, which her doctor said was normal.

Her delivery was going to be very different this time too. Eighteen years after Dominique was born, and in France, it was 1965 and natural childbirth was recommended, and they took Lamaze breathing classes to help deal with the pain. They showed a film of a woman in labor, and then finally delivering her baby, and Christophe thought it looked terrifying, but Gaëlle insisted that she wanted him to be there, and he had promised to stay with her.

'When Dominique was born, they weren't going to let Robert be in the room with me, but he stayed with me as long as he could, and a really stupid nurse didn't realize how far along I was, so he was there when she was born. The nurses were very shocked and thought it was a terrible idea to have him there, but I wanted him to be with me. And now everyone does it.' She smiled at Christophe, who admitted he was nervous but wanted to help her through it. She

301

wasn't sure about having it without drugs for the pain, but they were adamant that it was better for the baby than sedating the mother. They were more insistent about it in France than in the States.

She was going to a private clinic and would be staying for a week. It wasn't as luxurious as Doctors Hospital in New York, with her enormous suite, but it was medically sound and comfortable enough, and Christophe was going to be with her, and learn how to help take care of the baby. She wanted to nurse for as long as she could. She was going to take the baby with her for a month or two when she went back to work. Nursing had been discouraged when she had Dominique, it was out of fashion, but was becoming more accepted again. And Gaëlle was planning to do it, and Christophe's sister had told him it was good for the baby, so he was entirely in favor of it, and supportive of her.

They had their last Lamaze class three days before her due date, and she said the warm-up contractions had gotten stronger, but she knew they were nothing compared to the real ones. She still remembered.

Her bag was packed for the hospital, and every night they waited for labor to start. And a week after her due date, they were still waiting. They were talking about inducing her if it didn't come in the next week. And the midwife at the clinic had warned her that the delivery might be harder for her if they did. Gaëlle wasn't looking forward to it, and didn't want it induced, and Christophe got more nervous every day and wanted to stay home with her. But she sent him to his studio to work and told him not to worry. He was working late one night on a new score. Gaëlle was watching TV at home when her water broke, and she rushed to the bathroom, and saw that she was bleeding too, and the pains started in earnest this time within seconds. There was no gentle building up or slow increase in the strength of the contractions. They hit her with full force immediately, and she could hardly breathe or talk five minutes later. She called Christophe at the studio, and he didn't answer. She called the clinic, and they told her to come in as quickly as she could. She called him again, still no answer, and she assumed he was on his way home after finishing work for the night. She put her coat on, and sat on a chair in the entrance hall with a towel under her, so she'd be ready to go as soon as he walked in.

Twenty minutes later, there was no sign of him, he didn't answer at the studio, and she wondered if he had his earphones on, in which case he wouldn't hear her. The pains were so bad she could hardly stand up, and she felt enormous pressure with each contraction, and she knew the baby was coming soon. She called a cab to take her to the clinic, but she didn't want to go without Christophe. They both wanted to experience the birth together, and she didn't want him to miss it. She walked down the stairs doubled over, dragging her suitcase, and told the driver to take her to the studio, which was out of the way from the clinic.

'Is that a hospital?' the driver asked her

nervously about the address. He could see that she was in pain.

'No, it's my husband's office,' she said through clenched teeth, as he took off as quickly as he could.

'You're not having the baby now, are you? In my cab, I mean.'

'Not if you drive fast enough.' She promised him a big tip if they got there quickly. But when they got to the studio, she couldn't move, and she gave him the keys to the studio, and told him to go in and get Christophe. Five minutes later Christophe followed the driver out of the building at a dead run, and he got in next to her with a look of panic. The taxi driver had told him she was having the baby in the cab, and she looked as if she were. She was panting and puffing and breathing as they had told her to when the pains got really bad, as Christophe held her hand.

'Why didn't you call me?'

'I did,' she said between panting, 'you didn't answer.'

'I had my earphones on,' he said guiltily.

'I figured. I'm having the baby very soon,' she warned him, 'like now maybe,' she said as the cab pulled up in front of the clinic. She could recall feeling exactly the same kind of pressure right before Dominique had roared through her like an express train. Christophe paid the driver a huge tip, and he ran inside to get a nurse or a doctor or whoever he could find to help her.

'Wait till I get back!' he shouted at her, as though she could. And a minute later two attendants came out with a gurney and a nurse. She clutched Christophe's hand as they lifted her onto the gurney, and they wheeled her inside as quickly as they could. They had her in a delivery room in less than two minutes, took her clothes off, covered her with a drape, and checked her, as a doctor came into the room. The nurse was telling him that the baby's head was almost there, she was fully dilated, when Gaëlle screamed and asked them to give her something for the pain, she couldn't stand it anymore.

'You don't want that for your baby,' the nurse told her soothingly, and Gaëlle shouted at her.

'Yes, I do! I need it . . . this stupid panting doesn't work!' The contractions were excruciating. They put a monitor on her enormous belly, held in place with a wide elastic belt, and she pulled it off immediately. 'I can't breathe with that thing!' Christophe looked panicked, and before the doctor could tell her to, Gaëlle started to push. It appeared to be agonizing to Christophe, who wished they had never decided to have a baby. It seemed like a terrible idea now, as Gaëlle struggled to push with every contraction and screamed from the pain.

Ten minutes after she had started, a little face appeared between her legs and let out a wail. Christophe had never imagined it would be like this, so terrifying and so beautiful and so excruciating all at the same time, as Gaëlle continued to push. And they delivered the baby's shoulders, and then the body, and she came out then in a rapid whoosh, as the nurse said, 'It's a girl!' She was enormous and very long, and she had stopped crying and was staring at her parents as the doctor cut the cord. The nurse laid the baby on Gaëlle's chest as she and Christophe cried, looking at their baby, who was gazing at all of them as though wondering how she got there. It occurred to Christophe that suddenly there was another person in the room. The gift of life had never seemed as mystical to him.

'She looks like you,' he said, in awe of what he'd just seen.

'She looks like both of us.' The baby had blond hair and blue eyes just like them, and Gaëlle gently put her to her breast, and her father watched her in wonder as she nursed for the first time. It was all so simple and natural, although they had to do some repair work on Gaëlle after they took the baby to the nursery to check her and weigh her. Christophe went with the baby and came back in a few minutes. The placenta had been delivered, and they had given Gaëlle something for the pain by then. He reported that she weighed five kilos, just over ten pounds. 'She's even bigger than Dominique,' Gaëlle said groggily. 'We have to call her.' And Gaëlle did as soon as they wheeled her to a room, with Christophe pushing the baby in a bassinet beside her. They were suddenly a family. It truly was a miracle.

'You have a sister' were the first words Gaëlle said to her older daughter when she called her at the dorm, and luckily she was in, studying for exams. 'She's beautiful, and so were you when you were born.' She wanted her to feel part of it. 'I can't wait for you to see her.' She sounded happy and exhausted. It had been hard, but it was quick, even faster than the last time.

Dominique sounded distant and cold to cover an avalanche of emotions. 'Are you okay, Mom?' She was concerned for her mother in spite of herself, and there was a glimmer of the past in her voice, which Gaëlle heard with tenderness and hope.

'I'm fine. I'm a little sleepy right now, but I'll see you soon. And I love you.' Christophe hung up the phone for her, and Gaëlle dozed for a few minutes and then opened her eyes and smiled at him. 'Thank you for this wonderful baby, and for our family,' she whispered to him, and he bent to kiss her.

'Thank *you*.' He knew he would never forget the moment they had just shared. 'What's her name?' They had agreed on Daphne before she was born, and they both still liked it, now that they'd seen her. And her middle name was Rebekah, for Gaëlle's beloved friend.

They set up a bed for him next to her, and the baby went to the nursery for a while, to have her vitals checked again and drops put in her eyes. And Christophe gazed at his wife with more love than he had ever felt for any human, as Gaëlle drifted off to sleep with a smile. Christophe thought she looked like a Madonna as he watched his wife with tears in his eyes.

19

Gaëlle dressed the baby in a white flannel nightgown with a little pink sweater the night Dominique arrived from New York, and laid her in the bassinet, so she'd look like a little angel for her sister. Daphne was two weeks old, and they'd come home from the clinic the week before. Gaëlle was still sore and hobbling around, but mother and baby were thriving, and Christophe was doing everything he could to help. He didn't even want to go to the studio for once. He wanted to be home with them. He was in love with his wife and daughter.

She could hardly wait for Dominique to see her, and to hug her older daughter. She was looking forward to spending Christmas with her, although their life was still a little disrupted by the new baby. But Christophe had put up a tree, and Gaëlle had helped him decorate it. She was feeling well, and so excited by Daphne's arrival.

Dominique stared at her in the bassinet for a long time when she arrived from the airport, and touched her cheek with a careful finger. She had big blue eyes, skin like velvet, and a little rosebud mouth. She was a big beautiful baby with a lovely face.

'She's very pretty,' Dominique said as though she were unrelated to her, and Gaëlle could see she felt no bond to her yet. Her older daughter looked chic and pretty and very grown-up in her second year at Radcliffe, and seemed older than eighteen. It made Gaëlle realize how exciting it was to be starting all over again with a new baby. Dominique was a woman now, with a life and future all her own. Daphne would still be with them for a long time, although Gaëlle knew how quickly the years flew by.

'Would you like to hold her?' Gaëlle offered, and Dominique shook her head.

'I'm exhausted, I think I'll go to bed.' And a moment later, she had taken refuge in her familiar room, and Gaëlle nursed the baby as Christophe watched. He had left her alone while Dominique was in the room with her.

'How did it go?' He knew how desperately Gaëlle wanted to reconnect with her daughter and feel closer to her again.

'I think it's a little daunting at first,' Gaëlle said hopefully. From her perspective, who could resist a newborn, especially one as adorable as their baby girl? She was totally enamored with the baby, and so was Christophe. They would sit and watch her for hours. And she was sure Dominique would fall in love with her by the time she left.

'Did she hold her?' he asked, as the baby nursed peacefully at her mother's breast.

'Not yet. She touched her cheek.' Gaëlle smiled at him. She had thought it a promising sign. He wasn't convinced.

The next morning Dominique went out to see some of her old friends and came back in the afternoon. Gaëlle was nursing the baby when she walked in, with a pink cashmere blanket delicately covering her breast, and as soon as

Dominique realized what she was doing, she left the room and came back an hour later. She paid no attention to the sleeping infant, and talked to her mother about school. She loved Cambridge, and was still excited to be there. It was everything she had hoped it would be. And she mentioned that she was going to Argentina to visit a friend during spring break. Paris no longer seemed to be on her map as a vacation option, and she constantly had other plans. Gaëlle knew that that was typical in college, and Dominique had more opportunities to travel than her friends, and the ability to do so. It felt as though she had really flown the nest to the broader world. Gaëlle was grateful she had come to Paris for Christmas, but while listening to her daughter she sensed that after this, she wouldn't see her again until July in the Hamptons. They were planning to bring the baby with them this year. And Dominique didn't seem to care. But Gaëlle was sad that she saw Dominique only twice a year now, at Christmas and in July.

She was polite to Christophe this time but treated him with indifference. She acted like he was a houseguest, and whenever she saw the three of them together, she left the room. It was as though the sight of them was too painful for her, despite all her mother's efforts to include her and make her feel loved, which she rejected, and she never went near the baby again after the first night when she arrived.

'You know I love you just as much as ever, don't you?' her mother said gently, as Dominique started to leave while Gaëlle was nursing. 'I

310

have space in my heart for both of you, and Christophe.' Dominique nodded and left the room without a word. Nothing had changed. Dominique was even more removed than before, and resentful of her mother. And the baby was not a welcome addition to her. There were no outbursts this time, only ice. And no matter what Gaëlle did or said, Dominique made a point of not being part of their family. She chose to be the odd man out.

She left after a week, and went skiing in Val d'Isère with some of her old friends. It never occurred to her to ask her mother's permission, or if she minded. She made her own decisions now, and had the money to do so, and Gaëlle was disappointed when she left. The visit hadn't been as warm as she had hoped. Dominique didn't make it easy, and stayed aloof throughout, and said she was flying back to New York from Geneva. The week had gone by too quickly, and she kissed her mother goodbye but said nothing to Christophe, and didn't look at the baby again before she left. Christophe didn't say anything about it, but he could see how sad Gaëlle was afterward. She was crushed. The new baby had brought them not closer but farther apart.

'She doesn't want to repair our relationship, or be part of us,' she said to Christophe. Dominique acknowledged Gaëlle as her mother but wanted nothing to do with her husband or their child. Gaëlle had given her a very pretty bracelet for Christmas, and Dominique had given her a silk Hermès scarf, almost identical to the one Gaëlle had given to her assistant at the museum. And she had never asked once about her mother's work as curator. It seemed antiquated and irrelevant to her, to set up a home for people who had been dead for at least twenty years. She had no interest in the purpose of the museum, or the Strauss family and others like them, which her mother was so passionate about. The war had no meaning to Dominique, nor the new family her mother had formed. She had acted as though they were insignificant to her too. Dominique had become a disconnected person, unattached to anyone. And the only person who interested her was herself. And Gaëlle saw it too. It was harder and harder to make excuses for her. She seemed to have an aversion to being close to anyone. She had no desire to cross the bridge back to them.

★　★　★

Gaëlle went back to work in February, and had nearly regained her figure by then, although she had kept on a little weight, but Christophe thought it looked good on her. She took the baby to work with her and nursed her when she needed to. Their intern held her when Gaëlle had an important call or an interview, and Daphne slept in a basket in a corner of her mother's office. Watching her one day, Gaëlle remembered the babies she had transported during the war. She couldn't understand now how their mothers had been able to part with them. It was the ultimate act of love to send them away to safety with strangers.

And in March they went away with friends of Christophe's for the weekend. The husband was a well-known film producer he had worked with, and they were talking about a new project together with an American film company. Christophe had become increasingly respected in France, and he had received in the last year a major award for his movie score. Gaëlle was very proud of him. And he was being approached with one great project after another.

They were still living in the same apartment, and the owners kept extending their lease. They had no reason to move, they had all the space they needed, and Daphne's toys were everywhere, and a bassinet in every room. It was a happy home for them. Gaëlle had finally hired a nanny so she could go back to work full time, and didn't have to take the baby with her. Daphne was awake more, and it was hard to always bring her to work with her.

In April, they got a surprise that Gaëlle had hoped for but not expected. She discovered that she was pregnant again, and they were having another baby in November, right after Gaëlle's forty-second birthday.

'I'm going to be the oldest mother at their school,' she commented to Christophe, who was thrilled again, and Gaëlle wanted a boy this time to complete their family.

They christened Daphne a few days later, and Amandine was her godmother, and her two ruffian sons were fascinated by their new cousin and wanted to hold her whenever they saw her. Gaëlle felt like part of Christophe's family now,

313

and she genuinely liked her sister-in-law and had gotten closer to her. She talked to her about Dominique sometimes and how difficult it was to reach her. Their relationship, or lack of one, was heartbreaking for Gaëlle.

'She's a very withdrawn, unemotional person,' Gaëlle tried to explain to her, and she had gotten more so as she matured. Gaëlle's wise sister-in-law saw it more simply.

'I'm sure she's jealous of the baby and your new family. She feels shut out.'

'She shuts herself out,' Gaëlle said with regret. 'She feels I betrayed her father by marrying again. I think he would have understood it better than she does.' Dominique had just turned nineteen, and was finishing her sophomore year of Radcliffe and doing very well.

'Have you told her about the new baby?' Gaëlle shook her head, feeling guilty.

'I thought I'd wait till we see her in the summer.' She suspected that another baby would only make things worse between them. 'She'll have to come back here for Christmas again. I won't be able to travel yet with a new baby.' And she knew Dominique wouldn't like it. She had looked anxious to leave the whole time she had been there after Daphne was born. Babies clearly made her uncomfortable, and she always said she didn't want any. All she wanted was a career. She studied all the time, got excellent grades, and rarely dated. Her only passion was business. They hardly spoke to each other now. And the conversations were brief and superficial when they did. Dominique was busy at school and with her friends. Gaëlle was constantly running between Christophe, the baby, and her job. And she'd be even busier with a new baby. She had never been happier, and she and Christophe were very much in love, but Gaëlle felt more than ever as though Dominique had put up a wall between them, and was out of reach. It panicked Gaëlle but suited Dominique.

By the time they got to Southampton in July, Gaëlle was even bigger than with her last pregnancy. And when Dominique arrived, the first thing she saw was her mother holding seven-month-old Daphne in her arms, and it was obvious that there was another baby on the way. She was the symbol of motherhood and fertility. Dominique looked unnerved by the scene the moment she saw her.

'Don't you think it's a bit much to have a baby every year at your age?' Dominique said bluntly before she even said hello. 'What are you trying to prove? How young you are? You're forty-one years old. How many are you planning to have?' She made no move to hug her mother, as Gaëlle went to embrace her.

'At my age, we don't have time to wait. I'm sure this will be the last one.' Dominique's cursory embrace to her mother was anything but warm.

'You've become a baby factory,' Dominique said with a look of disgust. She remembered her mother as glamorous and elegant when she was married to her father when Dominique was a child. They went out a lot, and she wore pretty clothes. Now she wore jeans and sweatshirts,

315

boots and sneakers, and always had a baby in her belly or her arms. And Christophe's style was bohemian casual. His hair was long and disheveled when he was working. And like most men his age, particularly in the music business, he rarely shaved, unlike Robert, who had been impeccably groomed. To Dominique, it was all a symbol of how far her mother had fallen.

And to Gaëlle, Dominique seemed colder, haughtier, and acted more entitled every year. She had bought a very expensive vintage sports car, an old Jaguar, to drive at school, which Gaëlle thought was too showy. Dominique thought her mother and Christophe looked like slobs, which was not the case. They looked like successful intellectuals in their forties with a young child and a baby on the way.

Dominique thought everything had changed when her mother went back to France. She was no longer a chic New Yorker, but a member of the French bourgeoisie. And Dominique felt like there was no place for her in her mother's new family. She blamed Christophe for that. She dismissed her mother's virtues and pursuits as far less interesting than what she was learning at Radcliffe about business. And she couldn't wait to start graduate school in two years. She loved the time she spent at her father's firm in the summer. And they treated her like a princess. She learned a great deal when she worked there. To her, Wall Street was the epicenter of the world, not France.

Christophe didn't complain about the month they spent in Southampton. He knew it was important to Gaëlle to be with Dominique, but it was never enjoyable for him, nor to be ignored and snubbed by a spoiled brat, and watch his wife try to salvage and revive a relationship with a daughter who didn't care. It was painful to watch and always a relief when they left.

During the month they spent in Southampton, Christophe went into the city occasionally to meet with people he knew in the music business, and he came back energized with fresh ideas, which he discussed with Gaëlle. But there was always sadness in her eyes here, for the bond she couldn't form with her daughter, and the relationship they didn't have, and possibly never would.

When they left Southampton, they went to a house they rented in the South of France for August, in St. Jean Cap Ferrat, where they entertained friends, and spent time with each other and Daphne, and had much more fun. Gaëlle had invited Dominique, and she had declined. She preferred to stay in Southampton with friends of her own. But Louise joined them in the South, and other friends.

By the end of the summer, Gaëlle was huge again. And she was busy at the end of her pregnancy. They had just completed another room at the museum in October, and had received praise for it. Gaëlle had created something important, to honor the memory of those who had died in the Holocaust, and had received distinguished recognition for it from Holocaust museums all over Europe.

She turned forty-two a week before her due

317

date, and taking care of Daphne and tending to her work, she was exhausted every night.

They were at dinner with André and Geneviève this time at a restaurant when her water broke, and Christophe wanted her to go straight to the clinic, which she said was silly, she wasn't even having pains yet. She wanted to go home to pick up her bag, shower, and wait for the contractions to start. She insisted it might take hours.

'You almost had Daphne in the cab last time,' he reminded her.

'That's because you had your earphones on at the studio and I couldn't reach you.' She laughed. But she wasn't laughing an hour later, once they were home. And it hit her even more forcefully this time. She was in hard labor half an hour after it started, and Christophe almost had to carry her to his car. She had done it again, underestimated how quickly the baby would come. He drove as fast as he dared, and she was grabbing his arm with a look of terror as he sped toward the clinic. He wasn't sure if it was his driving or the pains and didn't ask as he kept his foot on the gas.

'It's much worse this time,' she said in a hoarse whisper, wondering what had made her think this would be a good idea again. It was so much more painful than she remembered, as they got to the clinic and the nurses rushed her inside to a room, while Christophe left his car outside parked at a crazy angle. 'I can't do it,' she said to one of the nurses, as they took her clothes off and put her feet in the stirrups. 'Make it stop,

318

I need drugs,' she gasped, 'it's really bad.' She was clinging to Christophe and trying to sit up. She didn't want to lie down, and she started to push when they told her not to. The doctor wasn't even there yet. 'Christophe, I can't!' she shouted at him, and as he supported her, she gave two enormous pushes, and their son was born. She hadn't even been at the clinic for ten minutes, and she was smiling through tears again as they looked down at their baby boy in awe. He looked just like his sister Daphne, and like them, with a halo of pale blond hair. He seemed even more like an angel than Daphne had, and the moment the nurse put him in his mother's arms, he wanted to nurse. He was a big, strong baby with a loud cry, and he seemed more like two months old as she held him and then handed him to his father, when he stopped nursing and went to sleep.

'We're not having any more babies,' Christophe said convincingly, as he held him tenderly and kissed the sleeping infant. 'Next time you won't make it out of the restaurant, and I'll have to deliver him myself.' Everyone in the delivery room laughed, and although it had been rugged for a few minutes, Gaëlle was saying it had been easy. But she recognized herself that two healthy babies were enough. They had been blessed. They named the baby Pierre, for Christophe's late father, and his middle name was Raphaël for hers.

Gaëlle called Dominique to tell her and couldn't reach her, so she sent her a telegram that her brother Pierre had arrived. She responded hours later with only 'Congratulations! Love, D.' And that was it.

They discovered, when they took the baby home a week later, that he had an enormous appetite, and Gaëlle spent all her time nursing. Daphne had just started walking, and within a week after she got home, Gaëlle was busy with both of them, and by the time Dominique arrived for Christmas, Gaëlle was either nursing or chasing Daphne, and exhausted and frantic all the time. And their nanny quit. Christophe was finishing a score for a movie and was working on another for TV, so had little time to help her. Dominique was appalled at the chaos of her mother's life with a newborn, a toddler, no nanny, and a job.

Gaëlle tried to make time for her older daughter, but one of the babies was always crying or needing to be fed, and Dominique looked annoyed and exasperated during her entire visit. She couldn't wait to leave.

'Do you ever do anything else, Mom, except change diapers and nurse?' she said tartly. It had been that way for more than a year now, and it made her feel even more disconnected from her mother. And she thought Christophe was a bore who changed diapers all the time. They were always holding one baby or the other, and Gaëlle liked taking care of them herself.

'Eventually, they'll grow up, I promise,' Gaëlle said apologetically, but she had given birth only a month before, and Dominique had no patience with it. She said she wondered how Christophe could stand it, and suggested that that was why he stayed at the studio till two A.M. 'He's finishing a score for a TV series and a movie,' Gaëlle explained, *and also avoiding Dominique,* which she didn't say. But in spite of Dominique's poor opinion of them, Christophe and Gaëlle were happy and in love with the new baby, and Daphne. Dominique's visit over Christmas was brief and cut short again, when she left for London after five days to meet up with friends. And Gaëlle apologized for how hectic it had been when she left. New babies had a way of turning things upside down. It looked like a day care center to Dominique and she nearly bolted out the door when she left.

'I hope this is your last one,' she said pointedly to Gaëlle when she kissed her goodbye. And there were tears in Gaëlle's eyes when Christophe saw her and tried to console her when Dominique was gone.

'I've lost my daughter,' she said miserably. She had two babies and had lost her oldest child.

'Maybe you never had her. You two are very different,' he said gently, but Gaëlle never wanted to believe that. She was always sure that one day they would reach common ground. But it happened less and less, and Christophe took her in his arms while she cried. He hoped that for her sake their children would be very different from her oldest child, and that one day Daphne and Pierre would give her the love and respect she deserved. Dominique hadn't so far, and he suspected that she never would.

20

Two small children a year apart turned out to be more of a juggling act than Gaëlle and Christophe had anticipated. His career took off exponentially after Pierre was born, Gaëlle was busy at the museum, and tried to spend time with the kids. Her life felt like a relay race, and she was always running behind. But they were happy times, the best in her life, Gaëlle always said.

The landmarks slipped by rapidly, and within a year both children were walking, running. They got to Southampton in July, but Dominique skipped Christmas with them the year after Pierre was born. She spent the holidays on a yacht in St. Bart's with friends instead, and Gaëlle and Christophe had a cozy Christmas with their children and Louise and hers at home in Paris, although Gaëlle missed seeing her oldest daughter, and tried to resign herself to it.

Time flew by, and it was a shock when Dominique's Radcliffe graduation was planned. Gaëlle and Christophe were excited to attend and decided to bring Pierre and Daphne with them. Daphne was two and a half and Pierre one and a half, in a double stroller they brought with them.

Louise thought Gaëlle was ambitious to take the younger children to the graduation, but she wanted all her children in one place for a change. Dominique hardly ever saw her younger half-brother and -sister, and Gaëlle assured Louise that she and Christophe could manage the little ones at the graduation, and Gaëlle wanted Dominique to see them.

Gaëlle had snacks and fruit juice for them to keep them quiet during the graduation ceremony, and she carried a huge bag with everything they needed, including food, diapers, and a change of clothes for each child. And Christophe kept them happy and quiet while Gaëlle took photos of Dominique in her cap and gown. It was a memorable moment, and Christophe took pictures of Gaëlle and Dominique together, while Pierre took off one of his sneakers and lost it in the crowd, and they spent half an hour looking for it before they went to Elsie's, just off Harvard Square, for lunch. Dominique joined her friends afterward, but they took her to dinner that night at Henry IV. She was leaving the next day for a summer internship in San Francisco at a venture capital firm, and she had been accepted to start her MBA program at Harvard in September. She had worked so diligently at her father's firm every summer that they had made an exception for her to attend without the usually required job experience.

She ran into one of her classmates when she was returning her rented cap and gown, when her fellow graduate commented, 'I didn't know you were French.' He had heard Christophe and Gaëlle speaking French to her, and the younger kids.

'I'm not. My mother is. I'm American,' she corrected him immediately. She felt no ties to France, or in recent years to her mother, but she spared him the explanation. She was fiercely annoyed that her mother had brought the younger children to graduation.

'Are you adopted?' he asked, confused.

'No. My mother went back to France and was kidnapped by aliens,' she said, referring to Christophe and their bourgeois lifestyle, which she found mortifying, and he laughed.

'Sounds interesting. Congratulations,' he said, referring to her diploma.

'You too,' she said, and disappeared into the crowd.

It was a relief for her when she left for San Francisco the next morning. She didn't have time to see her family again after dinner the night before. She was grateful that they had left Pierre and Daphne at the hotel with a babysitter, and they had an adult evening. They were skipping Southampton this year since she wouldn't be there, and were spending two months in St. Jean Cap Ferrat instead. She had no plans to see them again until Christmas. But at least they had stopped having babies. As far as Dominique was concerned, they could barely manage the two they had, who were always screaming, crying, running, had to be fed, needed a diaper change, or had just hit their heads. She didn't know how her mother stood it. Dominique thought they made having children look like a nightmare. Whenever she saw them, they confirmed Dominique's determination never to marry or have kids.

And as they drove to the airport, Gaëlle commented to Christophe that she didn't think Dominique would ever have children, she didn't have the patience for it, and barely looked at her half-brother and -sister when she was with them. 'I think she'll just be a career woman,' her mother said sadly, as she leaned over and kissed Daphne, who chortled happily at her mother and spoke a blue streak in French. Gaëlle was delighted to have these two younger children. She loved Dominique, but she finally realized that no matter how hard she tried, they would never be close, and in some way they would always be strangers. All she could hope now was that one day, as Dominique got older, they would wind up as friends. It was hard to accept that she didn't always understand her own daughter, couldn't get close to her because Dominique wouldn't let her, and they had so little in common. At times they didn't even like each other. She had stopped trying to pretend otherwise. Dominique was just too harsh and too different from Gaëlle.

Gaëlle was grateful for her life with Christophe and their babies. Every chapter and every age was different, and at forty-four, this was the one that suited her, and the only life she wanted. Her life in New York seemed like a distant dream now, and Robert a loving ghost from her past. And Dominique the phantom daughter she would chase forever, and perhaps never be able to reach after all.

Their summer in St. Jean Cap Ferrat after
Dominique's Radcliffe graduation was ideal for
Gaëlle and Christophe and the children, and so
much easier and more fun than Southampton.
They loved the house they rented, friends visited
from Paris, Christophe was relieved not to deal
with Dominique's acerbic comments, and Gaëlle
felt more at home in France now. She had been
back for six years, and her time in the States felt
like part of another life. For two months in the
South of France, they went to the beach, had
dinner in open-air restaurants while Daphne and
Pierre slept in their stroller, and talked with their
friends at the house late into the night. It was a
typical French summer. Thanks to Robert,
Gaëlle was able to provide extra advantages they
might not have had otherwise, and Christophe
was doing well too. The house they'd rented was
large and luxurious and had a pool. They had
many comforts in their life.

They had bought the apartment on Avenue
Foch the year before and remodeled it, and
rented a speedboat for the summer. They had an
enviable life they thoroughly enjoyed.

Gaëlle talked to Dominique several times in
San Francisco, and she loved her summer job
and thought it was a fun city. She had made
friends with a number of recent graduates
entering the MBA program at Stanford. But she
said she couldn't wait to get back to Harvard.
She was having a great summer. And so were
they.

They returned to Paris at the end of August, and Daphne started nursery school. She was turning three in December. And Pierre was still at home at almost two. The new nanny took him to the park every day, and Christophe and Gaëlle spent evenings and weekends with their children, and other families with children the same age. They were thinking of buying a weekend house in Normandy and were going to start looking soon.

At the end of September, a month after they got back, Pierre spiked a high fever, and Gaëlle suspected he had an earache. His crying woke her in the night, and she took his temperature. He had 105, and at five A.M. she called the doctor, and she said to bring him to the emergency room in the morning if he didn't improve. Gaëlle gave him two baby aspirin, and held him in her arms until he fell asleep, and in the morning when she woke with him still in her arms, his fever had climbed a degree higher. She wrapped him in a blanket immediately, and drove him to the hospital, while Christophe stayed home with Daphne. The nanny and housekeeper hadn't come in yet. And by the time she got to the hospital, Pierre's bright blue eyes were glassy, and half an hour later he slipped into a coma. They took him away immediately to do a spinal tap, while Gaëlle called Christophe hysterically, and they came to tell her he had meningitis. And by noon, as she stood alone in the halls of Necker Children's Hospital, it was all over. He had never regained consciousness, and they told her these things happen, and that children succumb to the disease very quickly. She looked dazed as she waited in the parking lot for Christophe to arrive, having left Daphne with the nanny the moment she arrived. Gaëlle was incoherent with grief as they stood and cried together, clinging to each other in despair.

The funeral was two days later, as they buried their son in a tiny white coffin with blue flowers on it. What had happened was incomprehensible, and Daphne was too young for Gaëlle to explain it to her. She kept asking for Pierre, and her nursery school class made drawings for them of Pierre going up to Heaven. Gaëlle couldn't even look at them when they sent them. She sat frozen in grief in their apartment, unable to move or care for her daughter. And Christophe was no better.

Gaëlle had called Dominique, sobbing uncontrollably, and asked her to come to Paris for the funeral. There had been a short silence and her voice was sympathetic, but her decision clear.

'I can't, Mom. I just started my MBA program. You don't get time off here. I can't fly to Paris for a few days.'

'For your brother's funeral?' her mother said angrily. And Dominique didn't say he wasn't her brother, or that she didn't consider him one. He was a foolish mistake her mother had made. They both were, in her opinion. She felt sorry for her mother, and even for Christophe, but she had long since decided that he and their children weren't her family. They were her mother's, and she couldn't take time off so early in the semester. She didn't come. And Gaëlle knew that even though she loved her, she would never forgive her.

Gaëlle felt as though she were in a daze in a silent, frozen world for months afterward. She and Christophe took turns crying over it, and sometimes they just sat and cried together. And they knew life would never be quite the same again. They had lost half their family, their only son, and in the spring Gaëlle was finally able to talk about him without sobbing, but she knew she would feel the loss forever. And her communications were sparse and chilly with Dominique. Gaëlle wasn't trying anymore.

They were walking in the park one day, and sat down by a lake with swans and geese, and she mentioned Rebekah to Christophe again, out of the blue. She hadn't mentioned her in a long time, but she'd been thinking of her, and Christophe remembered the story, and that losing her best friend was linked to why she had agreed to be the curator for the Strauss Museum. And then for the first time she told him about Jacob, who had climbed out the window and hidden behind the drain pipes, how she had hidden him in the shed, and taken him to safety. Her husband listened to her in stunned silence. She had never told him the story before, and after losing Pierre, he was deeply moved by it.

'Did you ever find out what happened to him?' He was suddenly haunted by a little boy she had saved twenty-seven years before. He would be a man now, if he had lived.

'No, I don't know,' she said softly, 'but there were others after him.' She told him about

329

Isabelle, the nine-year-old girl she had taken on the tractor, and the babies. 'I never counted, but there were a lot of them. I could never understand how people could send their children away with strangers, but it was the only way they could get them to safety.' She told him about the brave people of Le Chambon sur Lignon, the Huguenot pastors, and the OSE workers. 'I worked for the OSE till the end of the Occupation. I guess I must have transported over a hundred children, maybe more. I did it for Rebekah, because I couldn't save her, or Lotte, or her brothers.'

It was a whole new side of her he'd never known. Some of her war experiences had been too harrowing and too painful to talk about, including being accused as a traitor afterward.

'We all worked in secret, and all the units disbanded after the Liberation. Everyone disappeared and went back to wherever they were from before. We had done what we could. I never saw any of them again. We were all faceless strangers who did it for the children. We had our own reasons. For me, it was for Rebekah.'

'Why didn't you ever tell me about the children?' he asked, staring at her, bowled over by what she'd just told him. He knew about the paintings she had saved, but not the rest.

'I don't know. I can't talk about the war. It's too much . . . ' Words failed her for a moment.

He put his arms around her and held her, and she started to cry again. 'I saved all those children for so long, and I couldn't save one of my own.'

'You couldn't help it. You heard what the doctors said. Children his age almost never survive it.'

'They didn't survive the war either, but we saved a lot of them.' He nodded, thinking of what a remarkable woman she was. And after that, she told him about being accused of collaboration afterward, and that she couldn't prove otherwise. She said that all that mattered now was the lives of the children they'd saved, not what anyone thought or falsely accused her of. They sat talking for a long time in the park, as she told him many of her stories. And then they went home to Daphne. He was grateful they still had her, although he knew that for the rest of their lives they would never stop missing Pierre, every moment of every day. And now he knew too how heroic she had been in the war, and knowing that, he loved her all the more.

★ ★ ★

Because she was her mother, felt she should, and wanted to, Gaëlle went to Dominique's Harvard Business School graduation. She didn't bring Daphne, and Christophe refused to come. He still hadn't forgiven her for not attending Pierre's funeral. She had crossed the line for him, and they no longer went to Southampton. Gaëlle flew to Boston a few times a year to see her, when Dominique allowed it. But Dominique spent Thanksgiving with friends every year now, and found excuses not to come to Paris for Christmas. She hated the chaos in their house

331

with Daphne. To Gaëlle and Christophe, it was what Christmas was all about. Dominique had gone skiing in Aspen instead with friends from business school. And now she was graduating with a Harvard MBA, a major achievement, and Gaëlle was proud of her. She cried when she saw her in the procession to get her diploma, and it made her think of Pierre at Dominique's Radcliffe graduation, and made her heart ache for him again.

Dominique was pleased that her mother had come to her graduation, particularly alone. She was starting her job at her father's firm on Monday, and Gaëlle had dinner with her the night before she flew back to Paris. Dominique had big plans and intended to fulfill her promises to her father. She wanted to be just like him, but Gaëlle knew just how different she was from him. Robert had been a kind person, full of compassion. Their daughter wasn't. She was all sharp edges, a brilliant mind, and a razor tongue. But motherhood didn't depend on the good behavior of your children. You were their mother no matter what, for good or bad. By the time she graduated, and with her father's fortune, Dominique felt like an important person. The strength of her mother was that she never believed she was important. She had been part of a network of strangers who had joined forces in their country's darkest hour, and none of them could have done it alone, they needed one another. She knew that Dominique still didn't understand that about life. She thought she could do it all alone, and Gaëlle knew that no one could. Without the network of caring people, they could never have saved all those children.

Dominique was leaving Harvard believing she was destined for stardom on Wall Street. And Gaëlle hoped she would find her dreams one day, and the people who would help her accomplish them. But sacrificing those you loved, and not being there for them, was a lonely road and the wrong way to begin her journey. More than anything, Gaëlle felt sad for her daughter. Dominique still had a long way to go and much to learn if she was going to be a happy person. She would have to give of herself, not simply grace the world with her presence. But Gaëlle knew that she had to find her own way now. No one could teach her, or make her be what she didn't want to be, or didn't have in her heart.

When Gaëlle left the day after graduation, she told her how proud her father would have been of her, which was true, and then she kissed her goodbye, and promised to visit her in the fall in New York. She didn't urge her to come to Paris because she knew she wouldn't. And she thought about her on the flight home, wondering if they would ever be close. She didn't think so anymore. Gaëlle didn't mourn the relationship in recent years, and what was lacking. But she showed up for her, because she was her mother. And as she flew back to Paris, she knew her job was done. It was up to Dominique now to decide who she would become.

★ ★ ★

At thirty, six years after she got her MBA, Dominique was making her way on Wall Street and her dreams were coming true, or seemed to be, professionally. Her mother was happy for her, though she suspected she was no wiser about what truly mattered.

And ten years later, at forty, Dominique had achieved almost everything she wanted, and her mother wondered if her victories were hollow. She hadn't married, she had no children. She had no partner officially, although she had confided to her mother two years before, on one of Gaëlle's visits to New York to see her, that she'd had a married lover for twelve years, from twenty-six to thirty-eight. He had promised to leave his wife and never did, but she still thought he might, when his youngest son left for college, which was still six years away.

'Do you really want to wait that long? You'll have been with him for eighteen years by then,' Gaëlle said sensibly, touched that Dominique had confided in her, after two glasses of wine at dinner. 'What makes you think he'd leave her then? You're thirty-eight years old. You've given up your best years to him,' she reminded her. Dominique had spent twelve years in the waiting room of life hoping that her married lover would leave his wife, and Gaëlle suspected he probably never would. Dominique hadn't figured that out yet, and on a personal level, she had doomed herself to failure, on every front.

She had brought glory to her father's firm, with terrific investments and an instinctive sense for business. But when they saw each other,

334

Gaëlle could see in her eyes that she was lonely and still had no idea what was essential in life. All she thought about was business, and making deals. It seemed like an empty life to Gaëlle, but it was the one Dominique had always wanted, and now she had it. She had none of her father's kindness or her mother's warmth. And at forty, when Dominique's married lover still hadn't left his wife yet, the bitterness that had colored her life for years came out through her pores. It was the aura around her and had been since her father's death. She felt cheated by life to have lost him when she was so young. And it pained Gaëlle to see that her daughter was an unhappy woman, and always had been. And she still thought of no one but herself.

★   ★   ★

Daphne was twenty-two by then, when Dominique was forty, and she had just started medical school. The two sisters hadn't seen each other in nineteen years, and Daphne was the joy of her parents' existence. She married a fellow medical student a year later, at twenty-three, and their first baby, Delphine, was born a year after that, when Daphne was twenty-four. Gaëlle was sixty-five when she had her first grandchild, and the moment she saw her, minutes after she was born, she knew that Delphine was special. And Christophe could see it too. He adored her and loved spending time with her and taking her to the zoo. He always said that she was a remarkable child.

Christophe loved her twin brothers too, when they were born two years later. His grandchildren were the joy of his life, just as Daphne had been, and Pierre for his brief life.

Delphine was four when her grandfather fell ill, and she visited him whenever her mother would let her, and she was five when he succumbed to the illness, with Daphne and Gaëlle at his side. He told Gaëlle how much he loved her, closed his eyes, and went to sleep. They had shared a wonderful life to the very end.

Daphne called Dominique and told her, and was amazed when she came to the funeral. She flew to Paris and stayed at the Ritz. It was the first time the two sisters had seen each other in twenty-five years. Daphne was twenty-nine and Dominique was forty-seven. Gaëlle had just turned seventy. Dominique stayed in Paris for two days to attend the funeral, out of respect for her mother. She looked stiff and uncomfortable surrounded by a family she had avoided for more than half her life. She had the aura of success about her, and of power, but she had the look of a lonely, unhappy woman. She had never known the love of a man like Robert or Christophe, or of a child like Delphine, or her mother.

Delphine slipped her hand into her grandmother's at the funeral, and handed her a pink rose at the cemetery. She had the wisdom of the ages in her eyes. Gaëlle had seen eyes like that during the war. They were the children who were born to make a difference, had survived, and whom she had remembered forever.

336

And after the burial at the cemetery, Delphine rode back to town in the car with her grandmother, her mother, and her aunt Dominique whom she had never met before. 'She has sad eyes,' she commented to her grandmother later, and then went off to find her father and brothers, while her mother and aunt talked. They had a lot of years to cover in a short time. Dominique flew back to New York the next morning, promising to come back to visit soon. She was amazed by what an intelligent, interesting woman Daphne had turned out to be. She was just finishing her residency.

Dominique hugged her mother when she left — she had to go back for important meetings in New York. Gaëlle was glad she had come, even for two days.

And after that, life was very different without Christophe. It changed everything, and she had to learn to live alone again. She didn't want to be a burden to Daphne, and was grateful she had her work at the museum, her friend Louise, and her memories of thirty happy years with Christophe.

The years continued to pass too quickly, as Daphne established her practice and raised her children, Delphine and her brothers grew up, Gaëlle worked at the museum and saw Daphne and her family frequently. She and Daphne were always close, even more so after her father's death. And despite the renewed connection during the funeral, Dominique didn't come back to Paris. She couldn't. She was too busy making deals. Gaëlle still flew to New York to see her, though not as often, and she had a busy life too.

And three years after Christophe's death, Dominique's married lover left her for another woman, got divorced, and married the other woman. She had waited for him for twenty-four years. In some ways, her mother observed about her, and commented later to Daphne, Dominique got back as little as she gave. Her only kind gesture to her mother in all those years had been to attend Christophe's funeral.

Among Gaëlle's great pleasures now, without Christophe, was taking trips with Delphine. She and her granddaughter had a great time together. They were in Deauville the summer Delphine turned seventeen, when she told her about Rebekah.

'Is that why you work at the Strauss Museum?' Delphine asked her. She had always been fascinated by her grandmother, and admired her spirit, wisdom, and energy.

'Yes, it is, and for others like her.' She told Delphine about the piece of blue satin ribbon, and that she still had it in a drawer at home. And then she told her about all the other children, the places she had taken them to save them, and the countless people who had risked their lives to make a difference. 'You must always make a difference, Delphine. Not for yourself, but for others who can't do it without you.'

'I want to write a book about you one day,' Delphine said seriously. 'People should know about what you did.'

'I was only one person among many. None of us made a difference individually, but together we all did.' It was the true meaning of community.

'Did you ever get an award for it?' Delphine wanted to know.

'No.' And then she told her about being accused as a collaborator, and how she had saved paintings from being stolen by the Germans. She was part of the living history of her country, and listening to her, Delphine was more determined than ever to honor her grandmother one day and tell her story. She was a remarkable woman. Gaëlle was eighty-two then, and still full of excitement about life, and working at the museum.

When she went home, Delphine talked to her mother about what her grandmother had told her. Daphne said she vaguely remembered some of the stories of her mother's war experiences, but didn't know them all. 'She doesn't like to talk about it, but my father told me some of it when I was young.' She hadn't paid attention to it then, and wished now that she had, since her mother never spoke of it, except on rare occasions, as she just had to Delphine.

Delphine wrote to the Grand Chancellery of the Legion of Honor on her own eventually, with the details of her grandmother's story. They answered her and said that Gaëlle de Barbet had been accused of being a collaborator, and her name had never been cleared after the war, so she had never been decorated. They were matter-of-fact about it, and her grandmother had said as much herself.

She wrote to them again when her grandmother retired from the Strauss Museum five years later at eighty-seven, when Delphine was twenty-two, and she asked them to look into it again. They came back with the same response. Delphine was just finishing her studies in literature and history at the Sorbonne. She continued to pursue her grandmother's story doggedly, and asked her grandmother the name of the commandant who had given her the paintings to return to the Louvre, and Gaëlle told her. Her memory was as sharp and clear as it had ever been. But she told Delphine it would make no difference and didn't matter. She didn't need a decoration. The children's lives she had saved were enough.

Delphine searched the Internet for the German commandant and located his family. He had been dead for a long time by then, but they knew the story. She asked if he had ever mentioned having an affair with her grandmother, or being in love with her, and they said he never did. He had married again after the war, and had a second family after the one he had lost, and she asked them to write to the chancellery for her, telling them what they had told her, and they promised that they would.

She wrote her grandmother's story on the Internet, and Gaëlle was shocked when she did, and somewhat embarrassed, and she said something about it to Louise, that Delphine was obsessed with clearing her name all these years later.

'Good for her.' Louise was delighted. 'Maybe she can do for you what you never wanted to do yourself.'

And then the emails began coming in, from the children she had taken to safety. Some of them were still alive, and remembered Gaëlle, whose name they had never known, or had known her by the code name Marie-Ange. There were twenty-four of them who wrote to Delphine, and she submitted their letters as well.

She had written to the chancellery for thirteen years, but nothing had happened. And whether they gave Gaëlle an award or not, Delphine knew she would write a book about her. She had to. The story was too important not to. And she deserved to be vindicated, although Gaëlle always said it didn't matter. The children's lives that were saved were enough. She didn't need more than that and she'd been very touched by those who wrote to her on the Internet, thanks to Delphine and what she wrote to find them.

And then suddenly there it was. Her name was on the list on New Year's Day. So many years after Delphine had started writing to the chancellery, and had promised to clear her grandmother's name.

★ ★ ★

It was evening when Delphine finally reached her grandmother.

'Well? Did you see it?' she asked her, her voice filled with excitement.

'See what?' Gaëlle pretended not to know, but Delphine knew her better.

'Your name on the list,' she persisted, and her grandmother laughed.

'You're a stubborn girl,' Gaëlle said proudly. Delphine hadn't relented for all those years, and

341

she had grown up in the meantime. 'I always told your mother you were a special person.'

'Not as special as you are, Grandma. I haven't saved hundreds of children.'

'I just did what I knew I had to do.'

'So did I,' Delphine said happily. 'When are you going to have the ceremony?'

'I suppose they'll tell me what to do eventually. I've waited till I'm ninety-five, it won't kill me to wait a little longer.' They had rushed to call her a traitor and a collaborator, but no one had been in a hurry to call her a hero. Except her granddaughter.

'We'll all be there with you when it happens,' she promised. And Delphine knew it would be published in the newspaper and on the Internet.

They waited another month to give her the date when she would be decorated at the Elysée by the President of the Republic. Daphne saw it first this time, and called her sister in New York. They hadn't spoken to each other in twenty-five years, since Daphne's father died, and she had come back to Paris for the funeral but then lost the connection again.

'Our mother is being awarded the Legion of Honor,' Daphne told her when Dominique answered on her private line, and for a moment, she thought their mother had died.

'That's very impressive,' she said admiringly, wondering why Daphne had called her. Dominique was seventy-two now, and Daphne was fifty-four.

'You have to be there,' Daphne said urgently. 'You can't let her down.' She knew from what she read in the newspapers that her sister was still a powerful force on Wall Street and hadn't retired. It was who she was and all she had.

'I just had a knee replacement, and probably shouldn't make the trip.' Dominique sounded ill at ease and clearly didn't want to be asked to come. She preferred to remain at a distance, which was comfortable for her.

'I don't care,' Daphne said bluntly. 'She's ninety-five years old. How many important events in her life are you planning to miss? There aren't going to be any bigger ones than this.' She knew that rejection had been her sister's weapon of choice all her life. She had never been there for her mother when it mattered, except when she'd come for Christophe's funeral, but other than that she had never shown up. Gaëlle didn't talk about it, but Daphne could guess how much it hurt, and how disappointing it had been. 'My daughter fought hard to get her this decoration. The least you can do is show up. It's not a lot to ask,' Daphne said sternly, and for a moment, Dominique didn't answer.

'When is it?' she asked in a haunted voice, and Daphne told her, and she said she'd try, which Daphne knew meant nothing coming from her sister. She never tried. Only her mother did. And other than phone calls, Gaëlle had given up on Dominique long since. She had visited her in New York for so many years, until recently, and no longer did, but Dominique was too busy, and never came to Paris.

'Just be there. You don't have to talk to any of us. Just do it for her,' Daphne said, sounding fierce, which was unlike her. But someone had to do it.

'Did she ask you to call me?' Dominique wanted to know.

'No, she didn't,' Daphne said. And when she said that, Dominique knew she had to go, no matter how painful it was for her. Just like Christophe's funeral. There was no choice this time either. Gaëlle had been the mother she could never warm to, and hadn't tried, and she never knew why. Late in life she had realized that she had loved her father too much, and there had been nothing left for her mother. And Daphne was right. This was her last chance. One final gesture for a lifetime of failure to reach out, and heal the hurt she had caused.

★ ★ ★

The morning dawned bright and sunny. Daphne had bought the medal for her, the largest, most important-looking one they had. It was dark blue and white enamel, with green enamel leaves, a large white enamel star, and gold in the center. It hung from a scarlet ribbon, which they would attach to her suit or dress. And after the day of the award, she would wear a discreet red ribbon on her lapel, and a miniature of the medal on special occasions.

Delphine picked her grandmother up in her tiny car, which her energetic grandmother had no trouble getting into. Georges had said he'd come from his office.

Daphne and her husband were going in their

own car. Her brothers would come on their motorbikes. And Louise was going with her driver. The new director of the Strauss Museum had promised to be there, and the old one, and a representative of the Strauss family. André, Christophe's close friend, was coming — his wife Geneviève had died ten years before. Delphine's brothers' girlfriends had promised to come. The boys were proud of their grandmother too, but spent less time with her than their sister.

And Delphine had contacted the Louvre, told one of the curators the story, which he had verified, and the Louvre was sending a representative to attend the ceremony to honor her.

When they walked into the lobby of the Élysée, where the invitees were gathering and a band was playing, Delphine saw the group that had emailed her. They had formed an association fifty years before called The Survivors. They were the children whom Gaëlle and the members of the OSE had transported. All of them had been young children then, or babies, and now they were old people. They had come to pay their respects to Gaëlle, and to thank her for acts of courage that they had been too young to understand when they happened.

Delphine explained to her grandmother who they were, and Gaëlle went to shake hands with them and thank each one for coming. And many of them cried when they thanked her. Isabelle, the little girl who had ridden on the tractor, was there, and twenty others. One of them smiled broadly at Gaëlle, and looked nearly as old as she was.

Isabelle was eighty-six and excited to see her. 'I still remember you. You drove me on a borrowed tractor. We drove right past the soldiers, and you told me not to worry. You were as calm as can be. I never forgot it.' She had brought her grandchildren and greatgrandchildren with her, who thanked Gaëlle too. Isabelle said she'd had six children.

And then, as Gaëlle shook hands with them, Daphne and Delphine saw her. She was tall and thin, and had changed very little since Christophe's funeral. She just looked older, in a black Chanel suit with short gray hair. She walked in using a cane, but hung it over her arm once she entered. She didn't look like their mother, but she had the same dignified elegance, even if her coloring and features were different.

Dominique recognized Daphne immediately from her father's funeral and walked over to her, and then their mother saw her.

'What are you doing here?' Gaëlle asked Dominique in amazement. She hadn't told her about the decoration. She was sure she wouldn't come anyway.

'I understand you're being honored today,' Dominique said solemnly, and looking into her mother's eyes, she saw something she hadn't remembered. It was her compassion and forgiveness that had allowed her to survive the war, and go on to a good life afterward. Her mother had carried none of the betrayals with her. It made Dominique feel guilty just looking at Gaëlle. She had blamed her mother for so much, for her father's death, for having Daphne and her brother

346

Pierre, for marrying Christophe, even for the money she had inherited from Dominique's father. For most of her life, or all of it, she had decided it was all her mother's fault. It had been a heavy burden to carry and had left room in her heart for nothing else. And all of it showed on her face. She looked bitter and tired and older than her mother, who was still full of life, positive, and joyful.

'It's good to see you,' Gaëlle said quietly to Dominique. 'Thank you for coming.' She hugged her, and the familiar embrace brought tears to Dominique's eyes as she realized how much pain she had caused her for so long, and yet even in the way her mother reached out to her, Dominique could tell that her mother had forgiven her.

'I wouldn't miss it,' Dominique said in a voice filled with emotion. She was glad she had come, and smiled gratefully at Daphne for calling her, and introduced herself to Delphine, whom she hadn't seen since she was five. She congratulated her for her persistence to make this moment happen.

The crowd moved into the room where the ceremony was being held, once the doors opened, and Delphine tucked a hand into her grandmother's arm.

'Is that to steady you, or to help me?' Gaëlle teased her, and she and Louise winked at each other. 'I'm probably the oldest person in this room,' she said in a disparaging tone, and Delphine laughed.

'And the bravest. That's why we're all here today. For brave acts committed in battle.' The award was given for other reasons now, but the original purpose of the medal from Napoleonic times was to honor brave warriors on the battlefield. And brave she had been.

It only took the President a few minutes to pin the medal on her jacket. She had worn black so it would stand out. And then he pinned their medals on the other recipients, as the crowd watched and applauded each one. He made an impressive speech about their accomplishments, and each recipient made a brief one. Gaëlle's was typically humble and to the point, and at the end she thanked her family and friends for being there, and especially Delphine, who had fought so hard for her.

Listening to the President's speech had taken her back to those terrifying days of the war, when everyone thought they were going to die at any moment, and many had. They had stolen children from the enemy's clutches, and saved them, no matter the danger or risk to themselves, so the children could go on to lead good lives, and she hoped they had. If so, it was all worth it. And her own life had been worth the sorrows she'd survived. She'd been loved by two good men in her lifetime, and cherished their children. She smiled at Dominique afterward, and thanked her for coming. She knew it couldn't have been easy for her to face them again.

And for all those who had hurt her, she had forgiven them a long time before. The towns-people who had called her a traitor, the Germans who had killed her father. And if she herself had saved even one life, then it was all worth it. The rest didn't matter. And for those they couldn't save, like Rebekah and Lotte, the Feldmanns, and so many others, they were never forgotten.

Gaëlle left the room proudly, on her grand-daughter's arm, wearing her medal.

'When do we start the book, Grandma?' Delphine whispered, and her grandmother laughed and patted her hand.

'Tomorrow.' Delphine had earned it, and Gaëlle was looking forward to it. There was so much to tell. And she was finally ready to tell it.

BITTERSWEET
GRANNY DAN
JOURNEY
LONE EAGLE
LEAP OF FAITH
THE COTTAGE
SUNSET IN ST TROPEZ
DATING GAME
TOXIC BACHELORS
BIG GIRL
LEGACY
44 CHARLES STREET
HAPPY BIRTHDAY
HOTEL VENDOME
A GIFT OF HOPE
THE SINS OF THE MOTHER
PEGASUS
A PERFECT LIFE
RUSHING WATERS

Other titles published by Ulverscroft:

A PERFECT LIFE

Danielle Steel

An icon in the world of television news, Blaise McCarthy seems to have it all: beauty, intelligence and courage. But privately, there is a story she has protected for years . . . Blaise's daughter Salima, blinded by juvenile diabetes, now lives in a year-round boarding school with full-time assistance. When the school closes suddenly, Salima returns home to Blaise's New York apartment with her new carer, Simon. He rapidly shakes up their world, determined to help Salima find the independence she never thought possible. Then Blaise's personal and professional worlds collide: a young rival at work attempts to take over, and the well-guarded secrets of Blaise's home life are exposed. Suddenly her life is no longer perfect, but real. Can mother and daughter learn together how to face a world they can't control?

PEGASUS

Danielle Steel

In the German countryside, on the cusp of World War II, everything is about to change for two lifelong friends. As widowers, Nicolas and Alex are raising their children alone, but lead contented, peaceful lives — until a long-buried secret about Nicolas's ancestry threatens his family's safety. To survive, they must flee to America. The only treasures Nicolas and his sons can take are eight purebred horses. These magnificent creatures are their ticket to a new life, securing Nicolas a job with the famous Ringling Brothers Circus. There, he and the white stallion Pegasus become the centrepiece of the show. But as the years of war take their toll, Nicolas struggles to adapt to his new life, while Alex and his daughter face escalating danger in Europe. Then tragedy strikes on both sides of the ocean . . .

THE SINS OF THE MOTHER

Danielle Steel

Legendary businesswoman Olivia spends months each year planning a lavish holiday for her family to enjoy. More than anything, she hopes to express her love, and her regret at missing so much during her children's early years. But her younger daughter, Cassie, refuses the invitation altogether. Liz, her older daughter, is preoccupied. And her sons, John and Phillip, work for her, for better or worse, with wives who wish they didn't. This should be a summer to remember, but old resentments die hard. As each of them confronts the past, they find a mother who is strong enough to take more than her share of blame, and loving enough to accept them as they are. The question is: can they do the same for her?

A GIFT OF HOPE

Danielle Steel

Just months after the death of her beloved son, Danielle Steel found herself venturing out onto the streets with a small team of trusted friends to help the homeless of San Francisco, transforming the pain of loss into a campaign of service that enriched her life beyond anything she could have imagined. For eleven years, they worked under cover of darkness, distributing food, clothing, bedding, tools and toiletries to the city's most vulnerable citizens, seeking no publicity and remaining anonymous throughout. In this unflinchingly honest and deeply moving memoir, the author speaks publicly for the first time about their work among the most desperate members of society, and issues a heartfelt call for more effective action to aid this vast, deprived population.